Glory Days and Tragedy

Millennial Mind Publishing
An imprint of American Book Publishing
American Book Publishing
P.O. Box 65624
Salt Lake City, UT 84165
www.american-book.com
Printed in the United States of America on acid-free paper.

Glory Days and Tragedy

Designed by Karl Andrews, design@american-book.com

Publisher's Note: *This publication is designed to provide accurate and authoritative information in regard to the subject matter covered. It is sold or distributed with the understanding that the publisher and author is not engaged in rendering legal, accounting, or other professional service. If legal advice or other expert assistance is required, the services of a competent professional person in a consultation capacity should be sought.*

ISBN 1-58982-203-X

Prudent, Therold, Glory Days and Tragedy

Special Sales

These books are available at special discounts for bulk purchases. Special editions, including personalized covers, excerpts of existing books, and corporate imprints, can be created in large quantities for special needs. For more information e-mail orders@american-book.com, 801-486-8639.

Glory Days and Tragedy

By Therold Prudent

Dedicated to the memory of my childhood friend, George Phillip, along with all the boys who lost their lives in the great tragedy of '85.

To Kade, Nashota, and Asher:

*The fear of the Lord is the instruction of wisdom;
and before honour is humility.*

Proverbs 15:33

Preface

When I first set out to write this book, it was never my intention to make life in Gros Islet a big part of this project. My plan was to simply write about Kennedy's experience at sea, and to later pursue my dreams of writing a separate memoir of life in Gros Islet. But then, as the story began to evolve, and Kennedy and I began to reminisce about the good old days we had together, I became increasingly convinced that the time to tell the story of Gros Islet is now. As the book grew to paint a colorful picture of life in Gros Islet, I was eventually able to find a way to merge the harrowing experiences of death and ultimate survival suffered by some of her children at sea in 1985.

Therefore, I sincerely hope that the decision to combine the two will not only give the reader a better understanding of our community, but also that it will draw your attention to a period that so devastated our community emotionally.

Introduction

By the time it was finally over, George was dead! The year was 1985, during an ordeal at sea. In many respects, his death and those of his companions not only touched the hearts of an entire community, but they had also provided great insight as to how vulnerable human life can be.

Amidst the pain of this great tragedy, many were able to draw inspiration by marveling at the enduring nature of the human spirit, as one of George's shipmates cheated death and ultimately survived. In this story, you will come face to face with that individual and, like the people of Gros Islet, you will walk away astonished.

Prior to the time of the tragedy—seventeen years, to be exact—I had come to know George Phillip and his brother Kennedy on a very personal basis. We also had a good friend by the name of Ronnie Maxius, and from an early age we all seemed inseparable.

Therefore, the first part of this book recounts our earlier lives together in a St. Lucian town called Gros Islet. You will receive firsthand a clear understanding of the various local traditions, beliefs and other religious influences that would help shape our lives.

Later, as the story makes the transition to the tragedy at sea, there lies an even more intriguing journey than the one that we first started. Your emotions will be cast into a roller coaster mode of both empathy and sadness, but in the end, your spirits will be lifted.

Part One

Gros Islet

Rodney Bay and the Town of Gros Islet in the background. This picture was taken from Pigeon Point (formally Pigeon Island).

Endowed by nature with white sandy beaches, blue skies, and trees bearing coconut and breadfruit, this town radiates an ambience of tranquility. It lies on the northwestern coast of the Caribbean island of St. Lucia, and has for centuries been known as Gros Islet.

Pigeon Point from the shores of Gros Islet Town.

Gros Islet's modern history dates back to 1782, for it was from neighboring Pigeon Island on the dawn of April 8 of that year that the British set sail to pursue and defeat the French for possession of St. Lucia.

My earliest memories of Gros Islet have often evoked images from archaic times. But it is with the utmost pride and affection that I reminisce upon the once-antiquated settings of my hometown. Having been born in the sixties, I have always thought of myself as belonging to the last generation of that era. Those were the long nights of pitch darkness, street lanterns, and stories of evil spirits, commonly refereed to as *la-jah-bless*, which roamed the streets.

Mornings were usually greeted by the shrill cries of cocks crowing, the sights of older women on feast days dressed in their eighteenth-century formal garments, their "*Wob dwiyet,*" and the solitary proclamations of a town crier pervading the morning air. Then there were the frequent stops of Mr. Matiween and his donkey-cart, as they made the early morning rounds of garbage collection.

I remember also the configuration of those old, wooden houses, which were lined along the narrow, sandy streets. There was a uniformity about them. Most of the rooftops were triangular, and the entrance to each home was decorated with conch shells, which formed an arch-like structure on either side of the doorway. They were in fact ornaments wrapped in a shawl of secrecy that only the people of Gros Islet knew.

As a child I had been told many stories about the conch shell. But none was able to captivate my interest like the claims that they were once employed as weapons during the heyday of vigilantism in Gros Islet. Although I was much too young to have borne witness to those various conflicts, I am convinced that scores of alien vagabonds and ruffians were wounded and driven out of Gros Islet with the aid of the conch shell. To this day, that perception has not changed, and has remained as true as my profound convictions that within my veins flows the mixed blood of my African and Carib ancestors.

Life in Gros Islet was always filled with intrigue, but nothing there generates greater interest than we, the people of Gros Islet. For many generations we survived off the bounty of the sea by engaging in a thriving fishing industry, which became the epitome of our cultural pride. Every boy and girl, man and woman was a fisherman at heart. We were all bound together by this great economic influence, which symbolized our past, present, and future.

I can still recall the long stretch of boathouses, which were covered with dry coconut palms. There, under a blazing sun, the nets would be mended and fish pots crafted out of dry bamboo stalks. Occasionally, at the command of nature, a gentle breeze would rise from the sea. Then, like a most, powerful apparition, it seemed to cause the clouds to darken and the rain to fall. Although it's been years, these feelings of refreshment still cause my heart to stall in its beating.

Some of the best days were during the months of August and October. Those were the months when the sea was at its warmest, and a full moon indicated a jackfish invasion the following day.

By morning, the fishermen would race to the seashores with scores of volunteers, who often waited patiently for a glimpse of the invading jacks. Usually, a glare on the water with seagulls circling above was an indication of the exact location of the jackfish. Once the fish were spotted, the fishermen would set out in a canoe, spreading the entire net around the glare.

The accuracy and swiftness with which the nets were cast often left very little room for escape. Beneath the surface, a multitude of jackfish would be trapped within the confines of net.

Back on the shore, volunteers would form two parallel lines, each group holding onto a separate and lengthy rope which was secured to either end of the net. Simultaneously, they would engage in a quiet but vigorous hauling of the net until the entire catch was brought ashore.

Once this task was executed, an atmosphere of intense confusion would prevail. Volunteers could be seen shoving each other and shouting at the top of their lungs. Individually, they wanted to attract the attention of the net's owner, whose responsibility it was to ensure an adequate and fair distribution of the catch.

Normally, one could tell if the owner had become exasperated by the intricacies of the situation if his behavior became belligerent. It would take on the form of countless obscenities which were often hurled at those whom he perceived to have initiated the confusion. From long experience, this seemed to be the only way to quell the madness and reestablish an atmosphere of civility. Once this was achieved, everyone was rewarded accordingly, and the balance was carried over to the fish market to be sold.

Through the years, we the people of Gros Islet have also acquired a fair reputation for being politically vindictive. Our obsession with local politics has often led us to great lengths of hate and divisiveness. Our political behavior has become so notorious that petty jealousies, coupled with an unhealthy tendency to tarnish the images of aspiring local politicians, have become the hallmarks of our political activities. In that sense, we may have become the laughingstock of our entire nation. As if following an unspoken principle, we have never elected our peers to political office. As indigenous Gros Islians, we have learnt to accept the political status quo by consistently voting for outside representation. Anyone looking in from the outside would think that our political values reflect low self-esteem and dignity. But how could anyone judge us so harshly when there are so many other positive attributes within us that clearly indicate our unifying sentiments?

From earliest memory, we are known for our big hearts and humility. For in times of despair, tragedy, or death, one can be sure to receive a genuine outpouring of human compassion from even a most avowed enemy. In the tattered wreckage of our grief, we have served as pillars of strength for each other. Hence, our political blunders are forgiven through the legacy of compassion that we possess.

Yesterday

In a crowded sandy schoolyard on a sunny September morning in 1970, there we stood. All the boys were dressed in short khaki pants and khaki shirts, the prescribed school attire of the day. Not far away, perhaps fifty feet off, stood three large wooden buildings. The one to our left was the old convent. Straight ahead and to our right were the educational institutions that were to shape our academic future.

Although there were great differences in their architectural designs, we couldn't help but notice a distinct resemblance in their outward appearance. The gray color with which they were once painted had ceased to blend softly with the blue skies above. It had faded to an ugly whitewashed appearance, displaying the traces of time and neglect.

George, the oldest of we four, his brother Kennedy, Ronnie, and I had known each other ever since our preschool years. Way back then we had established a personal friendship that would later influence the greater part of our teenage years.

Our preschool teacher, Mrs. Florence Lastic, must have been proud of herself. She had accomplished the most tedious task of teaching us to count and to write our names. We used to bask in the recitation of the alphabet and in the beautiful chants of the nursery rhymes, with "Little Jack Horner" and "Pussy Cat Pussy Cat" our biggest favorites. But now those days were gone. The big day had arrived for our formal acceptance into the Gros Islet Infant School.

The anxieties of the moment sent waves of excitement tingling down our little spines. At about 8:25 A.M. Mother Theodore, the school principal, gracefully walked across from the old convent to the school directly ahead. She wore polished black moccasins which contrasted with her spotless white habit.

A sudden hush filled the restless air as my feet froze in their movement. The adrenaline jolted, pumped, and then kicked my respiration into a roller coaster mode. I knew then that the hour was fast approaching.

As I glanced slowly sideways, my eyes met those of my friends. Suspense shone in their eyes. Grappling for composure, Ronnie whispered something inaudible.

"What?" I said in a muffled voice.

He stared at George, then Kennedy, and then allowed himself a faint smile.

Suddenly, the sound of the bell came piercing through the silence. In the doorway, stern-faced, Mother Theodore kept rattling the bell. Quietly, as the many blasts of nerves ripped through our tiny bodies, we quivered in fear. After fifteen... twenty... perhaps thirty seconds, all was calm again.

Moments later, we were issued instructions for the morning assembly. The freshman class was to file to the front, followed by the senior students. Initially, we moved about in a scramble, but with some assistance from one of the teachers, we soon got it right. In the end, Ronnie and I were together, but George and his brother Kennedy had taken up positions in the row directly behind us.

As the gathering took shape, I once again laid eyes on Mother Theodore. This time she was pacing down the steps, and I noticed how the black wooden cross around her neck dangled wildly upon her chest. She was carrying a flat, wide book in her left hand, and a belt in the other. Like a ghost she whisked passed the front row, leaving behind an image of dread.

Suddenly, I heard it once, twice, and then three times. It was the whooping sound of the belt on flesh! A restless child had fallen victim to the ever-intolerant mother Theodore.

Her love for what I quietly regarded as excessive punishment and scolding were common knowledge to everyone. Therefore, I made no attempt to bear witness to the incident. Instead, I kept my head upright and my eyes focused directly ahead. Attracting her attention was the last thing on my mind.

The faint sobs of the child dwindled into thin air. All was quiet. I swallowed hard. It felt good. However, although I had relieved my throat of the gripping effects of anxiety, I shivered nervously with fear.

The event that followed wrested me from this nervous hell. In a breadfruit tree nearby, the tense silence had been broken. It was being replaced by the delightful sounds of the blackbirds. They were singing their morning hymns. Impressed, I listened. Then, in utter submission, I allowed my thoughts to drift melodically into the carefree world of the blackbirds.

The Assembly, Its Aftermath, and the First Day

The morning assembly was the embodiment of boredom, for it was long and tiring. It demanded of us our undivided attention, while reminding us of the dominating influences of the Catholic Church on the quality of our education. From that morning onwards, such religious terms as "limbo" and "purgatory" would be deeply entwined into all aspects of our academic lives.

In fact, the morning had begun with a call to prayer. Earnestly and fervently, yet reflecting of our childish ignorance, we recited what we thought were the correct words of the Our Father and Hail Mary. "Ah wah father, wah-at in heaven…" and "Hay-lee Mary, full of grace, the lord be sweedy."

After the prayers were offered, a great silence fell over the gathering. Mother Theodore was about to address us.

At first, she spoke in a tone of voice that was pleasing to the ear, but soon the address grew stale as she cautioned us about the importance of arriving early at school, and of the need to maintain a high level of academic discipline and excellence. According to Mother Theodore, school—as much as the family unit—was now an integral part of our lives, as it was going to be an experience that would guide us for years to come.

We all listened attentively, as those words fell on our ears with a very taunting effect. I noticed the frowns of disappointment on the countenances of most of the students, as we all sought to make sense of Mother Theodore's proclamation.

I guess, judging from the reaction to Mother Theodore's speech, that the problem was not so much with the idea of equating school to the family unit, but with the acceptance of "the dreaded mother" as an integral part of our new way of life. While it was true that at home we were sometimes disciplined rather harshly, it was mind-boggling to think that a nun had the same authority as our parents to beat us.

Was Mother Theodore that bad? Or had we allowed the personal prejudices of the older students towards her to influence and poison our minds? Regardless of how any of us felt, Mother Theodore would rule our external world.

When the assembly finally came to an end, there was a collective sigh of relief. The next thing I remember was the roll call, and students being escorted to their respective classes.

Of my companions, Ronnie was the first to go. On his way into the building, he almost tripped over the steps. I remember grinning broadly. There was laughter from the other students behind me.

Since the roll was being called in alphabetical order, George and Kennedy would go before me. Unlike Ronnie, they made it up the steps with very little difficulty. I soon followed, clutching my school bag tightly.

Once inside, I found the odor to be ghastly. It smelled like the droppings of pigeons. I thought they might have nested in the enclosed building during the long summer vacation.

As I shifted my eyes from one wall to another, I noticed the sky-blue color with which the walls were painted. There was a large crucifix hanging on the wall directly in front of me, and a few educational charts on the walls to my left and right. The ceiling above was supported by a number of huge rafters, most of which were covered with cobwebs. And from the looks of things, it seemed that our "new" school was designed as a large hall, with no partitions except the blackboards, which stood on easels.

Most of the desks and benches, which were made out of red cedar, looked drubbed and rugged with age. Some of them were covered with pen and pencil marks, and on a few, the legs were heading for collapse. As I proceeded deeper inside, I could hear the sound of the aging floorboards as they creaked beneath the weight of my tiny body.

Within a few minutes, we were all assigned to our individual classes. To my delight, George, Kennedy, Ronnie, and myself would remain together. I could tell by the expression on their faces that they felt the same way too, for they beamed with contentment.

Our new teacher was a tall and slender woman. She wore a short Afro and had healthy-looking brown skin. Her name was Ms. Sandra Verdant, the daughter of one of the finest bakers in town. From what I've been told, she is related to me somewhere down the line. But then, this really comes as no surprise to me, since just about everyone in Gros Islet is related to each other.

Those obvious realities at school, coupled with the strictness of our parents at home, obliged us to remain disciplined. Everyone understood that the slightest display of bad behavior would be quickly answered with deserved punishment.

As the morning proceeded, we became deeply engrossed in the affairs of school. There were books and pencils on all the desks, and our little eyes remained fixed on our teacher and the blackboard.

Occasionally, at our teacher's request, we would flip through some of the pages in search of an educational character or symbol. That concept would arrest our interest, gradually developing into something of a scholarly nature. Each child wanted to be the first to find the page containing the educational character or symbol. It was almost like being rewarded with honor.

The pioneering spirit which had begun to shape our new educational environment was invigorating. Most everyone I knew in class had begun to openly demonstrate an eagerness to learn.

At 12:00 noon on the first day of school, two bells tolled. The first chime of the midday hour came from the Catholic belfry nearby, which for many years has stood as a perfect symbol of time and the continuation of life in our community. The other was from our school.

Instantaneously, the entire class rose to its feet, and with hands clasped, eyes closed and heads bowed, we recited the prayer of "Grace Before Meals." After the prayer was offered, we all hurried out of the building and into the schoolyard.

Directly overhead, the blazing fury of the midday sun poured down upon us. For a short while, I tarried near the school gate with George, Kennedy, and Ronnie, waiting for my cousins Fedora and Cheryl. The girls soon made their way out of the schoolyard and I, in turn, bade goodbye to the boys. We walked home by way of Church Street, while George, Kennedy, and Ronnie followed Dauphin Street to their respective homes.

The walk to our home was less than five minutes long. Once we had made it there safely, there were plenty of stories to be told. Our grandmother, Irene, whom we affectionately referred to as "Iae," seemed to show much interest, judging from her facial expression and her periodic interruptions while dishing out our meals.

Seated in the front row, before leaving my Grandmother's home for school is my brother, Philip and cousin Cheryl. Fedora and I are in the back row.

I did not miss the opportunity to tell her of my dislike for Mother Theodore. I was hoping that she would get angry with Mother Theodore, so as to justify my own personal disdain for a nun who had until now done nothing to me.

That moment of anger would never arrive. For instead of reacting in the way which I had hoped, my grandmother simply said that everything would be all right. But even if my grandmother had agreed with me, there was something about her that gave me the impression that she was one of those who were bound to a quiet oath of religious loyalty. Speaking negatively about a nun, especially in the presence of one's grandchildren, was tantamount to sinning. She had an allegiance to protect, and that was to the Church.

My Granmother's early-twentieth-century wooden chattel at 73 Marie Therese Street is featured on a St. Lucian Stamp.

At about a quarter to one, we left my grandmother's early-twentieth-century wooden chattel at 73 Marie Therese Street. We made a quick right turn onto Parish, and were joined by our neighbor Sandra Modest. At the end of Parish Street, we made a quick right unto Notre Dame Street. We stopped to say hello to Mr. Cornelius Popo, the only shoemaker in town. Mr. Popes, as we affectionately referred to him, was a soft-spoken man with a gentleman's attitude. I personally enjoyed seeing him at work, and had a kind of addiction to the smell of his shoe polish. I loved to hang around him as he worked tirelessly in his tiny shop. But most of all, I always enjoyed listening to the old man as he hummed a number of his favorite tunes.

After our brief visit with Mr. Popes, we continued for about half a block up Notre Dame Street before turning left unto Church Street. On the corner was our old preschool. To our right was a famous pub where all the drunks gathered at intervals during the day to drink Madeira or a diluted form of 80-proof called Rheum Blanc. They were kept entertained by a small jukebox inside, where they drowned their sorrows to the music of Ray Charles.

Once we had arrived in the safety of the schoolyard, I left the girls to join George and Kennedy, who sat under a breadfruit tree. Ronnie joined us later, and we laughed and joked about some of the occurrences of the morning.

It wasn't long before our period of amusement came to an abrupt end. The school bell inside had signaled the resumption of classes. Hastily we headed up the steps and into one of the side entrances which led into our class.

The afternoon session began with a call to pray. Our heads bowed, eyes closed, hands clasped together, we recited the prayer of "Grace After Meals." Once the prayers had been offered, we were instructed to quietly take our respective seats.

Indeed, not a murmur could be heard as we each proceeded to sit down. It was a proud moment that demonstrated the strict discipline we had received from home.

As the afternoon progressed, a lesson was taught in Religious Knowledge. True to our Catholic upbringing, it was very clear that the religious indoctrination into the beliefs of the Church was inescapable. For many years, the Roman Catholic Church had remained the only acceptable form of religious authority in our community. Not even the government of the day dared to challenge the authority of the Church.

When we were told about the end of the world, and of how all the wicked would burn in the fires of Hell, those thoughts were traumatizing for us as children. I can't recall exactly how the lesson started, but it was very evident that Hell had captured our imagination and forced our curiosity to run wild. Besides Satan and other evildoers, everyone wanted to know whether little children could end up in the fires of Hell, and if so, what we should do to avert going to that dreadful place.

"Yes!" came the reply to the first question, followed by an immediate explanation of why some children would burn in the fires of Hell. According to our teacher, those of us who were disobedient to our parents at home, and who had cultivated habits of stealing and telling lies, would surely spend eternity in Hell with Satan and his angels.

Wow! "Here comes trouble" described the expression on everyone's face. It was terrifying enough to think of the concept of Hell, but worse to believe that you could be in that place keeping Satan company. That very afternoon, I must confess, the realities of Hell haunted us like mice sniffing for cheese. Everyone sat motionlessly in his or her seat as the teacher proceeded with the lesson. I felt as though my thoughts were moving at the speed of light. I was painstakingly trying to recreate an image inside my mind of who or what the Devil might really look like.

I had finally arrived at a mental effigy of a very tall beast with horns on his head. His skin was the color of tar, and there were large patches of hair over most of his body. A great quantity of dry coconut husks was attached to the Devil's back, and he was clothed from the waist down with dry banana leaves that extended to the ground. His feet were about the size of a diver's fin, and toenails jutted out from under the skin.

At that point, I was convinced that it was time to stop. I really did not want to create or see an image of the Devil's face. For surely, what I had imagined so far was terrifying enough. It may well have been that my perception of what the Devil might look like could have been greatly influenced by some of the costumes I had seen at the local carnival a few months before.

By the end of the lesson in religious studies, it was clear that none of us wanted to be in Hell with the Devil and his angels. Every child would be good, or so we thought at that moment.

That afternoon, the sentiments of the Religious Studies exercise would be carried over to the next class, Arts and Crafts. For even as our teacher slowly replaced the bold imprint of "Religious Knowledge" on the blackboard with "Arts and Crafts," there still remained the feeling of defiance aimed at renouncing the Devil, "and all his works and pomp."

At the request of our teacher, we each took out our drawing books and some crayons. Soon there were loads of colorful crayons lying on the desks. Not long after, we all began work on our individual paintings. We sketched a little here, and fixed a little over there, until the likeness of what we wanted to draw came into full view.

Eventually, the colors were added, which no doubt gave our artwork that "professional" look. Green, blue, black, red, orange, and pink were by far the most popular colors of the afternoon. In the end, a few students had produced artwork depicting boats, trees, houses, and motorcars. But none of the artwork was as innovative as the many portraits of Lucifer, which dominated the art scene in the classroom.

Some of the portraits of Lucifer depicted a man with a small round head, while others simply depicted him as an angry fellow with a very large head. However, nothing was as astounding as those depicting the Devil with an outweighed head over a tiny body.

There was also another component to the drawings that brought out a unanimous accord in everyone. It had to do with the fires of Hell. In other words, the rich and striking color of red over the Devil's head and under his feet meant that this beast, in whatever shape the students had drawn him, was for goodness' sake burning in Hell.

At about 2 P.M. that day we finally brought a remarkable end to the afternoon. Symbolically, we had won a serious victory over the Devil, which undoubtedly merited our giving thanks and praise to God in Heaven. As soon as closing prayers were offered, we jiggled our way through the narrow exit which led to the schoolyard.

Outside, the air was filled with the babble of students. The giant breadfruit trees nearby cast an enormous shadow over the entire yard. Out on the street ahead, I caught a glimpse of the postman delivering the afternoon mail as I hurried out of the schoolyard.

My cousins Cheryl and Fedora were already waiting on the sidewalk as I stepped out of the gate. I thought they were very fortunate to have gotten out through the front doors, which swung on giant hinges.

Not too far from where my cousins were waiting, I spotted George and Kennedy. They were surrounded by a small group of other students who all seemed curious about something that George was holding in his hands.

I still couldn't see because of the number of other students in front of me. I inched myself closer a bit until I was able to see what was going on. Indeed, what I saw was eye-catching. It was George's sketch, which I hadn't had a chance to see in class.

Personally, I was impressed, just like the other children; the drawing arrested my attention. It was a beautifully colored red boat, with a reflective background of a placid deep blue sea. Most attractive was the checkered black-and-white sail raised high above the boat, which almost seemed to make the portrait come alive. There were also petite images of what appeared to be sailors on board, and from the looks of things they were gingerly sailing over the sea.

As I studied the drawing for a little while longer, I also noticed how the image of a golden sun in the upper right hand corner mingled softly with what were presumably the flawlessly blue and ageless Caribbean skies above. George really had it going on, and soon loads of other thoughts flooded my mind.

As I bade goodbye to the boys for the last time that afternoon, I suddenly began to see a different side of George. It wasn't the usual perception of a loud individual with an aggressive character, but rather of one with the ability to recreate perfect images of things that our eyes had captured in the past. To me, George had suddenly been transformed into an extraordinary guy, one with lots of ingenuity and artistic expression. Overnight he became not only a friend, but also a kind of idol whom I strangely envied.

The Months Ahead

Growing up in Gros Islet during the early seventies was almost like growing up in an era of deplorable ignorance and backwardness. It was as though time had stood still. There were forty-eight hours in a day, and the concept of a week was only a deceptive psychological term used to prolong time. In our part of the world, there was always this hidden force or strange apparition whose responsibility it was to hold back the hands of time. Was this for real? Or was it the innocent and carefree nature of my childhood world, playing tricks on me? After we had been in school for about a month or two, it felt like eternity. As new knowledge was imparted daily, so were there vigorous challenges that confronted us. From the very onset, those challenges were proving to be difficult if not peculiar in nature. They included the ability to fully comprehend and to demonstrate superior competence in the various academic disciplines.

The change from our preschool years, when we were taught in a communal setting that included the simultaneous recitation of nursery rhymes by the entire class, required quick adaptation to our new educational environment.

We had to face up to the realities of our changing world. In essence, as we became increasingly aware of the purpose and importance of school, it enabled us to eventually piece together the mind-boggling puzzle commonly referred to as Education. There was a bottom line to this mystical term, and this meant judging an individual's academic progress through a rating system called "the big E."

The introduction of the concept of examination meant a lot. As students, our choice was very clear. We either had to work very hard to pass our exams, or suffer the humiliation of being known as a dunce or brainless child. Underachievers were never looked upon kindly in Gros Islet. Often, it meant being ridiculed by other students. In our class, there was an ongoing battle to avert this very sad and catastrophic experience. From very early on, it was clear that a few students were quickly establishing themselves as the *crème de la crème* of the intellectual environment in our class. Among the early prospects were our dear friend Ronnie and a stunning beauty named Debra Popo (no relation to Cornelius Popo, the shoemaker). There were also others like Patricia Joseph, Barbara Fessal, Phyllis Amos, Pollard Lucien, Armstrong Alexis, James Gaspard, Errol Albert, Ralph Octave, James Dupal, and Theodora Sylvester who made up the intellectual elite of our class.

For my part, although I never could quite be measured among the best, I always knew that I had the potential to excel academically. But that would have to wait. While reading and writing were my forte from an early age, mathematics was for me a boyish nightmare.

As for George and Kennedy, they were always on the flip side of the academic coin in my estimation. This isn't to suggest that I was the best of us in any intellectual sense, but that their interests were predominantly centered on the technical and creative aspects of our education.

For the greater part of our first year in school, their growing interest in Arts and Crafts, as well as boat building, was becoming increasingly obvious. I remember most explicitly their sighs of relief whenever the sessions for Arts and Crafts would begin. It always seemed like they had a desire to howl, but the boys were always smart enough to bottle up their emotions.

Whenever George and Kennedy were not drawing boats or other familiar emblems, they often talked about the art of boat building or topics in relation to the ocean. Their profound interest in that particular area could well have been attributed to their close proximity to the waters of the Caribbean Sea. As a matter of fact, their home was situated right on Bay Street, near the edges of the old Gros Islet sea wall. This alone accounted for a lot.

However, despite the great differences in what Ronnie and I liked academically, and what subjects George and Kennedy preferred, nothing could hinder our friendship. Ronnie, George, Kennedy, and I were a team, and that's how it would stay.

Our best moments together were always at about 10:30 each morning. This was by far the finest period of them all. Once we had stepped outside into the schoolyard, a few of the students would ignite the stillness of the yard with a loud cheer. Then gradually, like a tiny ripple on the water, the cheers would grow larger and louder until the whole yard exploded into the something like a street carnival.

I still can vividly recall the myriad band of students who chanted, pranced, and paraded within the confines of the yard. My God! This was a sight to see. For despite the fact that the words and chants were meaningless altogether, we all skipped concurrently to the "rhythm" of our own compositions.

Our chants were often composed of single lines, things that only a child could think of. And very soon we were singing "hit" songs that no radio station would ever play. The most popular of them all was one entitled "E Wish." Oh, how silly it felt to dance and prance to the chant of "E wish." But why would we care? As if it were only yesterday, I can still hear those mystifying words. They are ringing in my head with a deafening effect.

E WISH! E WISH! E WISH MAMA E WISH.

The Years Ahead

The passage of time in school would bring about greater changes in our lives, for not only were we a bit older and wiser, but there was also that common feeling that certain "childish" customs had to go. Soon, we did not think that it was either important or pleasurable to participate in the carnival-like atmosphere out in the schoolyard. Suddenly, we had lost complete interest in the "bacchanal," which had so expressively characterized our recreational period. Such pleasure, we were convinced, was better suited for rowdy little girls and boys, and most certainly not for older boys who felt like men.

At the sound of the bell each morning at about 10:30, George, Kennedy, Ronnie, and I would seek refuge under the shade of a Glory Cedar tree out in the schoolyard. It was situated in a far corner of the yard, directly behind a small shed, where peace and quiet were always abundant.

During those brief moments together, our conversations were largely of things pertaining to the ocean. They often included mysteries about ocean currents and the way they moved beneath the surface, to stories of sea devils (commonly referred to as "*Mon-day-Who*" in our local dialect).

It was always during those periods that George and Kennedy would prove to be among the greatest storytellers in matters of the sea, for unlike Ronnie and I, whose parents were not directly connected to the fishing industry, George and Kennedy's parents were very much a part of Gros Islet's largest means of economic survival: fishing.

Their father Elton, a career fisherman, had five brothers of the same profession. For many years, those six valorous men had faced the dangers of the sea, with seldom a concern for their safety. And now it seemed as though that knowledge and carefree attitude about the ocean was slowly being passed on to George and Kennedy. From an early age, it was very evident that one day the boys would follow in the footsteps of their father and uncles.

One morning an unexpected trip to the bathroom delayed our meeting for a few minutes. However, when I finally joined the boys in our usual spot under the Glory Cedar tree, I noticed how the shimmering sunlight fought to peek softly through its branches. It was a very lovely morning, and one in which it felt good to be alive.

George had just begun a new tale, and this one involved a pact between the famous *Mon-day-Who*—the sea devil—and an old fisherman who once lived in our town.

As the story goes, it was a cool and exceedingly dark Caribbean night. The moon and all the stars above had distanced themselves from our part of the earth. Occasionally, over the nearby Caribbean Sea, fireflies would illuminate the night. According to George, the lights weren't really those of fireflies, but of Caribbean witches who had made the waters their meeting place.

Strangely, on that night, the old fisherman decided that it was a perfect evening for fishing. After gearing himself with all the necessities for the fishing expedition, he quickly exited his home and headed for the shores.

As he walked through the lonely streets of our town, the loud barking of the dogs caught the interest of the town's people. In the clustered homes along the streets, curious residents lowered the mesh of their kerosene lamps before peeking through the tiny openings in the walls of their wooden homes.

Tonight was by no means the first time. On most nights they had watched him with guarded suspicion as he walked though the streets in the dead of the night. According to rumors, the old fisherman was in fact a wizard who had graduated with special honors among Gros Islet's finest sorcerers of his time. Those who knew him very well were never fooled by his simple appearance. In all sincerity, most of the townspeople feared him, for in those days, the common man would never have dared to mess with the sons or daughters of Beelzebub.

Later that night, after rowing his boat out to sea, he decided to cast his anchor at the precise point where the Caribbean Sea meets the Atlantic Ocean. In those strange and choppy waters, the mystique of ancient black magic would come alive.

As he sat quietly in the dark, he slowly reached into his pocket and pulled out a crystal bottle. The bottle had been filled with holy water from the fountain in the Gros Islet Catholic Church. He gently sprinkled the water around the boat, hoping that this ritual would yield something great.

Suddenly, there was a moment of turbulence in the waters around him as he summoned the sea devil to appear. Then, just as it seemed as though the waves would come rushing into his boat, the winds suddenly died down and there was a calm. In the darkness, a large shadowy figure had appeared on the left side of his boat. Face to face, the old fisherman and the *Mon-day-Who* had an open conversation, and a pact was made between the two.

The agreement was straightforward. Occasionally, the *Mon-day-Who* would deliver to him a boatload of fish in exchange for a white spotless chicken, or a living child whenever possible. However, should he ever renege upon his side of the bargain, he would lose his life at sea.

His regular contact with the *Mon-day-Who* soon became public knowledge in Gros Islet. On days when he returned ashore with a boatload of fishes, everyone knew that he had spoken with the *Mon-day-Who* that day.

In many homes throughout the town, there was a heightened feeling of anxiety and concern. Moreover, since everyone knew that the pact with the *Mon-day-Who* included giving a spotless chicken or a child in exchange for fish, they kept a watchful eye over their children. Throughout Gros Islet, children were cautioned to maintain a clear distance from the old fisherman. They were encouraged to return home as soon as it was sunset. A small group of community elders, who claimed to know a little about the art of sorcery, vowed to destroy the old fisherman. This went on for several months, but eventually the interest of the public waned.

It was by now almost two years into the pact, and still nothing significant had happened. Life in Gros Islet had returned to normal, or so the people thought.

It happened in the fiery month of July, when the northeast trade winds had quieted down and the sun scorched the land with an evil fury. This was also the commencement of the summer holidays, when all the children of Gros Islet had returned to the seashores. There, in the mystifying waters of the Caribbean Sea, the children had begun to savor countless days of swimming and fishing and building sand castles along the shores. Similar to previous years, the late December waves had come and gone, and had carried with them the many seashells and gravel-sized stones that the waves of September had stacked along our shores. It was summer now, and the seashells had returned. The soft, snow-white bed of sandy beaches meant that the children were going to have countless days of relaxation and fun.

Unfortunately, that summer would be interrupted by many strange activities in the waters and skies above Gros Islet. Occasionally, large patches of dark clouds would form a circle in the sky, and at times it almost seemed as though the portion of the sea the clouds had encircled would rage in a tempestuous motion. Normally, these activities would continue for a minute or two, and then suddenly the sun would appear from behind the dark clouds.

These very strange activities would continue throughout the summer. But coupled with all of those bizarre occurrences that had forced the children of Gros Islet to retreat from the shores was the fact that only one man dared to venture into the sea. He was purely demonic in all his activities, and had begun to take his only daughter out to sea.

Daily, as they cruised across the bay, the popular belief amongst the town people was that he would eventually offer his daughter as ransom to the *Mon-day-Who*. Some had even gone as far as to quietly accuse him of harboring evil sprits in his home, while others hoped that he might one day meet his end at sea.

To most people who had borne witness to these very weird circumstances, there was always the feeling that the truth would one day come to light. How long? No one could tell.

On the day that the *Mon-day-Who* finally came ashore, church bells rang throughout the entire town. At the Gros Islet Bay, where the townspeople had kept a quiet vigil for days, children gawked in total amazement as the grown-ups stood helplessly by.

The sudden ferocity with which the sea billowed caused the earth to quake beneath their feet. From a faraway distance across the sea, there were large patches of rain clouds hovering over the waters as throngs of sea birds took flight to sheltered places.

Amidst all of that stormy weather was the old fisherman. He was caught at sea and was struggling profusely with the billows and the undercurrents that held back his oars. To all whose eyes remained transfixed upon these rather strange occurrences, there was a feeling that he wouldn't survive the peril. It seemed certain that death was approaching, and it moved in pursuit of the fisherman.

As a crowd of people amassed along the shores, many watched in anticipation for what would occur next. But when it did, that moment would prove too much for some.

In a flash, the fisherman and his boat were tossed several feet into the air, then seemed to plummet in slow motion, hard upon the angry waves.

There was silence across the bay, as the impact of the fall had caused him to lose control of the oars. He had survived this one, but for how long?

The events that followed proved more frightening than before. The sea roared with added vengeance and swirled around the boat like a mighty whirlpool. The wild circular motion in the water was packed with jet streams, which rose high into the air with a punctuating effect. By then, it was clear to everyone what was beneath those jet streams. It was the *Mon-day-Who*, and it seemed to circle around in an effort to grab its prey.

A cry went out from the crowd as the incoming waves and rushing winds thrust the boat recklessly towards the shore. There was that sense of serious danger, as it seemed once again that the end had finally come for him. And so, as most in the crowd began to hold their breath in anticipation of the inevitable, they would be thoroughly surprised at what transpired next.

Amidst the towering jet streams and boisterous waves, the old fisherman began to undress. Soon he was tossing his shirt and undergarment into the sea.

A hush fell over the crowd of people, as suddenly the waters became calm and the whirlpool headed for the open seas. On that day, the old man outsmarted the sea devil. Legend has it that he never ventured into the sea again. Somewhere out there, where the pristine waters of the Caribbean Sea flow, the great *Mon-day-Who* still lies in wait for its prey!

A Crossroads in Our Lives

The year was 1973. Richard Nixon was sworn in as the 37th president of the United States, and ordered all U.S. troops to withdraw from Vietnam. Across the Atlantic, in good old England, Princess Anne and Captain Mark Phillips wed in London. Over in the United States, a blind musical genius named Stevie Wonder had done it again. He had produced a passionate ballad entitled "You are The Sunshine of My Life," which gave meaning to the joys of life in spite of its strains.

Here in the Caribbean, a new spirit of economic and political cooperation among the Caribbean states had led to the establishment of the Caribbean Community Market (Caricom). This was an exciting period, as the Rastafarian movement swept through the Caribbean and a deep Afro-centric consciousness in songs from Bob Marley and the Wailers burnt up the airwaves. The reggae classic "Stir it Up," from the album *Catch a Fire*, was by far the best.

For most of us, the year 1973 was not only one of hopeful renewal as we awaited the date of our First Communion, but it was also significant for reasons that pointed to the end of a very painful period in our lives.

The latter part of 1971 and most of 1972 held bitter memories for my friends and me. I was involved in a hit-and-run accident in which a crazy driver had left me for dead near a Texaco gas station. But one year later, in the summer of 1972, that very same driver would meet his death, as the steamroller on which he rode tipped over and crushed him to the ground.

That period of very sad experiences continued unabated. A few months after that tragic accident, we mourned the untimely passing of Mary "Christine" Evans, a classmate of ours.

To all of us whose lives she had touched, Christine was one of the most caring and unassuming students in the whole class. She was the daughter of a former schoolteacher (Lulu), who became a victim of alcohol consumption. For many years they had lived in the home of Lulu's mother, "Ma Door," in a remote part of Gros Islet called Derriere Labatwee. According to folklore, this area was once inhabited by evil sprits.

But what an extraordinary year '73 was turning out to be. The excitement over all the good things that were happening around the world, and especially the Caribbean, had given us reason to be thankful as young people. And so, as we prepared to face the new age of enlightenment and the opportunities it presented, we felt that the world was our domain.

Gros Islet and the rest of St. Lucia did not escape the rising tide of change in the Caribbean and around the world. And before long, what had begun as a quiet religious revolution years before, now had the trappings of a Protestant movement that was determined to challenge the teachings of the Roman Catholic Church.

Some had begun to openly challenge the religious doctrines of Roman Catholicism, dismissing such concepts as First Communion, Limbo, and Purgatory as teachings that were inconsistent with the Bible. For the first time ever, pocket copies of the New Testament were introduced into many homes, allowing families to explore the Bible firsthand.

Religiously each evening, Protestant preachers would gather on the street corners to proclaim what was termed "the good news of salvation." Those nightly religious crusades were not only interesting, but also had a marked difference from the dull and restrictive services in our church. The clapping of hands, guitars strumming loudly, and accordion music frolicking though the night air while "Christians" danced to melodic songs and choruses could never have been tolerated within the walls of the Catholic Church. Indeed, ours was a controlled environment where stillness was a virtue, and the only one with knowledge of the scriptures was the priest at the altar. Be it Seventh-Day Adventist, Baptist, or Pentecostal, there was always a common ending to those nightly crusades. The preacher would deliver a sermon and make an unpretentious appeal for new converts, while the rest of his following sang "Softly and Tenderly Jesus is Calling" in the background: "Come home, come home, ye who are weary come home."

It was very evident then that the brazen approaches of these "alien" spiritual organizations had stunned the local hierarchy of our Catholic Church. They seemed angry and lost as to how to handle the situation, and that annoyance soon manifested itself in the Sunday sermons.

It was a very difficult period for the Church, since it had never had to compete with any other religion for converts. In those days, not only did the people rely heavily on the Church's interpretation of the Bible without even having read it themselves, but many saw Catholicism as a national tradition.

Prior to 1973, the thought of reading the Bible was like an evil premonition. That period had played so much havoc exploiting the ignorance of a large number of people that you could not miss the popular beliefs, which seemed to suggest that reading the Bible could induce a state of insanity in those who were not authorized to do so.

For a growing number of supporters of the Bible, the religious myth associated with reading the Bible had finally been punctured. Contrary to earlier beliefs that studying the Bible would induce a state of derangement in its reader, there was now living proof that some had read it, and had remained strong in mind and will. Those very same people would go on to deliver hundreds of pocket-sized copies of the King James version to the homes of many people, enough to rock the Catholic establishment in our community.

Back in school, the growing resistance within the Catholic Church was astounding. It came in the form of an ultimatum, forbidding us from having any contacts with the "Christian" organizations. Any child who was caught reading "Christian" literature would be banned from the upcoming First Communion party. With this cessation of individual rights, it was clear that the church had not only won a significant victory, but also that it was well on its way to controlling the minds of its young subjects.

I must confess that the drastic measures adopted by the church not only piqued my curiosity, but also forced me to ponder deeply about the "dark and scandalous" concept of "Christianity." Since the term "Christian" in St. Lucia was often used to describe someone of a non-Catholic faith or denomination, it was evident to me that Catholics were not Christians.

The influences of the society at large did not help either, since from a very early age we were already being groomed to accept ignorance and bigotry. It was a society that demeaned women who had converted to "Christianity" by leading us to believe that they were hypocrites or *Vis yes* who often fornicated with the preacher or pastor.

Meanwhile, preparations for our First Communion were rigid. There were so many things to learn that at times many of us could not keep up. The constant emphasis was on forcing us to accept certain basic principles. The first rule of thumb was that Jesus had built the Catholic Church on a rock, and that rock was St. Peter, who was also the first Bishop of our Church.

In class, when the religious instructions were being taught, no one dared to share an opinion that was contrary to the Church's teachings. Moreover, since it was a great sense of pride and honor for a child to take his or her First Communion, it made no sense to say things that could have gotten one disbarred.

When Pope Paul VI was introduced to us in class, they made it very clear that he was the sole representative of God on Earth. He ruled from an ancient city called Rome and possessed great spiritual powers. In other words, though he was not God, there was something about him that demanded absolute respect and reverence for him.

I remember the feeling of astonishment that went through my entire being the first time I saw the Holy Father in a portrait hanging from a wall. Here was this white man looking directly down at me, with kindness and sanctity in his facial appearance.

My God! I thought to myself, if the Pope is white, and he is supposed to be the representative of God on earth, then Mother Theodore and our parish priest must have all descended directly from God. It was my general perception then that God was white, and Satan black.

And so, as I labored in vain to reconcile those stunning differences, I began to question weather being black had any virtue.

In reality, who could have blamed me for thinking that way when the early effigy of Satan, which the influences of Catholicism had embedded into our minds, was one of total darkness?

Even at the home of Auntie Fanso (an elderly and devoted Catholic woman who taught us to recite the Rosary), was a very sad and old portrait of Lucifer and his angels. In that portrait, Michael the archangel is depicted as light in complexion, and Lucifer and his angels are as dark as coal.

Then there were the other paintings, such as the famous portrait of Judgment Day, which bore a striking resemblance to the same archangel in Auntie Fanso's painting. This one appeared directly above a small altar in our church, and has continued to evoke a sense of dread. Amazingly, the artist who drew that painting decades ago had never taken into consideration that blacks might be eligible to enter Heaven. All those depicted in the portrait were of European descent, and they all stood before our great God with the express purpose of receiving a ticket into Heaven.

By late March of 1973, it was very clear that the Church might have succeeded in eradicating the creeping influence of "Christian doctrine" in our lives. We were halfway through the program that would lead us into receiving the Holy Eucharist, and no one could stop that. But no sooner had the religious problem been dealt with, than another one arose. Only this time, it had nothing to do with religion, but with the rights of parents to decide whether their children could participate in a newly established milk-feeding program.

Initially the program received broad acceptance from the community, but something would happen to change our parents' perception of it. There was an outbreak of diarrhea among the student population, and soon most of our parents began to attribute the ailment to the way in which the milk was being prepared. As Caribbean people, we weren't accustomed to drinking powdered milk that had been mixed with tap water without boiling. Everything, even milk, had to be warm. This wasn't how the program operated. Huge aluminum buckets were filled with water from a tap adjacent to the old convent and lined on a makeshift table in the yard. The powder was then deposited into the buckets, stirred with a wooden spoon until it had changed into a creamy substance, and served to us.

Back at home, although poverty was rampant throughout Gros Islet, any poor people (*Malaway*) exhibited a great sense of pride. The bottom line was that they'd prefer to serve their children bay leaf tea made from local leaves at home than subject them to this diarrhea-causing agent.

My parents, George and Kennedy's, and Ronnie's mom, along with countless others, were united in their stand. Individually, we were instructed to stay away from the lines, and we complied.

However, as the news got to Mother Theodore, she reacted angrily. It was obvious that she had grown so used to making decisions for other people's children that her pride was hurt.

Another part of the reason for her wounded pride is easily understood. She was part of a religious establishment with a history that displayed very little tolerance for dissent. Therefore, since she cared so deeply about the milk-feeding program, and felt that it was best for us, Mother Theodore was determined to impose her will on our parents. In her own narrow view of what was best for us, she must have felt that since the program had been sanctioned and financed by the United Nations to address starvation and malnutrition in Third World nations, parents should have been more appreciative of the program.

In reality, Mother Theodore was wrong, for while it was true that the ravages of civil war between Nigeria and its breakaway region of Biafra had plunged that African nation into starvation and famine, the same was not true of St. Lucia. We were poor, but not to the degree that we needed to be fed by the United Nations. Of course, there were many other kinds of assistance that we could have benefited from, but food was never our problem.

Disappointed but undaunted, Mother Theodore would show her resolve.

Children were rounded up from their classes, and forced into order lines out in the yard. Creating an atmosphere like a refugee camp was Mother Theodore's concept of acting in our best interest. The "milk," that white powered substance mixed with pure tap water, was good enough for us.

Usually, the petulant expressions on the faces of those students who had been served already gave the rest of us a nauseated feeling in our stomachs. It wasn't so much so the mixture that upset us, but those tiny dry particles of the powder that constantly floated up to the brim of our cups. They were awful-looking, and reminded us of the fresh vomit of newborn babes.

In time, and without any interference from our parents, we found a way to deal with the situation. The plan was to secretly scoop out the tiny particles of dry milk with a spoon, and add large quantities of sugar to our individual servings. As the news spread like wildfire among the student population, a growing number of other children happily joined the lines, much to the amazement of Mother Theodore.

George and Kennedy were the first to experiment with the new idea. Before leaving home for school, they would wrap small quantities of sugar into several pieces of brown paper and tuck them safely into their pockets. Soon, everyone followed suit, and before long, undetected raids on our mothers' sugar jars at home grew out of control.

Except for an occasional bout of diarrhea now and then, we were really living it up and having fun. Mother Theodore had won, but so had we!

Glory Days of Religion and Fun

The first time we fully understood the difference between Limbo and Purgatory we were out in the schoolyard. Limbo, we were told, was a place on the borders of Hell where some souls suffered for a while before going to heaven. Primarily, the souls that were received in Limbo were those of infants who had died before receiving the holy sacrament of baptism. In essence, because of the Original Sin which had been committed by Adam and Eve, not even infants would escape the wrath of God.

However, as these new and mind-boggling religious concepts continued to captivate our interest, a flood of questions would follow. Basically, the questions were not so much in regard to the concept of Hell because most of us were already acquainted with that phenomenon since way back in 1970. Rather, the questions had more do with what would become of us should we die now, since we were neither infants nor adults. Would we escape the wrath of God? And if not, what section of Hell would we occupy?

"Purgatory!" came the reply. "A place or state of temporary punishment." But unlike the concept of Limbo, where the period of penance for infants was shorter, God bless your soul if you ever got out of Purgatory within six months.

Personally, I pondered upon the meaning of Purgatory, and soon formulated my own opinion about it. To me, the concept of Purgatory was like a place where the souls of all sinners languish in near oblivion. Surely one would have to endure a lot of excruciating sufferings before he or she could achieve redemption into Paradise. As I pondered longer, I got the sense that the best definition for Purgatory was a place where all villains paid their dues to Lucifer.

On the Saturday that concluded that memorable week of religious studies, I made plans with George and Kennedy to meet at the seashore. Initially, we agreed to meet under a huge almond tree adjacent to the food and fish markets, but later decided against it. We would meet instead at the northern end of the bay, where a group of older boys were planning a roast made of breadfruit and salted pig snout.

As was the custom on Saturdays, the bay was flooded with children from as early as eleven that morning. In those days, there was very little pride in what was worn when going to the beach; people wore anything. In the absence of a good pair of swimming trunks, some of us had on ripped underpants, which often resembled a pair of giant eyes on either side of our buttocks. Whenever the breeze blew through those giant holes, our bare derrieres were always the first to feel its cooling effects. Usually, a girl who hadn't quite attained the age of puberty could be seen wearing gigantic grandmother panties up to her chest. Then there were the older teenage girls, who wore girdles and bras, and must have thought that they were putting the little girls to shame.

From a very short distance away I noticed the floating rafts out on the sea. The rafts, or *doe-rays* as we often referred to them in our local dialect, were carefully constructed out of either coconut or banana trunks. They were often bound together with strong rope and reinforced by several pieces of lightweight boards, which were fastened to the trunks to form the surface.

After I had walked briskly around the bay, I finally arrived at the meeting point where George and Kennedy, along with a few older boys, had gathered.

Among the older boys in the gathering was a fellow by name of Stanislaus Phulchere, who was also a very good friend of George and Kennedy. "Nourgearo," as everyone called him, was not related directly to me, but we shared the same uncle in the person of Mr. Bourbrun Phulchere. Also present was Augustine Joseph, better known to the residents of Gros Islet as "Cork-a-bet" or "one who lies with animals" in the English translation. True or not true, there were rumors in town that he had gained notoriety by having sexual relations with chickens, goats, pigs, cows, and several other creatures in the animal kingdom. Although Cork-a-bet never made any effort to disprove those vicious rumors, you could always tell that they affected him deeply. To those of us who knew him better, there were always suspicions, yet they were never enough to force us to end association with him.

Between Nourgearo and Cork-a-bet, they had assembled two huge pieces of rock, between which the breadfruit and salted pig snout would be roasted. But first, before the fire could be started, we were entrusted with the task of assembling large quantities of dry wood.

We ventured deep into a swampy and wooded area nearby and gathered a quantity of sticks and coconut palms, which were chopped and placed neatly between the rocks. Nourgearo then proceeded to make a padded ball out of dry coconut fiber, placed it carefully among the sticks, doused it with kerosene, and lit a match to it.

He waited a moment in anticipation but the fiber ball did not ignite. Sensing the temporary absence of the northeast trade winds, which commonly blew across the bay, Nourgearo lit another match, which finally set the fireball blazing into glory.

Excited about what had just transpired, we all retreated to a safe distance, leaving Nourgearo there alone to attend to the fire. The breadfruit were later gathered, placed on the heap of burning sticks, and covered with the dry coconut palms.

Back at the area to which we had retreated, the burning rays of the midday sun beat furiously upon our naked backs. Nourgearo had joined us by then, but would occasionally return to the fire to inspect the breadfruit with a wooden stake. He was always good at that, and it seemed that with time, he had gained an immeasurable amount of experience in roasting breadfruit. Often, the swiftness with which he rotated the breadfruit in the fire gave us the impression that his eyes had never left the fire.

To most of us, Nourgearo knew everything about the nuts and bolts of setting a fire, including the art of roasting breadfruit and pork. His intuition about how much fire was needed, or when a breadfruit was good enough, was always on target. As a result, he was crowned with a title whose literal translation is the King of Roast.

His final trip to inspect the breadfruit was memorable. It was as though he had received the gift of telepathy, which had taught him how to communicate with the breadfruit. In a kind of show-off fashion, with a screwy grin and his eyes bulging out of their sockets, he quickly scooped the breadfruit from the fire and onto the sand. He then spread a couple of fresh banana leaves over the sand, and used the wooden stake to gently roll them onto the leaves.

As we all waited, Nicholas Montoute, alias "Go Cho-Low," a relative of mine, had assumed the responsibility for roasting the salted pig snout. He had spent the last hour cleaning and slicing the meat into pieces. All that was left to do now was to deposit the pieces into an old black pot next to the fire.

Quietly, as he added a bit of oil into the pot, we all watched with eagerness. The pot was then lifted off the sand and placed onto the fire.

Over in the area where Nourgearo was tending to the breadfruit, Cork-a-bet had walked over to assist him. In a flash, he pulled out a rusty old dagger from his pocket, and held it firmly in the air.

There was a gasp of silence, and not an eyeball shifted. As our hearts began to race, the sight of Cork-a-bet with a dagger in his hands drove crazy thoughts through our heads.

Our reaction then was not only justified, but it was the only way we could have reacted. In those days, since good boys never carried weapons upon them, those who did always carried the stigma of vagabonds with criminal intentions. In the case of Cork-a-bet, while there were always speculations that he might have taken advantage of the animals, this young man had never assaulted another human being in his life. Aside from the mischievous disposition that gave others the chills whenever they saw him, he was a wayward but kind individual. A few moments passed, and soon most of us got over the initial shock. Cork-a-bet had not done anything unusual with the dagger, except to offer Nourgearo some help. The two took turns scraping the dark outer layer of the breadfruit until they looked almost brownish in appearance.

Near the flames, which rose steadily between the pillars of rocks, Cho-low was still very busy attending to the pot. He eventually removed the pot from the fire and gently set it on the sand. When it simmered down to his satisfaction, he took it over to where Nourgearo and Cork-a-bet were waiting.

We gathered around the banana leaves on the ground, in anticipation of our share of the roast. Cork-a-bet, still holding the dagger, was given the responsibility of testing the breadfruit.

With calm and accurate precision, he thrust the dagger through one of the breadfruit, and withdrew it slowly as if he had just slaughtered his prey. Cho-Low belted out a deep chuckle, and soon there were smiles on all of our faces.

Through the tiny opening in the breadfruit, a mouth-watering aroma rose steadily into the atmosphere, causing our stomachs to burn with hunger. It would soon be time to partake of the roast.

As was customary whenever older and younger boys gathered together for a roast, the older boys received the largest portion. Nourgearo sliced two of the largest breadfruit into four halves, securing one each for himself, Cork-a-bet, Cho-Low, and another fellow by the name of Kenny, alias "Lubar."

The remaining breadfruit were evenly divided among us younger boys, each receiving one quarter of the roast. Nourgearo then selected the choicest parts of the salted pig snout in the pot, leaving the rest of us at the mercy of Cork-a-bet, Cho-Low, and Lubar. They had each spread some oil and pig snout on their portion of breadfruit, forcing the rest of us to scout like Oliver Twist in an almost empty pot.

That would suffice, as we knew better than to complain. After we had satisfied our hunger, we all retreated into the nearby Caribbean Sea for a swim and an afternoon of aquatic pleasure.

The Holy Eucharist Cometh (Part I)

On Sundays, George, Kennedy, Ronnie, and I always sat in the front pew for the morning mass. The sacristan, Auntie Leo Lawrence (may she rest in peace), was always working alone at the altar prior to mass.

A dead silence would occupy the vacuum in the church as the early Sunday morning blusters blew directly through the open windows. Through the side entrances, the old but faithful ones would always trickle in. Strangely, but not at all atypically, some of those older folks had already attended the earlier mass.

Behind the pulpit stood a thick large curtain. It looked old and rugged. Time had drained it of its rich red luster, a reminder of the many decades that had passed since it was first hung. Right above the curtain was a fabulous portrait that depicted Jesus of Nazareth and his father Joseph working together.

Unlike any other Sunday, today is a very special one. We are exactly a week away from receiving the Holy Eucharist and all the rites that go with taking one's First Communion.

There are lots of fresh flowers at the altar, and the candleholders shine. Any minute now, the acolytes and priest will appear. They will be coming from directly behind that big ugly curtain, into the open where the entire congregation will rise to greet them.

It's been a few Sundays since I last heard the familiar voices of Mr. Farno Verdant, Ms. Mimi Ambrose, Ms. T-Phume and Uncle "Willow" Bravely Lucien coming from the choir upstairs. I really don't know why, but lately we are forced to listen to a young choir singing a mediocre version of the Negro Spiritual entitled "Lord I Am Blind."

Mr. John "Doso" Joseph, the church organist, must be feeling very lonely up there without the older folks. Unquestionably, he belongs in the same category as Mr. Farno Verdant and company. You've got to hear them together, especially when Ms. Mimi leads the choir in song, supported by Mr. Farno's deep, rumbling, and operatic voice.

I am seated near the middle aisle, and beside me are George, Kennedy, and Ronnie. We are all dressed like Steve Urkel from TV's *Family Matters*. Minus the glasses and suspenders, we are wearing those very tight, three-quarter-length trousers, with polished moccasins to match. As a matter of fact, the townspeople have a special name for those types of trousers. They are called "*see-my-zego*" or "*chee chit booye*" because of their resemblance to the barrel of a short gun. If any one was caught walking down the streets wearing *chee chit booye*, he would soon become a target for jokes. The other children would mockingly run for cover behind the street lamps and shout, "*chee chit booye, booye booye.*"

Those were awful-looking pants, symbols of an era gone by. Although they had been outdated by the new and incoming fashion of wide bottoms, our parents still regarded them as among the best in our small collection of clothes.

Seen in profile, I can't help but smile at those goofy-looking haircuts that some of the other boys in church have. Those haircuts are neither a testimony nor an inspiration to the newest fashions of our times. They look nothing like those tall, clean, jet-black Afros some of the older boys have. And, of course, although most of us would love to sport a mountaintop Afro like the trendsetters in our town (such as Pairsheen, Barabas, and Super Fly), neither our parents nor our school would allow it. To put it mildly, our haircuts resemble landing strips, the work of a no-nonsense barber.

I am cracking up inside, as more and more of these silly thoughts continue to flood my mind. I am also aware that I've got to be careful that no one sees me, but it's very difficult to stop myself. Often those types of haircuts were the trademark of the town's two oldest barbers, Mr. Simon and Mr. Lay-Lay. But one could always differentiate their work from that of others based on the rough edges around the ear. I know from experience, because I have been a recipient of those crazy hairdos, which were often referred to as *"pee-pee-rit."* It was because of those curtain-cutting scissors, the ones often used on dress patterns and hedges outside. Oh, how moms used to work them through our hair like a lawn mower on grass.

The Sunday mass is about to begin, and as a Catholic boy, I know better than to continue with these silly thoughts. Besides, distracting George, Kennedy, Ronnie, and the other children around us is the last thing I would ever want to do. There are severe consequences for "unholy" behavior, and a black Catholic child ought to think of those things beforehand. Occasionally, the officiating priest, in the middle of the mass, will head straight to the area where he might have perceived a disturbance. Guilty children are slapped across the face and forced to kneel at the altar for the duration of the mass.

Surprisingly, not a single parent has the courage to speak out against the physical abuse of their children by these white clerics. They have power over our parents and us, and they exercise it with impunity. Although I have never fully understood whether their actions were born out of racism, I always found this grand old tradition of abuse to be unacceptable to me as a child.

This morning, the officiating cleric is this young fellow from France. His name is Father "H," the reverend father I suppose. Father "H" is the newly appointed successor to the deceased Father Andre Hermouet, another French cleric like himself.

However, unlike Father Andre Hermouet, who had developed a large and protruding wine belly, Father "H" is symmetrical in appearance, and bears the enchanting features of a European male model in a magazine. He has a full head of curly hair, not a single sign of baldness, and the bluest pair of eyes, which could easily knock a woman off her feet.

Currently, his playboy features are not a distraction, as Father "H" has already demonstrated some early signs that he is sincere and may show tolerance for children. But you can never tell. Like his predecessors, once he gets to know Gros Islet, all of this may change one day.

I guess my pessimistic inklings are somehow rooted deeply in the past. I am referring to the handful of church gossips, the so-called religious elite, who always feel that it's their responsibility to tell a priest about the private lives of other worshipers. Funny, their own lives are no better, for they are riddled with the many half-truths that will be told to Father "H" in the confession box. Like a trashy stereo system that plays a broken record of gossip, one of those informers will inform on the rest.

I realize that I have to overcome this temporary lapse of religious pessimism. Besides, what business is it of mine if some chose to betray and sell out their community for the sake of petty recognition?

My mind is now refocused on the mass, and in true Catholic tradition, we go through the Penitential rite of "I confess to almighty God…," the Gloria and opening prayer, and the liturgy of the Word. The first and second readings are to follow.

As usual, a spellbound silence falls over the entire congregation as that moment arrives. The first reader, a congenial-looking schoolteacher from a quarter of Gros Islet called Grande Riviere, makes her way to the pulpit.

I don't think that I've ever seen her up there before, and there is something about her that draws my attention. This moment in church is also important, for it does allow some of the critics in the congregation to quietly pass judgment on what others are wearing, as well as their ability to read.

She draws near the microphone, and my heart leaps out of its cavity. The soft eloquence in her pronunciation of the words mirrors the beauty of the scriptural passage. She has made us all proud, and by the smiles on the faces of George and Kennedy, I know they feel the same way too.

As a rule, good readers and other academic achievers from our immediate community and its environs have always lifted our pride as a people. Moreover, with the ongoing rivalry between the people of Gros Islet and the people of St. Lucia's capital city of Castries, it is always a great joy to showcase a reader who is not overly accented, and is not excessive in their pronunciation of the words in the English Language.

We Gros Islians have a certain inferiority complex in relation to the people of Castries, St. Lucia's capital city. To them, our indulgence and love for St. Lucia's local dialect, called "Patois," places us in the category of "country bookies." Everyone is aware of this, and there are ongoing efforts to prove them wrong.

My attention is drawn once again to the pulpit, and I watch with glee as the reader gracefully descends the pulpit steps. Another reader has made her way to the altar for the second reading, but I am still interested in the first reader, who heads into the congregation.

Later that morning, as we go through the gospel and the homily, which is the open affirmation of loyalty to the Roman Catholic church, there seems to be much sincerity in what is being recited. "We believe in one God, the father, the Almighty, maker of Heaven and Earth, of all that is seen and unseen...we believe in the one holy Catholic and apostolic church...Amen."

A hush falls over the congregation as the last sounds of "Amen" drown in the air. Then, quietly, the ushers make their way to the back of the congregation to commence the offertory. Soft scuffles are heard throughout the congregation, as most of us dip into our little pockets in search of the offerings our parents gave us earlier. Rarely does anyone miss this moment, for it is perhaps the only time during the Mass that children feel free to quietly chitchat without fear of retribution.

Mind you, our contributions are small in comparison to the many stuffed white envelopes, which are visible in the baskets. *Mucho dinero* are the offerings of the proud, affluent folks who love to sit cross-legged in certain areas where they can be seen. I am sure they believe with all their hearts that their money will be able to secure a place for them in the kingdom of God.

As the ushers slowly approach our pew, those big round copper pennies of ours, the ones with the emblem of the Queen of England on one side of the coin and vines on the other, sink with a clamor to the bottom of the baskets. Like always, you could never miss them. Those clamoring sounds are always evidence of a poor man's contribution.

The ushers have just left, and they continue towards the altar. Once again, the youthful choir upstairs is having an awful time making sweet-sounding melodies out of this latest rendition.

With the ushers having finally approached the altar, the choir takes a much-needed rest. The collection baskets are handed over to a single usher, who takes the short walk up to the altar and lays them down.

"Blessed are you, Lord, God of all creation," says Father "H."

"Blessed be God forever," comes the response from the entire congregation.

My thoughts begin to wander again, and soon I find it almost impossible to keep my eyes affixed upon the altar. I guess I'm a bit confused by the habits that have become a kind of tradition in our church, and the way in which everyone simply falls in line in the recitation of repetitious lines that have by now lost their meaning. Apart from the homily, which fleetingly reminds us of the affirmation of loyalty to the Church, every other ritual of the Mass is observed without a clear sense or meaning as to why we do them. It is also clear that not too many grown-ups in the church know either. Often, it is easy to catch them reciting mere words, or giving lip service to God in church. Indeed, you couldn't miss the fact that most of those grown-ups conform to religious ignorance. As a child, it is almost impossible to escape the humorous thoughts that come with those cryptic religious practices, especially those requiem masses that are conducted in Latin. In fact, it is always an amazing sight to see how some of the old folks participate in those masses. They are used to repeating words in Latin, without the slightest idea of whether they are praising or cursing God. I guess that's how it's been, "*eso egoism, Keri Asome, domino bobisco,*" under the influence of a foreign religious power in Rome, on a distant, tropical island called St. Lucia.

I'm drawn back to the service as we offer each other the sign of peace. Willingly, I reach out to my friends, and they to me. From across the aisle, a few of the children and grown-ups alike have left their seats to extend well wishes to other members of the congregation. This is another part of the Mass that we love, for it is always a moment of great joy.

The cheerful smiles on the faces of most people as they either embrace or simply shake each other's hands, are about the closest thing to peace that you will ever see among some neighbors. As a rule, some hold enmity towards each other that often exists outside the church.

As the Mass moves into one of its most sacred stages, I catch a glimpse of the acolytes as they leave their seats and head to the front part of the altar. They each bow reverently, and proceed to kneel with their backs towards the congregation. Among the lot is a chubby-looking acolyte who goes by the nickname "Boom Boom" or "Ba-ba-lew." Like all the others, he is wearing an ultra-red cassock with a snow-white gown called a "*siply,*" or surplice, thrown over it.

Lately, he has become the most popular acolyte in the church. All of the children love him because of his name, and because we have included his mother's name into this particular song in church. I've often referred to this song as the "The Chorus of Unholy Pleasure." No one except we the children knew about it. We have never used the exact words in the official church hymnal, which makes this whole thing overly silly.

The Holy Eucharist Cometh (Part I)

Ba-ba-lew's mother, Ms. Fidelita Lord, a.k.a. "Ms. Fiday," a prominent restaurant owner in our community, is a devoted Catholic with a controversial side to her. She is an ardent advocate of the use of condoms, which she sells in her restaurant, and she doesn't care much that her social views are in conflict with the procreation views of the Church.

Since her crusade, the sale of condoms—or "Frenchies," as they are called locally—are on the rise. The church has condemned the sale of condoms, but Ms. Fiday continues to enjoy the support of the government, which has encouraged people like her to sell the things.

That concept, I think, is called "family planning," or so we've heard from the older boys on the streets. This subject is taboo, and not a thing for children. However, although we are not so knowledgeable in the concept of family planning, we are all confident of one thing. This controversial but fascinating little rubber toy which the older boys treasure so much, are to us simply balloons which can be blown into giant sizes. We all love to chase these mammoth balloons out in the streets, and it's always a pleasure to see them fly high in the sky like a kite.

I realize that my attention is slipping away from the Mass, and I feel the need to be more attentive. Back at the altar, as the priest finally breaks the bread, we are deeply moved not so much so by the trappings of this religious ritual, but for its symbolic meaning as the "Body of Christ."

Currently, George, Kennedy, Ronnie, and I, among others, are unable to partake of the "Body of Christ," but there is much hope that by this time next Sunday, we will have attained eligibility to receive the Holy Eucharist.

There is a moment of total silence, as the priest hoists the white, smooth, and full-moon-shaped "Body of Christ" high above the altar for all to see. Immediately, and in keeping with the ritual of the Mass, the sound of a bell rings out from the area around the altar.

For a moment, I keep my eyes fixated on the Body of Christ, and even envisage what it would feel like to take a bite out of that mysterious-looking bread. I soon lose my focus, and before long, my thoughts are drifting again to some of the silliest things imaginable.

I am thinking of this little old lady called Madeline, and her son Andrew Emanuel, who live in a small room in the presbytery nearby. Ms. Madeline, who served for many years as the housekeeper to the late Father Andre Hermouet, has been retained by the newly appointed Father "H."

The joke among the children is that she always bakes the finest "Body of Christ" whenever she is disappointed by her son's behavior. Poor Andrew has a lot to contend with. His mom hardly ever allows him to play out in the streets with the other boys, which makes him the butt of some of the cruelest jokes in town. Father Andre Hermouet, the proud owner of two huge Alsatian dogs, entrusted them into the care of Andrew. The creatures are often let loose in the yard, leading the town's children to conclude that these are about the only friends that Andrew really has. They will tease him so mercilessly that it often pains the heart.

Back at the altar, the priest has concluded the breaking of the bread, and has moved on to offer further thanks by commemorating the Blood of Christ in a golden chalice. But even as those sacred rites are being performed, I find myself drifting deeper and deeper into mischief. I am unable to feel sanctity inside, and not even George, who is closest to me, has detected this.

If the accounts are true, then that chalice is filled to the brim with plenty of red wine. It is imported from a special vineyard in France, the same kind of intoxicating stuff that, over a period of time, caused the abdomen of Father Andre Hermouet to swell.

I guess that Father "H" must be very careful if he is to avoid going down the same path as his predecessors. Right now, he has curly hair upon his head, and has a symmetrical figure that is evidence of his youthfulness. But I guarantee, after a few years of drinking that stuff, that there will be nothing symmetrical about his physical appearance, and those deep blue eyes of his will go red. I've always wondered why fermented grapes produce layers of thick and bulging red blood vessels, but I will have to wait my turn to find out.

As the remembrance celebration of the life of Christ continues upon the altar, I find myself desperately trying to retain focus, but cannot ward off the immense magnetism of distraction. As I allow my mind to wander, I occasionally glance over to look at both George and Kennedy, who unlike me seem very attentive.

God knows that I mean no disrespect at all, as it was never my intention to lose it like this. But then, how am I supposed to remain attentive when there are so many things around me that remain questionable? There is a vacuum, this great vacuum of religious secrecy, which always seems to elude me. I've always feared that one day it might swallow me whole.

Later, as the priest makes his way down the altar, my thoughts are drawn to the polished steps, which glow without a tint. They are made of pure marble, and I can tell that Father "H" sees a reflection of himself in them. It is a nice job. But the praise actually belongs to Auntie Leo Lawrence, and a few of her helpers from the Legion of Mary.

Father "H" may not know this, but those marble steps are from the contributions of many who had since died in extreme poverty, after donating all of their land and money to the Church. In fact, I have at times wished that someone would tell him about the sacrifices that were made, and about the many lives that were affected, instead of feeding him the gossip about the private lives of fellow parishioners. Maybe they can begin by telling him the story of Mr. Sylves, and how his mother had left her only son to languish as a pauper, after giving her property and all her money to the effort of constructing the Church. Sadly, today he lives in an old rundown shack on Notre Dame Street, which is also home to countless bats and mice. His only legitimate property on earth is an aged and malnourished dog, which follows him like a bodyguard around town.

Father "H" has now completed his descent, and is heading in the direction of a sacred shrine in the far right-hand corner of the church. There is a big statue of the Virgin Mary nearby, and above the shrine is a reproduction of Michaelangelo's famous portrait of Judgment Day.

Deep inside that shrine lies a secret, which only Father "H" and the parishioners know about. The "Body of Christ" is hidden in there, and it is in the form of hundreds of miniature versions of the bread that Father "H" has just eaten on the altar. They're all stacked up in another golden chalice, which has an inscription of the crucifix on the lid. The chalice and its contents are kept secured day and night under lock and key.

From the choir upstairs comes another rendition. It's "The Chorus of Unholy Pleasure," which includes the names of Baba-lew and Ms. Fidelity his mother, and an old acolyte named Burdick, a man we call "CaCa Lustee," who never seems able to outgrow "acolyte-hood."

The choir is busy singing the correct words to the song: "Sons of God, hear his holy word, gather round the table of the Lord," while we interject with "This is Burdick drinking wine, and we sing a song of joy, Ba-ba-lew! Ba-ba-lew! Ba-ba-lew Fidelity," as opposed to the church's version of "Allelu, Allelu, Alleluia!"

There is an undeclared rivalry between us and the choir upstairs, which has drowned our voices with the aid of the organ. Throughout the church, many people have begun to quietly line up to partake of the Holy Eucharist, and it is just a sight to see.

The majority have expressions of absolute seriousness on their faces. Of course, this is not at all atypical of loyal Catholics who are on their way to receive the Holy Eucharist. There are also those narcissistic-looking folks among the faithful, who have simply joined the lines with the express purpose of drawing attention to themselves.

Look at them now as they move towards the lines. Their walk is so well rehearsed, which gives me the impression that they might soon be off to a Miss Universe pageant. Some are wearing high heels, or *tick-ki-tocks*, as they are commonly referred to locally. And most of those *tick-ki-tocks* arrived in a concealed barrel from a relative or friend in either England or America. I am chuckling inside, which prompts George to ask what is so funny, but I refuse to tell him. In fact, I am so fascinated by the sight of the some of the women having difficulties walking with those *tick-ki-tocks* that I am about to die. Some of the dresses are also fascinating. They are those "one size fits all" garments, which either fit snugly and awkwardly on the heavyset ladies or have simply swallowed their new owners.

Returning my attention to the lines, I watch as more and more people continue to join in. It's going to be a daunting task for Father "H," I can tell that right now. He is standing near the middle aisle, with two acolytes in position. One is to his left, and the other to his right.

This is about the closest that I have ever been to Father "H" since his arrival here from France. Like all the other boys and girls, I can't help but stare directly at the Holy Father with great curiosity and fascination.

Mind you, he doesn't even seem to notice us, yet we idolize this complete stranger. Why should he anyway, when there are countless people with outstretched tongues before him? They are coming up to him in droves, and as quickly as one departs, another appears. Father "H," it seems, does have his work cut out for him today.

That moment lingers on with same repetitious actions of out-stretched tongues, and Father "H" carefully placing bread in the mouths of the faithful. But occasionally, that cycle is broken by "the wise" and not so humble, who prefer having the bread placed into the palms of their hands.

Among "the wise" is a very old woman who stands on the line with a pink and purple mushware (head-band) over her head. She is barefoot and seems to walk in a state of absolute mystical absorption. By this time, I'm not the only one who is distracted; so are George, Kennedy, Ronnie, and countless other children who know her quite well. In fact, the whole church knows about her, and what we know is not pretty at all. Today, in the house of the Lord, and in broad daylight, this proxy of the Devil is at work.

As she approaches the priest, he reluctantly deposits the bread into her outstretched hands. *Ah ha!* I think to myself, *some-one must have already informed Father "H" about her.* Slowly, she walks away, but she makes a stop at the statue of the Virgin

Mary. She kneels there in "prayer" while carefully wrapping the bread in a handkerchief.

From the choir upstairs, the reverberations of the organ rage on, and it almost feels as though bolts of lightning are descending upon the congregation. The choir is still singing "The Chorus of Unholy Pleasure," and so are we!

By now, the Communion lines are dwindling, but still the choir lingers on. In fact, there are just about eight or ten people left on the lines, which has prompted a concealed sigh of relief from Father "H."

Thus far, despite of my profound state of mental distraction, I have been very good. I have restrained myself to the point that not even George, Kennedy, or Ronnie are aware of the intense distraction that I have gone through. Apart from the sighting of the woman with the pink and purple mushware, and the "Chorus of Unholy Pleasure" that is still being sung, my state of mind has returned to normal. I dare not even tell them about the other thoughts that I have had with regards to some of the practices of the church, and will continue to keep it a secret.

Between the four of us, it is I who have questioned some of the religious practices of the church the most. I am not certain why I do, and no matter how hard I have tried, I've always found it difficult to feel totally devoted. I sometimes feel very guilty, but the level of guilt has never been enough to overcome the quiet resistance inside. Moreover, at my age, while I've never had a desire for any other religion, there is something that just isn't right.

Over at the statue of the Blessed Virgin Mary, the woman in the pink and purple mushware is still kneeling there. She remains in a state of near inertia, and seems unaware of the things that are happening around her. I guess the rule that defines paying homage to God is different from that of Satan.

That problem has always existed in certain quarters of our society, and it dates back to the days of slavery, when a blurry line separated religion from the occult. For while it is true today that the majority of our people have held fast to godly teachings, there are those who just can't seem to let go of the old tradition of mixing religion with black magic. As the natural cycles of sickness, death, and personal misfortune occur, these are often interpreted as "*Mal*" (an evil spell), from which only the Devil can offer protection.

Sadly, the woman in the pink and purple head tie is a prime example of one who sort of believes in God, but prefers being an agent of the Devil. There, in front of the statue, her lips are moving, but her eyes have turned to glass. They are as wide as those of an owl, as she supposedly pleads with the statue for deliverance from evil.

No one is deceived, as we all know very well that all she wants is more power to traumatize the innocent. I know from experience, for my friends and I almost became victims of her Satanic influences. With my own eyes, I have seen this living vampire at work.

Long before all of those evil things about her had come to light, she was actually a friend of ours, or so we thought. Every Sunday before the morning Mass, or whenever we were out walking on the streets, she would creep up on us and playfully rub her hands through our hair. At first, it really didn't seem odd that a woman of her age would consistently choose to behave as a child among children. But as word of her conniving and diabolical behavior got around, and the motives behind those vices (which were specifically aimed at retarding our ability to learn in school, and to perhaps cause us to amount to nothing in life), became widely understood, we made a mad dash to escape her.

Over, at the Communion lines, there is one person left. Father "H" offers the last serving of the Body of Christ, and heads once again to the sacred shine. As he makes his way though the narrow passage between the statue of Mary and a large pillar near the shrine, he does not pay any attention to the woman in the pink and purple mushware. The priest simply returns the golden chalice into the oven-like edifice, bows, and proceeds to walk back to the main altar.

Interestingly, just as he makes his way again between the statue and the pillar, she suddenly rises up to her feet, makes the sign of the cross, and begins walking back to her seat with the same aura of mysticism as when she first joined the Communion lines. Frankly, I don't know why the church has allowed those strange practices to proceed for so long, and why it has not insisted that the Body of Christ be consumed in the church, instead of being taken home for diabolical purposes. These satanic rituals are against the teachings of the church, but they have continued to this day.

All is well, as Satan looks proudly upon her with a smile. Once again, the two of them have succeeded in desecrating the house of the Lord. Strange, but not uncommon; it has always been a practice for God and Satan to do battle in this place. If you listen very carefully, you may even hear them in the rustling winds, and in the silence which grips the soul.

I am finally relieved of this appalling episode of religious acrimony as Father "H" finally takes his place behind the altar. As is customary at the end of each Communion service, Father "H" joins the ranks of his predecessors by taking a gulp of the old wine again. Only this time, it is diluted with water from a crystal decanter. The crumbs of bread which had fallen from the mouths of the worshippers and into the saucers of the acolytes, are also deposited into the chalice of water and wine.

It would only take a second, and before anyone could blink an eye, Father "H" has concluded his drinking. And in a scene reminiscent of a naughty child who has stolen a cookie from the cookie jar, he quietly wipes his mouth with a clean white towel, and places it gently over the chalice.

There is a brief silence at the altar, which signals the climax of the Mass. Father "H" slowly flips through the pages of a big book upon the altar and draws the microphone closer to him.

Father "H": THE LORD BE WITH YOU.
Response: AND ALSO WITH YOU.
Father "H": MAY ALMIGHTY GOD BLESS YOU, THE FATHER, THE SON, AND HOLY SPRIT.
Response: AMEN.
Father "H": THE MASS IS ENDED, GO IN PEACE.
Response: THANKS BE TO GOD.

The Holy Eucharist Cometh (Part II)

On the Sunday when we finally received the Holy Eucharist, it was as though the limited boundaries of our lives had suddenly found additional dimensions. That morning was not only fit for the coronation of a king or queen, but it was enhanced by the impeccable chimes of the church bells, which were heard throughout the town. The church was filled to capacity, overflowing to the outside with worshipers who had completely blocked the front exits.

This was the happiest day of our lives, and also a defining moment. As Catholics, in keeping with the principles of the Roman Catholic Church, we had arrived at the state of maturity in God's eyes, and we were old enough to renew the covenant of baptism.

Almost eight years before, our godparents (or sponsors, as they are known in the church) had interceded with God on our behalf. Thus God had granted to us a conditional pardon for the original sin committed by both Adam and Eve, until such time as we could represent ourselves.

Unlike the Sunday before, when I was gripped with quiet disobedience, I found it easier to contemplate holy things. Aided by the seriousness with which everyone regarded making one's First Communion, I had conditioned myself to feel the presence of the Lord in our midst.

A long silence fell over the congregation when it was our turn to join the Communion lines. It was our show, and unlike the many Sundays before, when we had been reduced to spectator status, it was the older people's turn to watch us was we walked by, accompanied by our sponsors.

Never before had I felt a greater sense of vindication and triumph over sin than at this special moment. In fact, given this pure state of mind that I was now in, not even the woman in the pink and purple mushware could have distracted me, if she'd cared to join the lines in defiance of the rules. By the time the choir and the congregation joined us in signing a hymn of triumph over sin, most of us had bottled up so much emotion that it felt as though a knife was cutting through our guts.

"Long ago I made a faithful solemn vow, but my sponsors— they lent their voice. The victory is won, and I do this of my own free choice."

Followed by the chorus:

"I renew all my promises now…and I do this of my own free choice."

As the procession made its way slowly down the aisles, I hardly gave any thought to my friends, who I was certain were somewhere in those lines. I guess with everyone paying so much attention to what their sponsors were busy whispering in their ear, this simply wasn't a time for boyish games.

My own acceptance of the Holy Eucharist was marked by total relief and inner jubilation. Father "H" slowly placed the bread upon my outstretched tongue, and before I could fully understand what had just transpired, I felt a light tap on my shoulders.

It was my godmother, Ms. Gerona "Amore" Ignatius, who was signaling me to move on. Slowly, we both headed back to our seats, where I knelt quietly in prayer.

Later, as the Mass concluded, we received lots of congratulatory wishes from our godparents, family, and friends who had attended. The mood was even more pleasing as some of us descended from the front steps of the church and went into the public square for a photo opportunity. Outside, the church bells rang in unison, in celebration and recognition of our special day.

Neither George nor Kennedy nor Ronnie were present at the public square. Therefore, I missed an early chance to chat a bit with them about the morning's proceedings. The closest I had been to them in church was two rows away. Our schoolteachers had approved this arrangement, for reasons that weren't quite clear.

The photo session would last no more than twenty minutes. Before long I was back at home, ready to enjoy the traditional First Communion soup. It was made from a mixture of fresh pumpkin and carrots, Irish potatoes, chopped beef, macaroni, chives, garlic, onions, butter, and a little salt to spice up the flavor.

That afternoon, as we gathered around a neatly set table with other members of my family, my mouth watered at the sight of the icing on the cake in the middle of the table. I knew that I would have to wait to have some, and nothing could change that fact.

Some of the grown-ups among us celebrated with a little wine, while filling my glass up to the brim with water. It wasn't funny at all, but what could I say?

By nightfall, since it was the tradition of the day to indulge in much larger festivities, many more family members and friends had gathered at our house. I was not permitted to participate, and would remain confined to my room for the rest of the evening.

Of course, this really wasn't what my mother would have chosen. However, she was bound to the oath of religious tradition, and wanted to be obedient like all other Catholics. Those values, although a gross misinterpretation of the Bible, may well have been the dictates of the earliest church on the island, since up until the early 1970s, many St. Lucians had never read the Bible. In fact, children who had just received the Holy Eucharist could not participate in any form of merriment. It was a sin, and any child who committed it risked losing his or her "Absolution."

A prime example of how the people adhered to those strict religious traditions was evident on the Friday and Saturday preceding the Sunday celebrations. On each of those days, after we had spent a total of five hours at the retreat in church, we were never permitted to play out on the streets, or to see the light of day once we had arrived home.

For most of us, those were not only excessively long and difficult days, but it also tested our patience as children. We were also prohibited from bathing in the sea, and forced to obey a number of other unwritten rules, such as not listening to music on the radio, and not dancing or participating in any activities that might appear to be festive. For the most part, those were very difficult rules to keep up with.

I was still awake in my bed when the music finally died down. It must have been shortly after midnight. The guests had departed, leaving my mother alone to straighten up the place.

Indeed, that period in itself was particularly painful for me, since I—more than anyone else—understood the sacrifice and effort that my mother had put into the celebrations, for while it was true that I had come of age religiously, it had come at a great financial cost to her.

In those days, poor people tended to spend beyond their means; it was a common practice, perpetuated by fear of being looked down upon by others in the community. Although my family was by no means among the poorest of the poor in Gros Islet, I knew that money was always hard to come by. Moreover, the burden of buying shoes, a suit, meat, and alcoholic beverages for the celebration of a child's First Communion was a daunting task in itself.

It would be quite awhile before my mother could finally retire to bed. Finally, as the lights went out in the living room, I could almost follow her footsteps as she walked in a state of exhaustion into her room.

The following morning, just before sunrise, we were back to the grind. My brother and I each took turns sponging ourselves in a white pail which was filled with cold tap water that had been warmed for our comfort with water from a kettle.

By eight o'clock, we were out of the house. I later joined up with George and Kennedy, who were also on their way to school.

There were lots of stories to be told, but in the end, it was obvious that their experiences were no different from mine. Like my mom, their mom had spent her life's savings, and like me, they had remained confined to their rooms during the evening festivities.

On the following Sunday, exactly seven days after our First Communion celebrations, we received our scapulars in accordance with principles set forth by the Church. The scapulars are religious rope necklaces, with two miniature cushions attached to opposite ends. Members of the Legion of Mary frequently wear them, and in recent times it has become widely associated with members of that secret society known as "The Lodge" in our town. There are also the larger and longer versions that are inscribed with unknown religious symbols. Probably Latin. They fall like cushions on the chest and the back of those who wear them. For our part, we had always been led to believe that a scapular posses certain mystical powers. According to legend, they were specifically designed to protect little children from all evil, and I assumed that this included the woman in the pink and purple mushware. No longer would she and the Devil be allowed to exercise any dominion over our lives, for once the powers of the scapular had kicked in, we were bound to achieve this glorious victory over all that was evil. In essence, we had suddenly arrived at the stage of "religious invincibility."

However, in spite of the aura of mysticism which the scapular possessed, that in itself could not have afforded us absolute protection from evil. The old folks had taught us a prayer, one that was intended to increase the powers of the scapular: "*Escapilliar, glow benny, bordia do-vair, bordia dareye.*"

Indeed, these were powerful words, or so we were taught. They were so powerful that when said while wearing the scapular, we swore they had the power to remove mountains, bind Satan, and ship him like a rocket to the moon. But were we kidding ourselves? You bet not.

The Visions That Changed Our Lives

Although the years had run before us, my friendship with George and Kennedy remained unbroken. We were now approximately eleven years old, but the years since our First Communion had not come and gone without controversy. At the early age of eleven, I was forced to completely sever ties with the Roman Catholic Church. Sadly, it was not of my own doing, but I became a victim of the brash Catholic mentality of that era.

It all started in the summer of 1975, when my mother began to have a series of terrifying dreams. Later she recounted those strange and seemingly unnatural experiences to a family member, who initially thought that my mom was being visited by evil sprits.

As the weeks went by, the dreams continued. In one of them, my mother claimed to have seen an image of Christ with outstretched hands, and in another there was a shimmering light in the formation of a crucifix, which appeared on the walls of our home. In that very same dream, as she touched the crucifix, it suddenly disappeared from the wall.

Within days of that dream, something led her to dismiss the notion that these strange phenomena were the work of evil sprits. Therefore, to ascertain the truth, she began a Novena, a Roman

Catholic practice in which candles are left burning for a specific period of time while prayers or requests are made to God.

She soon received an answer, and it came in the form of another dream. An angel visited her that night, and instructed her to consecrate her life to God through baptism.

"What baptism?" she asked the angel. "I was baptized as a child, and I don't understand what you mean."

"Think about it," the angel responded, and disappeared from the dream.

On the following morning, at about the break of day, my mother awakened in her bed in a state of confusion. She did not understand this latest dream, since the concept of baptism in the Catholic sense meant that she had already been baptized as an infant. Moreover, being the very staunch Catholic woman that she was, the thought of "re-baptism" sounded nothing but ridiculous.

To date, the only group of people who believed in that concept were those from the foolish evangelical denominations around town. They were known to make a mockery of the holy sacrament of baptism by keeping all new converts submerged under water until they had responded yes to the pastor's taunting of, "Do you see God?"

To my mom, the Catholic prescription of infant baptism conflicted greatly with the advice of the angel. And so, as the sprit of conflict hovered around her, she decided that it was time to pay Father "H" a visit.

Their meeting together did not go quite as she expected. In the end, she still felt a spiritual void inside, which was later destined to change all of our lives. While Father "H" felt convinced that it was the sprit of the Lord that had appeared to her in her dreams, he did not agree to her request for re-baptism.

His position was firm. He had been raised in the Catholic faith, where baptism was a one-time thing. Moreover, as a Catholic priest, it behooved him to uphold the principles of the Church. He advised her to continue to pray about it, and he would do likewise.

With each passing day, her yearning for baptism grew. Soon it became a thing over which she had no control, nor could it wait.

During that period, she had another dream. This time she was instructed to visit Ms. Fedora Pamphile, known as "Fidoe," who was the assistant town nurse, and who had for many years championed the cause of the Seventh Day Adventist movement in Gros Islet. She was among the earliest "Christians" known to us, and lived only a stone's throw away from the Catholic church. As a "Semdays" (the local term used to describe a Seventh-Day Adventist follower), Fidoe was like the rock of Gibraltar when it came to the observance of her faith.

Their meetings together yielded some serious consequences for us all. Soon my mother was attending Bible studies in Fidoe's home, and before long she was baptized into the Seventh Day Adventist faith.

Exercising that personal and inalienable right to chose her own spiritual destiny greatly offended Father "H" and a host of other people in the Church. But it affected my grandmother the most. One Saturday morning, she literally attempted to order my mother out of the small wooden Seventh Day Adventist church down on Church Street. In fact, her "Christian-phobic" reaction was clear. She just couldn't accept the fact that her daughter had joined this ridiculous group of people.

At that time, I did empathize with my grandmother because of the close-knit society in which we lived. But I did not feel the same towards Father "H," who by then had transformed from a saintly priest into a beast. He had become full of himself and very angry over my mother's decision. His anger led him to commit acts of abusive behavior in his attempt to prove who was righteous and who wasn't.

My brother and I would soon experience the wrath of Father "H." Since my mother had not forced us to choose her newfound religion over the Catholic faith, we opted to remain Catholics, and to also serve the Church as acolytes (which we were prior to her conversion).

As was our custom on a Sunday, we had all gathered with the other boys in the Sacristy. When Father "H" arrived, he headed straight for the closet where his robe was hanging. That morning, as he had done so many Sundays before, he hardly paid any attention to us. However, as he turned around to adjust his robe, he spotted my brother and myself among the group of acolytes present.

Suddenly, his demeanor changed and anger flashed across his face. "Get out! Get out! Get out!" he shouted at both of us. "And don't come back here again."

We were still standing there in absolute shock when Father "H" decided to walk over and violently yank the cassocks from our tiny bodies. There were tears in my eyes as I struggled helplessly to free myself from his reach and the cassock. When it was all over, my brother and I hurried through a side door which led into an open coconut field outside. We then followed a tiny footpath and headed on for home.

I was the first to enter through the aluminum gate that secured our yard. My mother, who was busy doing her Sunday laundry, was very surprised to see us back so soon. We recounted the events of the morning, only to see her fall into a state of shock, and then anger.

"If the Bible says to suffer the little children to come unto me, for theirs is the Kingdom of Heaven, what priest has the right to cast them away?" she said.

I was not familiar with that part of the scriptures which my mom had just quoted, but already my own anger was building inside. In fact, at four foot five, and with a skinny frame that weighed no more than ninety pounds, my first instinct was to return to the Sacristy and simply kick Father "H" around like a soccer ball. I wanted to kill this white man for the pain and humiliation he had inflicted upon my brother and me.

However, in spite of my mother's anger, this certainly was not her idea of how the situation should be handled. She counseled us to leave it in the hands of Jesus, which baffled me at the time. Jesus was not there to protect us, so how in the world did she expect us to leave the matter to Him?

During our discussion, I thought a bit about what it would have been like to be a Catholic in France. Was the Church always right? And if so, would I have accepted as normal the incident that just occurred this morning?

For the next few days, there still wasn't any pressure from my mom to join her religion. Moreover, although we were very angry with Father "H," there was nothing attractive about my mother's religion to entice us to join.

During that period, we also met with a number of grown-up sympathizers who, while secretly acknowledging that the approach Father "H" had taken was wrong, did not have the courage to speak out on our behalf. In the end, our lack of enthusiasm for my mother's religion, along with the fear of being ridiculed by our friends, brought us back from the brink of renouncing the Catholic Church.

I received a lot of support from both George and Kennedy, who continued to be my friends during those trying times. However, despite our determination to remain Catholics, Father "H" did all in his power to exert pressure upon us. He was not satisfied with firing us as acolytes, and wanted to force us out of the Church completely.

His abominable behavior continued unabated, to the point where he would deny us the opportunity to partake of the Holy Eucharist at the Sunday masses. All the while, not a single person came to our defense.

A few months later, when I had become of age to receive the sacrament of Confirmation, he yanked my name off the list of those who were eligible. I had finally arrived at the point when I felt that there was no use in remaining a Catholic, but my grandfather, Mr. Ernest Montoute, would not allow me to accept defeat.

Having spent the greater part of his life in England, a society where people were more enlightened, he decided that it was time to pay a visit to Father "H." I accompanied him to the vesper service one evening, and we sat near where Father "H" usually made his exit at the end of the services.

That evening, as we waited, he finally walked down the corner aisle and passed us without a word. "Father!" my grandfather called out to him in a calm but firm voice. "I'd move to have a word with you."

Turning to face my grandfather, who by virtue of his height towered over Father "H," the two engaged in a spirited conversation. In the end, it was clear that Father "H" would not change his mind. And so, unable to remain in a church where we were no longer welcome, my brother and I, at the tender ages of eleven and ten, made the painful but bold decision to renounce Catholicism.

An Unbreakable Friendship

Fortunately, in spite of the religiously motivated turbulence around me, I was able to maintain my friendship with George and Kennedy. We were now a trio, since our dear friend Ronnie Maxius had migrated to Barbados to join his mom.

A lot had also occurred in the years that had just passed. We had moved to a larger and more modern school in an area of Gros Islet called Massade, and shortly afterwards, the decision was made to demolish the old wooden school in the center of town, leaving the old convent to stand on its own.

Also during that period and in the years that followed, both George and Kennedy had begun to realize their life-long dreams of becoming fishermen. Like their father and uncles before them, the boys were driven by an intense obsession with the sea.

I remember vividly their very first expedition. Routinely, at the approaching sunset, I always sat alone at the beach in quiet conversation with my God.

That afternoon, as the boat left the shore, I delighted to see George and Kennedy aboard. There were also two older fishermen on board. One was positioned behind the engine, the other near the bow, and George and Kennedy were near the center.

This would continue for several weeks, and in time both George and Kennedy, under the watchful eye of the older fishermen, each took turns in steering the boat out to sea and back.

Normally, since their tasks only included setting the nets and attending to the fish pots, they were often back ashore within forty-five minutes to an hour. By then, the sun would appear as a huge orange ball in the sky as it descended into the sea. With the night quickly falling over the waters, they would sometimes pull the boat up to the boathouse and head for the public bathroom near the northern end of the bay for their evening shower.

Customarily at about 7:30 each evening, we all used to converge on the step of the old society hall for an evening of conversation. There were always scores of other teenage boys, and evenings together were for the most part interesting.

Right across the street and not too far from the society hall was an English-style pub where the owner, Mr. Herbert Scott, used to entertain his patrons with some of the most popular records of that era. They included songs by Tom Jones and Engelbert Humperdinck, and all night long, "Blue Spanish Eyes," "Love Me With All Your Heart," "It's Not Unusual," "Please Release Me," and "Green, Green Grass of Home" would keep them drinking.

From the steps outside, we used to watch and laugh as a few of the drunks sat near the window with their heads tilted backwards in a doze. But for the most part, we engaged in a number of serious discussions whose topics usually ranged from sports to religion to politics, and, on rare occasions, girls.

However, despite of our many areas of interest, none was as entertaining as the game of cricket. In fact, we used to marvel in awe at the number of young and exciting players who had joined the international cricket leagues during that period.

From India to Pakistan, Australia, New Zealand, England and the West Indies, they had set the cricket world on fire. They included big names like Vivian Richards, Ian and Greg Chapel, Roy Fredericks and Gordon Greenidge, Jeff Thompson and Denis Lily, Andy Roberts and Michael Holding, Sunil Gavasca and "Wasim" Rager, Alvin Kalichrun and Gus Logie, just to name a few.

Often, those discussions would continue through the evening, up until about 9:00 or 9:30, which was about the time that the effects of physical exhaustion, coupled with the coolness of the night air, drove us home to sleep.

Sunday afternoons were usually among the best days of our lives. We used to gather in an open field that was once the site of a polluted swamp. To most of us, this area was simply called the Mahung. There was still a vast mosquito population out there, which bred secretly under the leaves of hundreds of wild plants known locally as "tabac-jab" or "devil's tobacco." And to top it all, the Mahung was located directly behind a cemetery, where a large canal separated it from the adjacent residences out in my neighborhood of Tou Tigre or Tiger Hole.

In fact, getting across the canal was always the most difficult thing of all. It was filled with polluted water, which often contained human waste or the remains of a dead dog or other animal. To avoid direct contact with the water, we placed two huge coconut logs across the full width of the canal as a passageway, which we crossed while holding our breath to avoid the stench.

In spite of the terrible odor that came from the canal and pigsties nearby, we all loved the Mahung because of the hard work we had put into transforming that area into our own personal playground. And soon, there were plans on the way to host some of the best cricket matches that any avid teenage cricketer could love.

The Mahung: Our old playground with lots of "Devil Tobacco" trees in the background.

We had established a local cricket league, which consisted of two separate teams from our respective neighborhoods. Since George and Kennedy lived closer to the waters of the Caribbean Sea, they teamed up with Nourgearo to form a ball club which they christened Seagulls. Also, bending the rules a bit, they offered membership to two brothers by the name of Claudius and Terry Daniel, and also to Cork-A-Bet who resided in my neighborhood of Tou Tigre.

The old swamp that formed the western boundary of the playground.

Their decision to lure some of the boys from Tou Tigre into their club had caused a temporary strain in my relationship with both George and Kennedy. I was especially angry with George, or "Dis-Yute" as Nourgearo often referred to him. I was convinced that George was directly responsible for hatching the plot.

Putting together a team of our own in Tou Tigre, where miserable old women spend their days quarreling and cursing each other, was an arduous task. Therefore, amidst much frustration, I eventually settled for a group of boys, most of whom were my relatives.

They included Victor "Natty" and Kenneth "Pussycat" Morille; my brother Phillip; and Stanley "Shallow," Skey "Goo-lue," Lambert "Fiet," and Andrew McPhee. We later selected Rollence Mathurin, known as "your your"; Thomas St. Hill, called "Thompty"; and Sylvester Eugene, a.k.a. "Lala-leel," who was Cork-a-bet's youngest brother.

The next task was to select a name for our club. After a tedious process of elimination, we finally decided on Three Stars, which was borrowed from a brand of popular matchsticks.

Our first encounter with the Seagulls was on a warm Sunday afternoon. They had arrived with a small entourage comprised mostly of people who lived in the Bay area. Some had taken refuge under some "Sip" trees nearby, while others simply sat alongside a few of our supporters in a makeshift spectators' stand made up of a few coconut trunks on the ground.

As is customary with the game of cricket, Nourgearo and I (the two captains) took the coin toss, as the players and spectators waited patiently in the pavilion. Nourgearo won the toss and elected to bat. Without further ado, I was joined on the field by my teammates. There was a tense silence as I began to place men at strategic locations throughout the field.

The crowd applauded loudly as Kennedy and Claudius, the two opening batsmen for Seagulls; made their way unto the field. Claudius had tucked his shirt carefully into his pants, which were secured firmly by a knot that was commonly referred to in our local dialect as a "*bar-boo-chet*." Kennedy had on dark pants, a white jersey, and a golfer's cap.

The two soon settled down at the wicket, signaling the commencement of the game. As I handed the ball to my cousin Stanley McPhee, everyone could tell by his demeanor and flashy smile that the game was on.

Stanley's first delivery to Kennedy was rather hostile. The ball flew past his face like a bullet from an automatic rifle, and into the hands of our wicket keeper, Skey McPhee.

I could tell that Kennedy was visibly shaken, and I quietly enjoyed every moment of it. This was payback for "cheating," and I just could not wait for the moment when it would be George's turn at the wicket.

For the next several minutes into the attack, Stanley continued to terrorize Kennedy while drawing smiles from his teammates and jeers from the Seagulls and their supporters. We were having the desired effect, and I felt a sense of invincibility.

Feeling the pressure and humiliation that Stanley had thrust upon him, Kennedy tried his best to adapt. Before long, he got a lucky strike, only to see the ball cut short by Lala-leel in the covers position.

This also signaled the end of Stanley's spell, at which point the ball was handed to Lala-leel for a series of deliveries to Claudius.

Unlike Stanley with his swift deliveries, Lala-leel was a medium-pace bowler with a predictable delivery. Claudius took full advantage of the situation. He struck two fours and a six in the course of three deliveries, which seemed to leave Lala-leel a bit shaken.

There were celebrations in the stands as I walked over to chat with Lala-leel. I wanted to impress upon him that I still had lots of confidence in him, and that things were still looking up.

After our brief conversation together, he managed a faint smile while fastening a rope around his visibly torn trousers. With the ball held firmly in his hands, he walked back to the mark in preparation for another delivery.

The moments prior to the next delivery were filled with apprehension. I wanted a miracle that would exonerate my friend and finally ease him out of the early humiliation that he had suffered at the hands of Claudius. I knew that it would come, so I just kept waiting.

From the spectators' stand nearby, things were beginning to look a little bit ugly. The earlier silence that Stanley had forced upon Seagulls and their following had now been replaced with laughter and ridicule.

I was surprised to discover that George was among the lot, and that troubled me greatly. By the time Lala-leel finally made his fourth delivery, there was so much distraction that it broke everyone's concentration. In fact, the immense laughter, the short pauses, and the sarcastic roaring taunts of "one, two, three, and fooooouuuuuurrrrr" caused me to lose my patience with them.

Their behavior was not only offensive, but it just drove me nuts. I wanted to curse them out, but there was something holding me back. Being a born-again Christian on a playing field dominated by Catholics behooved me to be at my best. "Christians" do not curse, I said to myself, and I tried really hard to avoid that pit.

For a while, it seemed that I would be able to maintain my cool if only I could learn to ignore them. But that was short-lived. I was drawn into a war of words with George and some of the Seagulls players.

It started at the end of the over, shortly after Claudius had struck another four off the bowling of Lala-leel. George and company were chanting something, which sounded like, "Bang bang, bing bang, pinky linky," and making all sorts of foolish noises and gestures.

I had arrived at the peak of anger and just couldn't stomach this any more. Without even thinking, I pointed my middle finger in the air, signaling my indignation with the situation. Skey and Lambert soon followed, and before long, George and company were returning the obscene gesture as we cursed each other out like loose cannons.

There was now a storm out on the field that no one could stop. I then decided to walk off the field, and so did all of my teammates. Initially, Thompty, Victor, and Nourgearo tried their best to mediate the situation, but George and I just kept mouthing at each other like stubborn mules that just would not listen.

Several moments passed, and suddenly not a word. However, although a period of calm had prevailed, the bitterness between us remained.

We soon returned to the field, and I realized there and then that my relationship with the Phillip brothers, George and Kennedy, had been deeply strained. For while it was true that I had not quarreled directly with Kennedy, he gave me those very cold stares which accurately conveyed that he had quietly chosen sides in the fray. This continued for some time, but I was determined to ignore him.

In fact, whenever Kennedy attempted to cut me down to size with his eyes, I responded with a silly grin on my face. I guess I had regained some of my "Christianity," which I shouldn't have lost in the first place.

This reaction on my part did the trick. Very soon, all the cold stares were replaced by focus and a genuine desire to play the game.

By then, both Stanley and Lala-leel were performing so admirably with the ball that you could not miss the smiles on all of our faces. Lala-leel had gone on to retire both Claudius and Kennedy, while Stanley occasionally terrorized our opponents with swift deliveries and bouncers.

A load had been finally lifted off my shoulders as I watched in amazement at this turn of events. I was convinced that we were gaining the upper hand, and wanted to do all in my power to inspire our team to victory. In fact, if only I could radiate a serious level of confidence, I knew then that my teammates would feed off my sudden burst of energy and determination. I was the captain and I longed to do the best I could.

Stanley went on to dislodge Terry (a.k.a. Short Ass) and Roger "Ma Martin," which ultimately resulted in the introduction of Lambert "Fiet" and myself on the attack. I wanted to give Stanley and Lala-leel a breather, and prayed that Lambert and I could rise to the occasion.

Lambert would operate from the eastern end of the grounds, and I from the west. We had a strategy in mind, and that was to trick the batsman into committing himself to making careless swipes at the ball. Since our deliveries were similar, and also not up to the pace of either Stanley or Lala-leel, we all were convinced that this was the approach most likely to work.

It was George's and Rickey Daniel's turn at the wicket when Lambert and I began the operation. Boy, was I happy to see George. When it became George's turn to face me at the other end, I was not only prepared, but also determined to settle our sporting differences. I also wanted so much to demonstrate that he was just a big-mouth shouting from the stands, and also felt that this was my chance to humiliate him a bit.

As hoped for, his performance with the bat drew laughter from my teammates, and some fun in the pavilion. George simply could not compose himself enough to score some runs for his team. Every swing at the ball was wild and awkward, which made me chuckle at the fact that not even Tarzan would welcome George into his jungle. In fact, by our local definition of one who batted awkwardly, George was a real *Neg Marron* (runaway slave).

However, the most thrilling moment of all came when I decided that it was time to dislodge George. Fearing that George might lose his grip on the bat, I quickly positioned some of my teammates in the outfield, hoping to avoid possible injuries.

Lala-leel and Rollence "Your Your" were the only ones left within a reasonable distance of George. Since they were good catchers and also quick on their feet, we did not have to worry much for their safety. In any event, two things could happen. If George were to lose the handle on his bat, or if the ball were to pop up from his bat, they were quick enough to either move away or run forward to take the catch.

It was finally time to execute our plan, and the idea was to simply surprise George with a "Peepindo." A Peepindo is a simulation of a very fast moving delivery, which actually turns into a slow, bouncing pitch after it has left the baller's hand. It can sometimes travel at speeds from anywhere between two to five miles an hour and, in the process, causes the batsman to lose his focus. Waiting for a Peepindo to arrive can often be frustrating to the batsman. The ball can sometimes come to an abrupt halt midway between baller and the batsman.

As I walked slowly to the mark from where I would commence my delivery, I sniggered at the idea of bowling to George. How I couldn't wait to see the expression of astonishment on his face. As a matter of fact, the sight of his thick lower lip, whenever it dangled over his chin as it was doing now, was always a sign of his frustration. I was having fun, and God knows that I could hardly contain myself. With the winds blowing briskly behind me, I started my run up like Hercules. I delivered a classic Peepindo, which took forever to get to George.

His lips had finally dropped, and he appeared restless and anxious. But the most amusing thing about it all was the manner in which his legs were spread far apart, and his entire back hunched forward like that of a camel which was trying to draw air through its buttocks. We were all dying inside, but the best was yet to come.

With his bat held high up in the air, and his eyes fixated on the ball, George took a wild swing at the ball, and in the process shattered his entire wicket.

There was laughter all around as he made his way back towards the coconut stands. We had finally silenced the big-mouth of Seagulls, but the memories of his poor performance with the bat lingered on.

The events following George's untimely dismissal proved favorable to our team. Lambert went on to dismiss Ricky, Cho-low, and Luba at the other end, paving the way for Nourgearo and Cork-a-bet to try their luck at the wicket.

However, by the time Nourgearo and Cork-a-bet arrived on the scene, we had switched back to Stanley and Lala-leel. Nourgearo and Cork-a-bet would go on to score some additional runs for their team, but this was about all the fun they would have. Stanley dislodged Nourgearo, and Lala-leel went on to take care of his brother Cork-a-bet at the other end. Soon the remaining Seagulls batting line would collapse at the hands of Stanley, paving the way for our turn with the bat.

As we left the field and headed back to the stands, the open show of elation from my teammates gave me a special feeling inside. Moreover, since the Seagulls had not scored much, we believed that it was possible to win the game, and to draw first blood in the rivalry between neighborhood teams.

Initially, I selected the duo of Skey and Kenneth to represent Three Stars as its opening act, but I soon changed my mind. On the advice of Thompty and Stanley, we rearranged the batting order to showcase Victor and Kenneth Morille, then Skey, Thompty and myself, in that order.

Nourgearo and the rest of his team were already settled on the field by the time Victor and Kenny left the stands. We had even them dubbed them the Ian and Greg Chapel of Three Stars, patterned after the names of two real live brothers who were superstars on the Australian cricket team.

Suddenly, there was loud applause, as we called, "Okay, Ian," meaning Kenneth, and "all right, Greg," meaning Victor. Also adding to the hype was the fact that Victor was a natural born left-handed batsman, while Kenneth, like the rest of us, batted right-handed. This, we thought, was bound to frustrate Seagulls and inevitably cause them to lose their patience and focus.

In fact, judging from past experience in the game of cricket, it was always a psychological burden for any team to deal with an opposing duo of left- and right-handed batsmen. This was what we hoped to capitalize on. Seagulls had selected Cork-a-bet as their opening act, and as usual he looked intimidating. Quietly, as he took the last drag from a locally manufactured brand of cigarettes called Diamonds, he measured his run and dug his heels into the ground for demarcation. He was like a mean machine, and everyone could tell.

Secretly, this was alarming us. But we could ill afford to give Cork-a-bet the impression that we were scared. Therefore, we were determined to put up a bold front, since this was the only way to deceive him.

Of the two Three Star batsmen at the wicket, Kenneth would be the first to face a very hostile Cork-a-bet. In anticipation of the worst, we quickly encouraged him with lines such as, "You can do it, Ian" and "Okay, Ian."

Cork-a-bet's first delivery to Kenneth was as expected: swift and with a deadly sting. It was aimed directly at Kenny's head, which for the first time led me to believe that Cork-a-bet was capable of harming another human being.

Kenneth ducked just in time, as the ball missed his head by an inch. There was silence as we awaited a reaction from him, but none would come. He appeared calm and collected under the pressure, and was ready once again to receive another menacing delivery from Cork-a-bet.

Surprisingly, Cork-a-bet's second delivery to Kenneth was far more decent than the first. It moved at the speed of light, but lacked the intent to harm. Shifting his left foot forward, Kenny drove the ball gracefully to covers, only to see it quickly picked up by Terry.

"Short Ass," as we loved to refer to Terry because of his height, was always an exceptional fielder. He moved like a tiger on the field, had lots of power in his arms, and could easily hit a bulls-eye in an instant. Kenneth and Victor, aware of his skills, made the decision to remain still. As the game progressed, neither Kenneth nor Victor was able to score much off Cork-a-bet's deliveries, but they would have better luck with Nourgearo, who operated from the eastern end of the grounds.

Nourgearo was a good bowler, but not as good or menacing as Cork-a-bet and Stanley. His deliveries were often predictable, and he usually offered his opponents a chance to score.

Out on the field, the left- and right-handed duo of Victor and Kenneth seemed to pose a challenge to both Nourgearo and Cork-a-bet. We weren't scoring many runs, but they couldn't find a way to dislodge us either.

Nourgearo made the decision to temporarily remove himself and Cork-a-bet from the bowling attack by introducing George and Kennedy. He wanted results, and he hoped that George and Kennedy could deliver.

Although George and Kennedy, like Lambert and myself, were by no means first-class bowlers, they made their captain proud. George sent Victor packing, and Kennedy took care of Kenneth at the other end.

In part, their success was highly dependent on their individual style of balling. George's rhythm of delivery, while not patterned after the classic Peepindo, often made a few bumps before reaching the batsman. On the other hand, Kennedy always had an inert or lethargic style of delivery which always keeps the recipient guessing.

With the departure of Victor and Kenneth, George and Kennedy were soon given a rest. Nourgearo had reintroduced himself and Cork-a-bet on the attack, only this time operating from the cemetery end of the grounds, while Cork-a-bet plotted his terror from the west. He went on to bowl out Thompty after just a short spell, and soon I joined Skey at the wicket.

I must honestly say that having to face the bowling of Cork-a-bet was a hellish experience. Moreover, with the late afternoon sun looking deep into my eyes, I knew that there were going to be problems ahead.

Cork-a-bet loved it! And everything about him told you exactly how much.

In fact, when it was finally my turn to bat, I trembled nervously. I was so petrified of being struck in the face that I became physically sick. I knew I was being a wimp, but the thought of receiving a black eye at the hand of Cork-a-bet was not amusing at all. Besides, I had seen it happen to other people—not from the bowling of Cork-a-bet, but at some of the games at the official community grounds at Massade in Gros Islet. Men who had been struck in the face with the ball looked like monkeys with their black eyes. And popping "Phensics," a local brand of pain-killing tablets, while rubbing around the eyes with Iodex did very little to ease their misery. I had an idea, and it was to simply move away from the ball as quickly as I could if I saw it coming. As Cork-a-bet threw a number of menacing deliveries to me, there were times when I had to duck, and other times when I only knew that I had not been struck once the ball was safely in the hands of their keeper, Luba. However, Cork-a-bet's fifth delivery to me was a treat, and recognizing it for what it was, I quickly took advantage of it by scoring a single run.

At the other end of the pitch, if my open display of cowardice was any indication of how my batting partner Skey felt, then it was easy for any one to have been fooled. He appeared fearless, and if he was at all terrified of Cork-a-bet, he really did a good job of concealing it.

He would soon prove his worth, and convincingly so. As Cork-a-bet delivered his final ball of the over, Skey hammered it high over the deep end of the boundary for a six.

The crowd roared from the stands as the ball sailed overhead. Skey had lifted us to magical heights, and everyone admired his courage.

However, with the end of that period, it became my turn to face the bowling of Nourgearo. At the left field, where George was positioned, I did not see a smile. He looked me smack in the face and did not show any of the disdain that had characterized our earlier argument. I guess we had both moved on and just wanted to be able to concentrate on the game.

Dealing with Nourgearo's deliveries was a comfort to the soul. I scored a couple of runs and had similar successes with him. However, by the end of the spell, it became my turn once again to face Cork-a-bet.

There was a long moment of silence as I settled down to face the "devil." I could tell that he had grown angrier by the way he repeatedly spat on the ground. He had also summoned Kennedy and Short Ass to the covers position, which gave me that sick feeling that Hell was about to descend on me.

A rocket flew pass my bum, and into the hands of Luba. I had survived this one, but things were just getting toastier. Then came the second delivery, which never even touched the ground. It was a classic Yorker, which landed on the face of my bat and fell to the ground. By then Terry was all over the ball.

Sensing the pressure I was under, Skey walked over to converse with me for a while. His advice to me was simple. I was to keep my eye on the ball, my foot grounded, and then attempt a mighty swing at the ball. And so, with Skey having walked away, I attempted to do just that.

The impact was swift and painful, as the ball unexpectedly struck me right in the back of the neck. I heard the chuckles, and then the roar of laughter, which suddenly came from every quarter. I wanted to appear angry, but couldn't keep up the pretense, since even Skey had this silly smirk on his face. It was a grand affair, and suddenly I became the laughingstock of everyone. I had to find a way out of this one.

Gently rubbing the back of my neck to ease the pain, I was determined not to give Cork-a-bet and his teammates the benefit of thinking that my confidence had been shattered. I wanted to appear courageous, and felt that the only way to do so was to take another swing at the ball. Maybe this time, I would finally be lucky.

The next delivery was a memorable one. As the ball left his hand, I positioned myself to hammer it over the western end of the boundary. Instead, the ball flew past my knee and shattered my wicket. I was through, but the laughter from the field and the stands had only just begun.

As I walked back to the coconut stands, feeling a bit disgraced by Cork-a-bet, I had a deep sense of personal defeat that I had never felt before. It wasn't easy at all, especially having to work through the scornful stares and evasive look on the face of Cork-a-bet. It was, for me, a humbling experience that very few teenagers would quietly accept.

In the aftermath of my dismissal we watched as the rest of our team collapsed. It was evident then that we just couldn't hold up to the bowling of Cork-a-bet. Therefore, with the last of our teammates at the wicket (Stanley and Lala-leel), the inevitability of defeat hung high over our heads.

Admittedly, and more so than with anyone else, the impending loss was a crushing blow to my ego. It had reduced me to shreds, and my silence didn't do much to conceal my defeated self.

I also noticed the blunt expressions on the faces of my teammates, and it hurt badly. In fact, the silence that permeated itself within our camp was much greater than words could have described.

Obviously, the boys of Tiger Hole had conceded defeat. For now, until the next game when we would have a chance to try again, we were forced to accept our new title as the underdogs in the newly established league. The Seagulls would go on to rout us out completely in the second inning, which ended at sundown.

Horse Racing

There was never a Sunday afternoon without sports. And soon, as we began to experiment with various forms of entertainment other than cricket, we began to attract more and more teenage boys to the Mahung. Whenever we weren't battling the Seagulls for first place in a cricket match, we spent our leisure time together organizing "Horse Racing."

During that period I had also begun to discover some of my talents, and soon rose to the top as the main organizer of most of these events. I was full of life, and had a burning passion to transform our neighborhood and community into an oasis of entertainment. I always had a plan and knew exactly how to make things happen. And so, with the help of the other boys, Sunday afternoon in Gros Islet would never be the same again.

We reeled in the excitement of putting on a simulation of jockeys on horseback at the races. A broomstick tucked between our legs, with two cardboard designs of a horse's head attached to it, did the trick for most of us. Then there was a rope or strap that we tied around the "horse's" neck, which served as a bridle for total control.

The racetrack was a work of art. It was constructed on a large plot of land that extended to the eastern boundary of our cricket playing grounds. It was covered with brown dirt and had patches of grass all over. We had also constructed a stable of dry coconut palms, and a small pavilion with magnificent views of the long and winding racetrack with the hills in the background.

I remember vividly the strenuous preparations that went into its construction, and the huge amount of time we spent trying to get our very first event off the ground.

We had spent the entire week before cutting and gathering dry sticks throughout the Mahung, and all day Saturday, which was the eve of the race, Lala-leel and I had worked tirelessly until dark to put the finishing touches together.

However, early that Sunday morning, while the dew was still visible on the grass, Lala-leel and I took the opportunity to visit the track for a final inspection. After all the hard work that had gone into constructing the tracks, and the efforts to ensure that things went off without a hitch, we were absolutely devastated to discover the amount of damage done to the track during the night before. What we saw was not only shocking, but it made us very angry. A large number of the sticks we had erected as demarcation for the tracks and the inner lanes had been knocked to the ground.

"Who could have done such an evil thing?" I cried in indignation. But just as I was about to point the finger at a few suspects, Lala-leel made an astonishing discovery. He pointed to the fresh animal excrement on the ground, and at the hoof marks near the damaged area. They all led in one direction, and that was to the many pigsties nearby. Obviously, at some point during the night, while they scavenged through the open fields, the pigs' paths had crossed the tracks.

Our anger soon turned to dejection, once acceptance of that theory settled in our minds. As we quickly moved to repair the tracks, Lala-leel, in search of a spade, hurried to a nearby site where his parents (Ufita and Jenyo) labored making charcoal on weekdays.

He later returned with a rusty old spade which we used to scoop the excrement off the ground. As we hastily went about accomplishing the task, we were able to finish in record speed and head back home for some needed rest.

At about a little past noon, although the first race was not scheduled to begin until 2:30, quite a few of the jockeys were arriving on "horseback." Among the early-bird riders were my best friends George and Kennedy Phillip. They had arrived with such an air of seriousness about the race that I could not help but smile. As a matter of fact, they both had tamarind whips in their hands, and occasionally flogged their "horses" in order to keep them moving. It was really a sight to see, and I could tell by the colorful designs attached to the broomsticks to depict the horses' heads that today was shaping up to be no ordinary one.

There was much enthusiasm when I finally announced that riders could opt for early registration and a chance to test the racetrack. Everyone present came forward, and Lala-leel and I collected a quarter from each jockey.

The warm-ups were exhilarating, and drove us to laughter. Some of the boys who seized on the opportunity to test the tracks tucked their broomstick horses safely between their legs and did a simulation of a horse's gallop by moving their hips from side to side.

By 1:35 P.M. I had registered a total of twenty-one jockeys, and still they kept on coming. There were far more than we had anticipated, and very soon Lala-leel made a suggestion that I quickly agreed to. We decided to up the registration fee a bit, by charging thirty cents for all registration after 1:40 P.M. and fifty cents for any jockey who, in our estimation, came from an affluent family in Gros Islet. What was fifty cents for a boy whose parents could have afforded much more?

Among those whom we regarded as being affluent were two brothers by the names of David and Crusoe Moise. I was astounded by their presence, since they hardly ever came to any events that were hosted in the Mahung. I was especially happy to see Dave, whom I've always considered to be a good friend. We had once served together as acolytes, and at other times when we weren't involved in the activities of the church, I spent countless afternoons with him and his brother Crusoe as they assisted their father in the pub he owned. Dave was always generous, and although we might have been too young to hang out among the patrons in the pub, he always gave me a free soda, or "aerated," which I sipped on while he served the patrons who often got their fix on cheap Madeira and white rum.

The final minutes leading up to the first race were very exciting. There were countless teenage boys on horseback, pouring with perspiration and eager for a chance to run away with the top prize.

In all, there were five scheduled races, four of which were open to all registered jockeys. The fifth race would feature only the first-place winners of the four previous races. The rules were very clear, and we thought that everyone understood. However, unlike the final race, which was structured on the basis of "winner takes it all," first, second, and third prizes would be rewarded in all of the first four races. All first-prize winners would receive three ice pops, two ice pops would go to the second-place winners, and there would be one ice pop for each of the third-place winners. There were also a few rewards for Lala-leel and myself, as the main organizers of the event. We agreed that we each would receive an ice pop at the end of every race.

We had also set aside a whole bag of ice pops to be offered as the grand prize to the winner of the fifth and final race. It was also hinted that whoever the winner was, he should be generous enough to offer Lala-leel and me an additional ice pop out of the bag.

With the terms agreed upon, we looked forward to every minute of the upcoming event. To ensure that there was no confusion and that all jockeys were accounted for, I jotted the names of everyone, their horses, and the amount which each had paid onto a clean sheet of paper. When I was done, the list followed this format:

1. George Phillip - Good Friday 25¢
2. Kennedy Phillip - Lady Grey 25¢
3. David Moise - Stalin 50¢

And so forth.

A second list was drawn and pasted to what was left of a nearby coconut tree trunk. We were moving at full speed, and before anyone knew it the tension in the air was rising as from an active volcano. With no more than fifteen minutes left before the first race, I went over the rules for the last time.

Each race required a total of four laps, and anyone who attempted to violate the rules would be disqualified. Jockeys were expected to keep their horses tucked between their legs, and no exceptions would be made.

Suddenly everyone was pointing to the finish line, where a multicolored flag hung from a pole There was a loud chuckle. Initially, I couldn't tell what the joke was all about, but I soon would.

They were laughing at the stiffness of the flag in the open breeze, and at its peculiar shape. Part of the flag was cut out of blue denim and polyester cloth, which I had collected from the local tailor shop. However, once the laughter had died out, we all continued with utmost seriousness.

At approximately 2:00 P.M. all the jockeys and their horses took positions at the starting line. George and Kennedy were positioned to the extreme left of the track, followed by Roger (Ma Martin), a very boastful fellow. Terry and Claudius were all ready to go, and so were Dave and Crusoe and the whole lot.

It was hard to contain the excitement as I walked over for a final inspection. Not an eye blinked as I slowly passed by. I was satisfied, and the thought that everyone had taken the events so seriously brought a special joy to my heart.

As I moved away to a safe distance, a prevailing silence suddenly fell over the track. I was looking at my watch, which must have sent jitters into hearts of every participant.

By then, all eyes were transfixed upon me, and waiting for that moment when the command of go would be sounded. However, while I secretly enjoyed being in a position of authority, I also could not help noticing the posture of some of the jockeys, who stood on their tiptoes with their legs trembling beneath them from the involuntary movement of nerves.

George and Kennedy were among the lot, and with their tamarind whips held high above their heads, it was obvious that they were prepared to whip their horses to victory. By then, the whistle was out of my pocket and into my hand. Not an eye blinked.

I held the whistle firmly to my lips and blew forcefully through it. The frenzy began!

The events that followed were total chaos. One of the jockeys tripped forward and fell to the ground. Others directly behind him fell over him, and soon there was a huge scramble. However, once the affected had gotten up, more confusion ensued. Some had taken off with horses not belonging to them, which set up a storm of confusion.

Also, in defiance of the rules, Roger, who was among those who had fallen to the ground, had finished the first lap without a horse. He did grab his horse off of the ground at the beginning of the second lap, which sparked off a great controversy when he finally ended in first place.

He then demanded that I declare him the winner, which prompted an immediate objection from the other boys. Most of them wanted Ricky declared the winner, since he had actually concluded all the rounds with his horse securely tucked between his legs.

I took a moment to confer with Lala-leel, and in the end, we both decided in favor of Ricky. The rules were clear, and not only had they mandated that all jockeys complete a total of four laps, they also required them to finish all laps with their horses tucked between their legs. While it was true that Roger had completed a total of four rounds, he had done so through dishonest means.

My decision did not suffice for Roger, who along with a few of his pals demanded that they be refunded their registration fee. Initially, I put up stiff resistance, but soon gave in to their demands.

What happened next proved that Roger's departure was a blessing in disguise. Not only had we gotten rid of Roger and his pals, but our disappointment was short-lived. Thanks to the generosity of David Moise, we were soon able to replace the dollar which had been returned to Roger and his pals. We were also glad to be able to cover the cost of the grand prize, without having to dip into the $3.00 profit which we had hoped to invest in a future event.

With these unexpected problems safely behind us, we quickly moved on to the other races, which all went by without a hitch. Everyone was overjoyed, and the great spirit of friendship that filled the air with laughter was indicative of the huge success we had achieved together. As the conversation and laughter continued into the late afternoon, George and Kennedy began to hatch their own plans to host the next event at the bay.

Obviously, by the tone of the conversation, they wanted to be in charge of things. I did not object, although I would have preferred that events remained in the Mahung. However, by the time the evening finally cast its shadows upon us, it was clear that the other event would be hosted at the bay.

This new idea in itself had a particular appeal to most of the boys; compared to the hard, dark, and arid earth in the Mahung, the bay afforded the luxury of white sand and a refreshing sea breeze. Moreover, since more people in Gros Islet frequented the bay, it could easily attract a larger group of spectators.

By Friday afternoon of the following week, George and Kennedy had completed the new racing track, which was modeled after the one that Lala-leel and I had constructed in the Mahung. The one visible difference was that it extended from the old sea wall and down to the waterline where the waves beat gently against the shore. They had also constructed a few booths near the southern entrance of the food market, and had shifted their boat, *Charlie Josie*, to another location to make space.

George, posing with his boat—Charlie Josie.

I was astounded to see the way they had transformed the area, and I knew right there and then that George and Kenny were indeed planning an exquisite gala. It seemed that their intent was to take horse racing to an unimaginable level.

That Sunday afternoon would confirm the reality of their vision, as the provocative and hunger-inducing aroma of fishcakes in deep frying pans rose steadily into the air. There was also a keen sense of organization, which was manifested by the presence of many hired hands who assisted around the tracks and under the booths. They were mostly elderly women and fishmongers who didn't hope to earn much, but were willing to give of their time and effort to an event hosted by the sons of a fisherman.

From both ends of the street, spectators trickled in. Soon the crowd had grown to great proportions. There were also a number of jockeys all over the place, and the numbers seemed to double with each passing moment. It was obvious that they had invested much publicity into making this thing a grand community affair.

As I forced my way closer to the tracks, I stumbled into a small group of fishermen, who all appeared drunk long before the event even started. They were also engaged in a very heated argument, which seemed to have made one of them very upset.

The dispute centered on the terms of a bet, between one fellow who went by the name of Jim Pow, and another named Pintac. They had agreed to buy each other a shot of Denross, a local rum, if the horses on which they had wagered placed first in any of the races. But Pintac had apparently changed his mind and attempted to pressure Jim Pow into renegotiating the terms of the bet. He wanted to up the ante to a shot of Whitehorse whiskey, a suggestion that triggered a storm between the two. This new condition was certainly not one that Jim Pow was willing to accept. He did not have much money left, but he refused to admit that he just couldn't afford to pay for whiskey. Therefore, instead of appearing broke, he insulted Pintac by saying that a shot of whiskey was too expensive to waste on him.

What an afternoon this was turning out to be. A simple sporting affair, first conceived on the barren lands of the Mahung, had suddenly found itself at center stage in our community. What was most thrilling about the whole thing was the manner in which the people had embraced it. Looking back, I don't think that I could recall a period in Gros Islet when so many adults had come out to support the creative ideas of young people. And that, to me, was refreshing.

Having inched my way to a spot that was almost comfortable, I finally caught a glimpse of George and Kennedy. They were doing some last-minute preparations, and they sure looked busy. George was wearing a pair of shorts and an Afro shirt, and he had a red bandana tied to his forehead. Kennedy was dressed in simple T-shirt and shorts, with a white bandana around his forehead.

At the starting point, where a huge line of demarcation was drawn in the sand, some of the jockeys had already begun to position themselves. The majority had covered their faces with cardboard masks which had small incisions dug into the area around the nose and eyes. All the masks were fastened with rubber bands that were fitted tightly around their heads.

They had also painted their broomstick horses, and had even replaced the original cardboard heads with wooden ones. There was a marked difference, and it was as if the horses had come alive.

The mood was really one of tremendous excitement, and there were occasional bursts of laughter and shouts from the crowd. Most of the people seemed fascinated by the strange costumes worn by some of the boys. Some had old ruffled satin trousers that dazzled in the afternoon sun, while others wore torn outfits that must have been tucked away for years as bedding under the old coconut-fiber mattresses in their homes.

As the moment grew closer, special feelings of exhilaration filled the air. By then, the crowd had drawn in closer, forming a human chain around the track. They had gathered from the streets right down to the waterline.

While all of this was going on, a few of the jockeys, unaware that some of their colleagues had already begun positioning themselves at the starting lines, took the liberty to show off their horses around the track. Most were galloping in style, and it was apparent from the continuous eruption of laughter and applause that there were favorites among them.

A state of order was brought to the parading of the horses around the track, and for a short while everyone returned to the starting line and stood at attention. But even as it seemed as though no one would move till the order of go had come, things soon broke out into a posturing match. As the jockeys pushed and shoved each other for advantage in line, the crowed roared with laughter at the spectacle that had unfolded.

I was also caught in the excitement of the moment, biting mercilessly upon my lower lip until it hurt. Then, suddenly and without warning, the conch shells sounded like trumpets, and off they went.

The softness of the sand presented an enormous challenge to all as their feet sank deeply into the ground. With each stride forward, one could easily tell by the expressions on their faces that a lot of energy was being exerted. The crowed roared and roared, but in the end, only a handful of jockeys were able to make it past the finish line.

Throughout the course of the afternoon, the fierceness of the competition continued right down to the last race. As the day came to an end, I walked over to congratulate George and Kennedy for a job well done. We promised to collaborate with each other on future events, and reminisced a bit on the good fortunes of the afternoon. Once again, everyone was pleased, and during the course of our conversation together, other bright ideas, such as the establishment of a soccer league, were discussed.

A Tragedy Foretold (Part I)

Unknown to most of us at the time, that last Sunday was a fitting farewell to the long personal friendship that we shared. As the weeks went by, I saw very little of George and Kennedy.

A blanket of silence had fallen over the Mahung, and life at the bay soon returned to normal. It was as though the restless actions of our childhood days had been finally laid to rest in a dark and imaginary coffin.

On the very few occasions when our paths crossed, we basically greeted each other with a friendly wave, had short conversations, and went about our business. During that period, George and Kennedy had befriended a new set of boys who had arrived on St. Lucia from the neighboring French island of Martinique. Their father, like George and Kennedy's father, was also a fisherman, and it soon become obvious to all that they had struck up a real friendship. In fact, whenever they weren't together with the French boys, George and Kennedy were often busy doing carpentry work, which of course they were also very good at.

**George (L) with Kennedy, after a painting job inside
their Bay Street Home.**

However, in spite of all the changes that had taken place in
their lives, there was something that would never change. Their
love and devotion for the sea and fishing would remain with
them like an old-fashioned religion. As they grew older, their
destiny became entwined with sea exploration, and all of the

mysterious things that make the sea so wonderful. Soon they were making voyages from St. Lucia to Martinique, and a whole new world opened up to them.

I vividly recall the setting one warm August afternoon just before their first voyage to Martinique. There were blue skies above, and the sea appeared to lie as still as a newborn babe.

George and Kennedy, along with the French boys, had spent most of the afternoon securing their belongings in plastic containers that would later be loaded onto two large fishing boats. Monsieur Timotay, the father of the French boys, and his eldest son Patrick would each captain one of the two boats.

I was seated under a huge plum tree near the home that Mr. Timotay had rented for his family while in St. Lucia. I guess I had found myself there because of the tremendous publicity that the voyage had generated throughout Gros Islet.

As the containers were loaded into the boats one by one, I watched in silence and thought of the fascinating new world out there awaiting George and Kennedy Phillip. By reason of Martinique's geographical proximity to St. Lucia, we had heard a lot about it. They say that its capital, Fort De France, is like a miniature version of Paris under the Caribbean sun. It has breathtaking expressways and overpasses, and the cost of living there is just great.

Martinique's comparatively successful development could be directly attributed to the brutal but unselfish rule of French colonialism. They had taken time to establish a modern society out here in the Caribbean, while the British had turned St. Lucia into one of its harlots, sucking dry its slave labor in order to support an aristocratic lifestyle back in England.

At about 4:30 that afternoon, as each passenger climbed into the boats, I noticed that George and Kennedy had chosen to

ride with Mr. Timotay. Three of his youngest sons had also accompanied George and Kennedy aboard, and they seemed to
burst with excitement at the thought of crossing the channel
again into their native island of Martinique.

After the two parties had found comfortable places on board
the boats, I shifted my attention again to George and Kennedy.
They had received from Mr. Timotay two oversized yellow fisherman's cloaks, which seemed to have swallowed them whole.
Mr. Timotay and his sons, accustomed to the dangers of the
channel, wore dark sweaters, and wide-brimmed sombrero-type
hats over their heads.

By then the engines were all turned on, and the propellers of
the 75-horsepower Yamahas sliced through the peaceful waters
of the bay with a thunderous roar. Everything was now in place,
and like a magical moment, the voyage began.

I was down at the water's edge, and so were numerous other
people who had come to bid them farewell. We waved goodbye
amidst the roaring sound of the engines, the stern of each boat
lowered with the increased speed, as the bows soared over the
water like eagles in flight. They were all pointed in a northwest-
erly direction, and had taken aim for the open seas.

It was a thrilling moment for everyone present, with the fanfare of farewells and the roaring of the engines as they blasted
from behind the boats. Within a few minutes of their departure
they had completely crossed the large body of water known as
the Gros Islet bay. With the droning sounds of the engines fading slowly, the boats eventually disappeared behind the histori-
cally acclaimed landmass once proudly referred to as Pigeon Island.

Part Two

A Tragedy Foretold (Part II)

It was several weeks later when I bumped into George and Kennedy. They had just returned home the night before, and from all accounts their vacation in Martinique was a blast. They had even picked up a French accent, and did not hesitate to show off their acquired accents and French Creole vocabulary. The best phrases among them were "*La bar*" (down there), "*T Bollum*" (small boy), "*Fume Collayqet*" (prostitute), and even referring to every male person as "*Monsieur.*"

They would return again to Martinique on several other occasions, but without any of the fanfare and curiosity that had surrounded their first trip. By now everyone had grown pretty much accustomed to seeing them depart for Martinique, and basically went about their own business.

It was also during that period that they finally came into their own as fishermen. They had acquired a great deal of experience, and like their father and uncles before them, they had found their place in a long lineage of men who had a profound attachment to the ocean. Sadly, and unknown to either of them, their interest in the ocean that began when they were children would in effect seal their fate.

A Countdown To Tragedy

Friday, February 14, 1985, the winds whistle over an open pasture where the waters of the Gros Islet Marina flow deep into the land. At the water's edge, a fishing vessel, manned by six youths, is quietly set afloat into the Marina. The captain and co-captain are no more than twenty years old, while the rest of the crew range in age from thirteen to nineteen.

For three of the youngest crewmen aboard, the earlier part of the day had been filled with events of an unpleasant nature. Their unruly behavior in school, and a foolish desire to live a wayward life, had caused their teacher to toss them outside.

Three hours later, they were roaming the banks of the Marina in search of adventure. Spurred by these ambitions, thirteen-year-old Christopher "Baby" Clovis, his cousin Dominic "Peter" Edwin, and fourteen-year-old George "Jones" Bruneau jumped in the boat, in spite of strict warnings to stay ashore.

"IN GOD WE TRUST," are the spiritual words of confidence that appear boldly near the right side of the bow as the boat steams down the open Marina. It is not only the name of the boat, but also a fisherman's prayer, and that of millions of other people throughout the world.

A yellow stripe of paint along the sides separates the colors of red and green. The boat, twenty-two feet long and six feet wide, is powered by a forty-eight-horse engine, which feeds hungrily off the gas in a red metal container. The bow is narrow and ends in a triangular formation, but the stern appears oblong to the naked eye. There are a total of four wooden seats spread out across the boat, each configured differently depending on its location.

As the craft pushes past a thirty-foot German yacht anchored near the mouth of the Marina, pleasant waves are exchanged with those on board. The boat then continues in a westerly direction, and into the open sea.

Far ahead, under the scorching rays of the early afternoon sun, lie miles and miles of treacherous seas. These are the unguarded waters where the blue sharks roam, and peculiar currents dictate the course of most vessels. There is a tiny landmark out there, a rock that sits all by itself in the middle of the sea. The locals refer to it as La Wash, and this is exactly where the boat is headed.

Aboard, the mood is rather festive, as three of the older crewmen are engaged in a rather interesting conversation. Captain Evans "Perry" Charles, a tall and slender young man with knock-knees, converses with his cousins George and Kennedy. They have plans for the evening to attend the calypso finals in downtown Castries. Therefore, they are hoping to return ashore as early as possible.

From all accounts, lots of people will attend. And like George, Kennedy, and their cousin Perry, they will be coming from all over the island. With the expected mad rush for seats, it would be a silly mistake to not arrive early for the show.

As the boat advances deeper and deeper into the sea, it gently rises and tumbles against the choppy waters. There is an uncharacteristically long silence among the younger crew, who back ashore would ordinarily be loud and restless.

Out on the sea, the sun's hard rays mirror off the glassy ocean. The waters are so clear that it's impossible to miss the gentle slopes of the coral reefs, spread wide along the ocean floor. It's the home of the blue sharks and countless other cold-blooded and aquatic vertebrates.

Approximately two hundred yards off La Wash, this clandestine sanctuary covered with seabird guano, the boat comes to a drifting halt. Out there the air is particularly dry and heavy, and the fresh sultry scent rushes through the nostrils and makes their eyes water and their noses drip like molten syrup.

There's a scramble aboard as the weight of the crew tilts the boat slightly. The younger crew holds on tightly, and gives a sigh of relief when it finally stops.

The first of two fishing nets is carefully lowered into the water, and everyone waits patiently for it to sink to the ocean floor. There's a sharp swishing sound, as the last of the net leaves the boat, and the buoy shoots back to the surface like a rubber bullet. It then rides high upon the choppy seas, even with the weight of the net below. The next stop is a little further west of La Wash, where the winds blow precariously over the summit of the rock. It's also an area where the currents usually swell to dangerous proportions, yet every fisherman loves that spot for the potential rewards of a big catch.

The engine is turned on and the boat is guided calmly towards that area. They receive some help from the undercurrents, which help to steer the boat easily onwards.

However, as the second net is hoisted into the water, there is a sudden movement on board. The boat tilts to the right, then left, and back to the right.

It brings laughter to the younger crew, who in the aftermath of that rocking motion spend the time mimicking what has just transpired. But Perry, George, and Kennedy are not laughing. They just do not understand what was so funny.

It is almost time to start up the engine again, and to finally head back to shore. There is a whopping sound, and then another. This isn't unusual to anyone aboard. It is a familiar sound, and one that always follows the exertion of force when the engine's cord is pulled.

Perry eagerly waits for the engine to fire off with a blast, but nothing happens. There are a few seconds of silence between each of the whopping sounds, which is followed by another, and another.

Bending calmly forward, as if to clear an object from beneath his seat, George appears almost at one with the peace around him. In the seat directly behind, Kennedy is slumped with his back resting comfortably against the side, waiting patiently for the sound of the engine.

A minute or two goes by and still the humming sound of the engine is not heard. Way towards the back, Perry's patience is wearing thin. With one leg on the seat and the other on the floorboard, Perry struggles tirelessly to get the engine started.

Among the younger crew, who are all squished together in the front seat, the laughter has died out. There is a great silence that grows long and troubling. The boat has begun to drift, but no one takes notice. George has moved towards the back to assist Perry, and so has Kennedy.

An hour goes by, and still no sign of life from the engine. In fact, the monster, which only hours before fed hungrily off a few gallons of gas, now hangs from the stern of the boat, a worthless piece of metal.

George has a plan to row the boat back ashore. With the help of Kennedy and Perry, he attempts to do so.

It is proving to be difficult, much more difficult than they had anticipated. The currents are flowing in a southerly direction, and they latch onto the boat like a mighty anchor. In fact, with every push forward, the current pulls the boat one notch backwards. It is becoming pretty difficult, but still they try.

Another hour or so has now gone by, and there are worries on board as the dark of night begins to fall upon them. Perry would like to dump the engine into the sea to lighten the boat, but he is afraid to do so at this early stage. He discusses the matter with George and Kennedy, but neither one can bring themselves to do it.

With each passing moment, their efforts are waning. They are really tired now, as the effects of physical exhaustion haunt them like a ghost. Then, with pained backs, blistered hands, and the realization that not much was gained through their efforts, they allow the boat to drift in the darkness, at the mercy of the currents.

There are faint sobs in the front seat, where the crippling effects of fear have made the younger crew inconsolable. The evening breeze does not help either; it blows with a shivering coolness, brushing contemptuously against their naked backs.

Quietly, as the current moves the boat along, not a word is said. In the distance, and through the darkness which surrounds them like a maximum security prison, an array of dazzling lights, presumably that of the city of Castries, evokes thoughts of the calypso finals they'd hoped to attend. There's a dark lonely feeling, and it cuts away at the walls of their stomachs. This feeling is deeply rooted in the uncertainty that lies ahead, and of course the dimming hopes of being rescued tonight.

No one says a word, but in Kennedy's mind, there is a feeling of hope for tomorrow. His belief is that, should the morning come and find them still alive, someone will rescue them from this clear and present danger.

He feels a need to speak, but since no one has said a word, he keeps his mouth shut. As the silence grows louder, and the air around them grows cooler, he shivers a bit but continues to hold his peace.

Unable to deal with the pervading silence, Perry is the first to speak out. He predicts that by morning the tide will have rolled the boat back up north, making it easier for any search party from Gros Islet to spot them. But even as he tries to reassure everyone that things will be okay, there is a gentle agitation in his voice that no one can miss.

George latches onto Perry's theory, and backs him in encouraging the younger crew to remain strong through the night. Deep inside, he also feels assured that the bond and familiarity they have formed with the sea will guide them to safety on the following day.

However, as the darkness becomes prolonged into an endless night, sleep seems almost as far away as the shimmering lights in the distance. Also, the relentless bites from bloodthirsty mosquitoes torture them in the silence, as if they were already dead.

Shortly after midnight, the boat is positioned about fifty miles off the southern shore of a St. Lucian town, presumably Soufriere. This is an area where the peaks of St. Lucia's two majestic mountains (The Pitons) meet the heavens, and the town of Soufriere sits deep down in a canyon, as if looking up in awe at God's creation.

There is a feeling on board that the area is Soufriere. But the concealing effects of the darkness create a shadowy image of a great St. Lucian phenomenon that is sparsely lit by night, but tells an exquisite story of itself by day.

From the starless heavens overhead, intermittent raindrops have begun to fall. The sea, sensing the changing weather above, begins to move the boat in a rocking motion. There is a bit of fear among the younger crew, but George is able to calm them down. The sea continues to pummel the boat, but so far everyone is safe.

Perhaps an hour later, the rains finally die down, releasing the tension from their drenched bodies. Then there are the gentle sounds of the sea as it beats tirelessly but tamely against the boat, filling their senses with hope of tomorrow.

Thus far, the boat has withstood the test of perilous seas, and has carried them safely, despite the odds. She is very strong, and no one can ever doubt that the water-repellent gumwood from which her hull was constructed is what has kept the painted floorboards firm beneath their feet.

It's way past one in the morning, and still no one has shut his eyes to sleep. They have kept an all-night vigil, and under a blanket of dark clouds, they are waiting patiently for the morning to arrive.

At about a quarter past four, as the first sign of daybreak shoots across the horizon, they catch a hazy view of a landmass of hills and mountains in the very far distance. Then, gradually, as the fading darkness progresses into day, they become overjoyed upon discovering that Pigeon Point is still visible, in spite of the distance.

Perry was right, and although the distance is too great to attempt to swim ashore, they feel comforted by the distant views of a familiar area.

The News (Part I)

I was sitting under the late afternoon shade of an almond tree when I first heard the news. It must have been twenty past five or thereabouts when an old fisherman friend who prefers going by the alias "Laboo Lay Vay" delivered the shocking news. He heard it from the mouth of Nourgearo, who was sitting on the steps of York's café with a group of other boys.

Laboo had not grasped the story, since he was just passing by, but he had gleaned from Nourgearo that the boys had been missing since the day before. Yesterday, which was Friday, they had departed from the Marina, and had not been heard from since then.

I immediately left Laboo and began pacing up the small block up Bay Street and onto Dauphine Street where York's café is situated at the corner of Marie Therese. There was a small crowd at that intersection, but they were closer to the Special Corner variety store, opposite York's café.

Suddenly, my heart sank, and I could tell immediately by the attentiveness of the crowd that there was truth to Laboo's story. It had reached a pivotal point of crisis, and there were no ifs or buts about it.

I overheard Nourgearo almost tearfully recalling the events of the day and telling the crowd of people that from as early as 6:00 P.M. yesterday, he had a strong suspicion that something had gone terribly wrong. In fact, the last time he had spoken to George and Kennedy was at about 12 noon the day before. They had briefly talked about the calypso show that evening, but would first have to make their regular outing to sea later in the afternoon, and upon their return, head for Castries.

However, at about 6:30 that evening, when it became obvious that they had not returned, he urged a younger friend by the name Grantly Dupal (a.k.a. Bick) to take the short ride to the Marina on his bike to see whether or not the boys had returned.

Bick was back within fifteen minutes, and as the bike came to a screeching halt, he yelled out "no sign" to Nourgearo, who was sitting at the edge of the old sea wall. "Jah!" Nourgearo responded in a troubled voice, and hurried down to the shores where a few other fishermen were wrapping up their day's work.

With very little hesitation he told of his suspicions, but none of them were convinced that anything had happened to the boys. Moreover, knowing George and Kennedy as they did, and the area where they had gone to set the nets, it was impossible for them to be lost at sea. Convinced that he had failed to persuade the fishermen, and also upset at their dismissive attitude, Nourgearo left the boathouse in a state of melancholy, which quickly changed to anger.

He retreated quietly to the comfort of a small shack he owned on Bay Street, which was adjacent to the home of George and Kennedy Phillip. As he lay face-up across the bed with his arms folded upon his chest, he found himself haunted by a strange feeling, petrified by the darkness, which was swiftly closing over the bay. Amidst the occasional sightings of low-flying bats which flew quickly past his open window, there was a weakness in his body. It was as though he no longer knew who he was, yet he could neither cry nor come to grips with what was really happening to him.

From the yard next door, he could still hear the voices of the ghetto youths as they chanted out to "Jah" (God) during the evening meditation. This was always their method of escape, and their only way to register their opposition and defiance to the perceived injustices of a bourgeois community, or what was termed a "Bald-Head Society." "Jah" knew that they needed it badly, as the pain and hardships were at times too much to bear.

Later, as the sweet scent of Sinsemilla (Marijuana) filled the evening air, there was suddenly a hush over the entire yard. Rapt in mental anguish, Nourgearo struggled in vain to overcome his state of emotional despair. He frantically moved his eyes around the four walls of his shack, and couldn't seem to find an answer. He knew that there were dangers looming out there for his friends, and the darkness of night would not help them either.

On the following morning, Saturday, at about 5 A.M., Nourgearo hurried barefoot from the shack to the waterfront. He began to search for clues or a signal that the boys might still be out there somewhere. His eyes were hurting, and although they were red and puffy from lack of sleep, still he tried.

However, as he scanned across the misty bay for signs of the boat, he discovered nothing unusual. The coolness of the gray firmament, which stood before him as an accomplice in the disappearance of the boat, held only a body of unanswered questions. Where were George and Kennedy, he wondered in silence, and why hadn't Perry and the others returned ashore the evening before? These mysteries, and a nagging premonition that something had gone wrong, finally drove Nourgearo to take matters into his own hands. His idea was to assemble a list of people who might be willing to participate in a search party. But for now he would return to his shack, and wait for the sunrise to fully appear.

Going quickly though a list of names in his head, he realized that there was someone whom he could count on. That person was none other than Mr. Thaddeus Montoute, a well-known community activist who had time and time again proven to be a pillar of support in our community. "Taddy" had also assisted tremendously by reestablishing a deep appreciation for sports throughout Gros Islet, and was definitely the kind of fellow that anyone would want around in times like these. His experience in the Boy Scouts, and later the Cadet Corps, was particularly appealing to Nourgearo, and from the looks of things, Nourgearo had no doubt that he had built a body of contacts that were capable of offering even greater assistance. Feeling confident that he would be able to pull off his plan if Taddy was willing to stand by his side, Nourgearo decided to wait up until 6:45, hoping that by then the Montoute family would be off their beds. His idea was simple. He would present the problem to Taddy and request his help.

At exactly 6:45 that morning, he was over at the small colonial home on Marie Therese Street, where the Montoutes resided. From the open window towards the left side of the house, it was evident to him that someone was up. Therefore, quietly walking up to the front door, he tapped softly upon it, and stepped back anxiously for someone to answer.

A minute or so passed after the first tap; no one came to the door. Feeling the need to alert someone inside of his presence, Nourgearo tapped a bit louder, while raising his voice in "Good morning, good morning."

**Members of the Gros Islet Primary School soccer team
with their teacher and coach. Standing in the back row
(L) is Lenard "Spider" Montoute, "Baby" is (fourth
from left). Peter Clovis is (second from left) kneeling in
the front row.**

Lenard "Spider" Montoute, the younger brother of Thaddeus Montoute, answered the door. He looked a bit craggy, and with his typically laid back Saturday morning persona, seemed ready to question Nourgearo's early morning visit. However, before he even had the chance to fully step out of the door, Nourgearo got straight to the point.

Spider's expression became somber. He thought he had heard what Nourgearo had just said, but it did not make much sense at all. He asked again, and this time it really sunk in. He was saddened by the news of George and Kennedy, but was particularly shocked to learn that Baby and Peter were among those missing.

Incidentally, that fateful Friday afternoon, Spider was the school teacher who had sought to discipline the youths. After an entire morning of disturbance and unruly behavior, he had finally lost his patience with them. He had asked them to temporarily leave the class, but they had decided to call it a day. Their idea was always to be the bad boys of the class, and they often took great pleasure in testing their teacher's patience.

But even then, despite of their lack of interest in academia, there was a close and respectful relationship with Spider outside of the classroom. As a matter of fact, besides being their teacher on an academic level, he was also the coach of the high school soccer team. They had achieved good things together. That year they had not only played their best soccer, but they had also gone on to win the Interschool National Championship. Baby was the biggest star of that victorious soccer team. This very pesky-mannered, four-foot-five, dark-skinned boy had some exceptional skills when it came to playing soccer.

There was a tense moment of silence outside as Nourgearo waited impatiently for Spider to hurry back in to fetch Taddy. Although Nourgearo wasn't sure how Taddy would react to the news, he was hopeful for Taddy's help.

By the time Spider and Taddy returned to the door, it was a forgone conclusion as to what role Taddy would play. All Nourgearo had to do was give a brief account of the situation, and this in itself was enough to cement Taddy's willingness to participate.

They wasted little time in getting started, and before long Taddy was on the phone trying to make contact with the St. Lucia Coast Guard. He was finally able to reach someone at the other end, and there was a brief conversation. When it was over, it was clear that they would be heading down to Castries that morning.

A party of three—which included Taddy, Nourgearo, and another prominent community activist named Kenty "Carter" Pamphile—traveled from Gros Islet to Castries. There, they would accompany the Coast Guard to sea, and perhaps point them to the location where the boys had gone to tend their nets.

At about 10:00 that morning they were down at the Castries Harbor and were joined by a Constable Sealy. They finally boarded the *Defender* at about 10:30, and waited patiently through the final preparations before launch.

The *Defender* is one of a kind, and perhaps the only vessel owned by the St. Lucian Coast Guard. It was donated to us by the People's Republic of China, but many critics of the government often argue that the vessel is more of a defender in name than in deed. They seriously believe that it is incapable of finding missing persons at sea, and if there were ever a story where the *Defender* carried out a rescue at sea, one can bet that it would be treated as one of the biggest stunts since Christopher Columbus's claim that he discovered St. Lucia. Nevertheless, the *Defender* does have its supporters among St. Lucians.

It was a smooth and peaceful ride out to sea as the *Defender* left the harbor. There were panoramic views of the lush coastal terrain in the background, and of the rolling mountains and hills that give our island its impeccable beauty.

Once the *Defender* had made it way past the harbor's entrance, the captain decided to steer the vessel south, instead of north towards Gros Islet.

Norgearo's outward calm belied his inward uneasiness, as the *Defender* raced along the southern coast. Before long, they approached the area around Hess Oil Refineries, which sits as a symbol of American corporate power on a sun-soaked Caribbean island.

Not a word was said as the vessel continued to run along the southern coast, and it seemed for a while that everything was fine. But then, as an endless silence grew to fill the minutes, so did the irritable feeling of uneasiness that was bottled up inside of Nourgearo. Deep down inside he felt that need to comment, but restrained himself from doing so. Slowly, with each passing moment, his uneasiness grew into outrage. Approaching the point where he felt that he couldn't control his thoughts, he tried desperately for a moment longer to suppress those feelings. There was no doubt that his anger was directed at the captain, who he believed was leading them on a wild goose chase. Driven by his convictions, he finally spoke his mind as they neared the forty-fifth minute of the search.

There was fire in his eyes as his eyeballs rolled in discontent. "Man, you're going the f----- wrong way, and I done checked that already. All morning long the current has been moving up north, and you still can't see that."

"What are you talking about?" the captain responded testily. "Do you know anything about the sea?"

There was a brief pause, and then he went off again on Nourgearo, but this time in our local dialect of French patois and back again to English.

"*Hot say boug sa la, tou jour quire hot connet plea passer lot moon.*" (You guys always believe that you know more than other people.) "But when I look at you fellas, you know nothing."

148

"F--- you," Nourgearo quickly shot back, and gave the captain a vicious look. He then retreated from the confrontation, but not without a parting word.

The air was punctuated by an uncanny silence, as the captain pretended to ignore Nourgearo. With his sights kept forward, he steered the *Defender* over the rolling waves.

Every furlong forward heaped a ton of weight on Nourgearo's already strained emotional state. He could not believe that this was happening. Here he was sitting on a boat, with a captain whom he increasingly despised, and on a search to nowhere.

As he remained there in the silence, his mind wandered to some of the things that were said during the bitter exchange. For most of his life, and as far back as he could remember, he had never stooped to any man, especially when he was convinced that he was right. But now look at what had happened. This guy, the captain, had questioned his knowledge of the sea.

As the only son of an old fisherman who had since retired, Nourgearo felt that he had learnt a lot from his father, and was crafty enough in the ways of the sea. Moreover, given his reputation as a good swimmer, there must have been something that he could have shared on this search.

It was now well past an hour into the search, and there had not been a sign of the boys. All the while, Nourgearo was growing increasingly wary of the situation. He had all but conceded that it was time to return ashore, but was willing to give himself some time before making that request. Moreover, his loyalty to the boys forced him to question his own attitude. What if he was wrong, and the boys were not somewhere up north? Would he be able to live with himself if he were to prematurely bring an end to this search?

For an extended period, he was very quiet and kept a vigil over the waters. But just when it seemed as though he had finally rid himself of the urge to end the search, that feeling returned.

Calmly, he made his request to the captain, and he was surprised to find the man receptive to the idea. Since their search had not yielded anything, there really wasn't any reason to continue.

There was a sigh of relief from all aboard as the vessel turned around and hopped and dropped a bit over the waves. No one wanted a further escalation, and for now, they preferred to set out for the comfort of the shore, where clear minds would prevail and another plan could be devised.

But even though it was understood the decision to return ashore was from general consensus, there was a visible expression of sadness, which painted a picture of how disappointed Nourgearo was with the turn of events.

Deep down inside, he wished that the *Defender* had headed north, and that the argument with the captain had not happened. He chastised himself and entertained doubts about his decision to second-guess the captain.

In his mind, he retraced the events of the day before, attempting to piece together theories of what might have transpired at sea. Perhaps there was an accident, and perhaps that boat had sunk. But if this was so, there was no way for Kennedy, George, or even Perry to have not made it ashore.

He was suddenly thinking like a madman, as he once again allowed his thoughts to wander. Maybe they had made shore in a remote part of the island, and were having difficulty in making their way back home over land.

Finally, as the *Defender* made its way into the harbor, he tried to pull his thoughts together, but couldn't quite concentrate. He would never be at peace, not until the fate of the boys had been fully established.

The News (Part II)

Nourgearo was just about finished recounting his tale when I left the gathering and hurried on home.

Glancing momentarily at the digital timepiece with the chrome bangle upon my wrist, I noticed that it had stopped. Normally, something like that would really infuriate me, but the thought of what had just happened to George and the boys at sea was far more important. Even if it was very obvious that I had been dubbed into paying thirty Eastern Caribbean dollars for the watch, I still had a lot to be thankful for. I was alive.

The house was in total darkness when I finally arrived home. And in the left-hand corner of the balcony, where my mother usually kept some potted plants, I saw the scintillating eyes of our cat Francine, staring right at me in the dark.

It had been a couple days since the last time I'd seen her. She was upset with my mother for moving the tiny creatures she had given birth to under the bed. In fact, there was a big controversy between my mother and Francine. No sooner had my mother transferred the kittens than Francine decided to take them right back. This time, my mother decided to put all of them into the kitchen outside. Although it was clear that Francine had been defeated, she accepted it grudgingly.

Tonight I was in no mood for any of Francine's foolish antics. Therefore I turned away and entered through the front door. The switch was not very difficult to find. With a single backhand motion, I turned on the light in the living room.

The large wooden clock on the wall read 7:25 P.M. Soon it would be time for me to leave again. In about fifteen minutes or so, I must be over at Pairsheen's house to commence our nightly musical rehearsal. At this time, I was all into music. I was the "leader" of a rock band called the Universal Stars. We wrote and arranged all of our songs, and we were very much committed to improving the music. However, although I was certain of success in the future, there was one thing that we had to overcome. We constantly fought over money, and this was something I felt must change.

My eyes were back on the clock as I carelessly stuck my head into the fridge and pulled out some butter and cheese. From the silver-plated bread pan on the table, I snatched a loaf that had been sitting there since last Thursday evening.

The loaf in my hands felt like a rock. Moreover, the crust was so sharp that I swore I might choke on it. Not wishing to do any harm to myself, I decided to throw it right back into the pan.

I turned quickly and returned the butter and cheese to their place, I began to sift through the refrigerator for something else to eat. There were a few bananas on the bottom shelf, and some fried fish and avocado in a bowl. I was hungry, but my appetite and schedule would not allow me to sit around and enjoy any of these things.

Me as a teenager in 1984, posing for an individual picture on Dauphine Street (Gros Islet's main Street). I was
then a member of the local Rock Group, The Universal
Stars. In the background (R) is the Special Corner Variety Store, and directly opposite is York's Café'. The
Caribbean sea is at the end of the street).

Therefore, turning away from the freezer, I slammed the door a bit harder than usual. "Ooops!" I said to myself, thinking fleetingly of what my mother might have said were she present.

Stumbling a bit into my bedroom, I grabbed my guitar, which was lying close to my pillow, and headed out of the room.

The clock in the living room read 7:35 as I stepped outside. Out in the balcony, among the potted plants, I didn't see a trace of Francine. Although there was a street lamp near the house, for the most part the block was always permeated with darkness.

At the corner of Notre Dame and Parish Street, and also at the intersection of Notre Dame with Dauphine, the street lamps were far brighter. I turned left onto Dauphine and went halfway up the block. I decided to make a stop at the local baker to purchase some bread with butter and cheese for dinner.

The baker, whom everyone affectionately refers to as "Brother," was a very good friend of mine. At times, when I found myself with nothing much to do, this area was the perfect place to discuss religion and politics.

A light rain began to drizzle softly on my head at about the time I left the tiny bakery. Overhead and high up in the heavens, a blanket of gray clouds covered the night skies. Therefore, I hastened my steps a bit and quickly turned right onto Bridge Street and down the block.

My godmother, Ms. Jerona "Amore" Ignatius, was sitting comfortably on her veranda. As usual, I said good night and turned left onto St. George street, where the darkness of night covered that lonely block.

I was now a few yards away from Pairsheen's home, where the full width of the street measured no more than fifteen feet. The homes on either side of the street were clustered so tightly that it almost felt as though I was trespassing on private property.

As I neared the wooden gate that led into the yard, I was greeted with a wag of a tail against my leg by Pairsheen's beautiful brown dog. Looking over the gate, I could see the floodlights in the shed outside.

Webster "Webe" Gustave, our drummer, was seated on a wooden stool, and we jammed fists as I entered the shed. I liked Webe very much, because he had a great sense of dedication to the music and hardly complained about a thing.

The concrete floor in the shed was littered with scraps of wood that were left over from Pairsheen's work during the day. In the far corner of the shed was an incomplete cabinet, which was being supported by a stool. On the narrow work table, which stretched the full length of the shed, were some tools, a paint brush, and three cans of varnish.

As I quietly took my seat on top of some bricks that were stacked neatly in the shed, I couldn't help but catch the sound of the running water behind me. In the midst of all the silence, I suddenly felt a strange and eerie feeling inside. I was aware of what triggered it, and couldn't help myself. Ever since I'd left the area around York Café and Special Corner, God knows how hard I tried not to think about what Nourgearo had said. But now it had finally caught up with me. I just could not help but think of the terrible situation that George and company had fallen into.

For the next ten to fifteen minutes, it seemed as though the night had gone to sleep. There was not much being said between myself and Webe, who sat patiently on the stool with his face in his hands.

Suddenly, from the darkness outside, the sound of the running water died out. Pairsheen had concluded his evening shower. He howled over to us and checked inside the house for a change of clothes.

It was about that time that Francis "Parker" Quito, our lead guitarist, bumped into the shed with his guitar tucked under his arm. Parker, a tall and slender chap, always had a quiet disposition. Judging by his mild manner out on the streets, you could not tell that this man was able to turn the guitar into a mean machine. He was, in my estimation, a quiet musical genius of sorts. Together with the outgoing personality of his cousin Pairsheen, who played the bass guitar in the group, the two tried to keep the musical legacy of their parents alive.

Parker, who shares the same father as my cousin Victor, was but a child when his father passed away in 1971. He died in an auto accident in St. Croix, U.S. Virgin Islands, on his way to a performance that never took place.

As usual, Parker took his seat on an old straw chair beside me and searched in his pocket for his trademark plectrum, which was carved out of an empty Clorox bottle. Once he located the pick, he quietly pulled himself together and strummed softly and melodiously upon the strings of his guitar.

Incidentally, the chords he has chosen to play are all favorites of mine. I have always found the combination of G, A, E-minor, and C to be not only melodious, but melancholy at times. Softly, as he strummed his guitar, I also picked up on the tune. Parker was playing an instrumental version of our latest composition ("A Hero"), which I had written less than seventy-two hours before.

The sun is shining yet we're not hot
What's all gone wrong I'd like to know,
Why has the sun become so cold?
It's broad daylight and there's still no heat

[Chorus]

A hero is dying somewhere right now
And is dying now with pain in his heart
Where in the world is he dying?

The words and the music ignited emotions of sadness inside of me. I found myself quietly singing the song in my mind while Parker strummed and picked away at the chords on his guitar. I was being drawn into a world of my own, and in that world I had George and Kennedy on my mind.

Although this song was not written with George and Kennedy in mind, I couldn't help but feel a certain connection between the individual in my song and the boys whom I once idolized and respected as kids. It is true, and in spite of some of the striking differences in our personalities and in our individual approaches to life, George and Kennedy had made a serious impression upon me as a child.

As kids, they had acquired a certain level of independence that most kids their age had not yet attained. From early on, they distinguished themselves from the rest of their peers by proving how easily they could make a livelihood from the sea. George and Kennedy were always skillful with their hands, but it was their creative minds that I admired the most.

I was feeling all teary-eyed as Pairsheen walked into the shed. He was dressed in a pair of blue shorts and a T-shirt, with a pair of rubber slippers on his feet.

On the work table across the floor lay an acoustic guitar that Pairsheen had literally transformed into a bass guitar. It was painted in a dark glossy finish, but the color was unrecognizable through the great quantity of sawdust all over its body.

Just as he had done on so many evenings before, Pairsheen reached under the worktable, and grabbed a rag to dust off his guitar. Unfortunately, tonight not even the old cotton rag was clean enough to do the job. It too, was covered with sawdust, which forced Pairsheen to race out of the shed and into the small concrete kitchen in search of another.

It was at that very moment that "Boom Boom" walked in. He was not a member of the band, but remained very supportive of the group since its formation. Not only did he know the words to all of our songs, but he also knew how to play the guitar. Although he lived directly opposite Pairsheen, we never thought of him as being serious enough to join the band.

There was a long moment of silence on my part, as my mind flashed back to the ordeal that George and Kennedy were facing at sea. Oh, how I wished that no harm would befall them, and that there was something that I, or anyone else for that matter, could do to bring them safely home.

With Boom Boom in the shed, I started to reminisce a bit about the early days, and all of the naughty fun that George, Kennedy, and I had enjoyed with the other kids inside the Catholic church.

Boom Boom or "Ba-ba-lew," as he is commonly known throughout Gros Islet, happened to be that very same acolyte whom we'd silently made fun of by adding his name and that of his mother (Ms. Fiday) to the song "Chorus of Unholy Pleasure." He had really grown into a fine young man, and had discarded his cassock and churchly ways for the image of a *petit bourgeois*.

As I briefly pondered upon those innocent yet crazy days of our childhood, I took some solace in my memories of the past. About that time, Pairsheen re-entered the shed and proceeded to dust off his guitar with the new rag.

I had suddenly lost my enthusiasm for the rehearsal, but was too afraid to say so. Knowing Pairsheen, and how upset he got when others did not apply themselves musically, I did not want to be the guilty one. In the next week or so we were scheduled to play on stage with the likes of Luther Francois and Malcolm "Locks" McGowan. Therefore, it was imperative that all the arrangements to our songs were completed.

As usual, the task of arranging the original compositions, which I had written, was left to Pairsheen. He possessed great skill in that area, and could always perfect the roughest parts of any songs.

To us, Pairsheen was like a god of music who felt every musical vibe, saw every musical imperfection, and had the answers to everything musical. Even that could not stave off the fights between the two of us, especially when I perceived that he had radically changed my songs.

Incidentally, the song we were about to work on that evening was the same one Parker had been strumming on his guitar earlier. I had originally intended for "A Hero" to be played in a slow rock fashion, but Pairsheen had other plans. He wanted it wild and crazy, with something of a Mick Jagger, Rolling Stones rhythm. I relented on this one, and what a noble gesture this was.

Within half an hour of experimentation with that new sound, Pairsheen had formulated an appropriate bass rhythm, which he termed "The Pairsheen Style." With his left leg positioned forward and the right split to the back, he moved in a robotic fashion to a fast-paced rhythm. Over and over again, we attempted to master the intricacies of that arrangement, and before long, not only had we gotten it right, but we also had Boom Boom on his feet, dancing for joy.

He reached into his back pocket and pulled out a joint. And before I could follow what was happening, he had struck a match and set the end of the joint ablaze. It did not take very long for the smell of that forbidden herb to fill the air and the smoke to fill the shed. Boom Boom took another drag, and another one, and soon there was a blanket of thick smoke over his face. He was by now in Satan's grip, and a long way from his innocent days as an acolyte in the Catholic Church.

By now, with several patches of smoke hanging like clouds around the entire shed, I was not only becoming dizzy, but I had an irritating lump in my throat. Yet in spite of that second-hand high, I just kept the tempo going.

Unfortunately, this wasn't my first experience with a second-hand high, and certainly not the last. I guess as long as I am exposed to the music, I will continue to involuntarily inhale that potent stuff, which makes others feel like "a boat on a river," floating below "marmalade skies."

As the joint made its way around the shed, it bypassed Webster and I, who religiously declined. We had already received our kick from the second-hand smoke, and had no physical need to partake of that miracle grass wrapped in white paper.

From here onwards, the music got louder and better. It was also pretty difficult, but I was doing my best to keep pace with those who had voluntarily inhaled the transforming grass. It was like riding in a fast car, and every change from one chord to another presented an exciting challenge. But then, I wasn't about to stop either, for you never did in the middle of an important chord rotation.

At about 10:00 that evening, we decided to call it a night. Parker, Webe, and I walked out of the yard, leaving Pairsheen and Boom Boom alone to discuss how good the session had been.

The entire portion of St. George that stretches from St. John's to Bridge Street seemed dark and deserted. Therefore, it was a kind of welcoming relief when I arrived at Bridge Street and the light from the lamp pole cast its brightness upon us. There, we bade each other good night, and Webster continued west on St. George towards Notre Dame, while Parker turned left and I turned right on Bridge Street in the direction of our respective homes.

The coolness of the night air felt a little brisk as it stroked my face. I continued along to the place where Bridge and Dauphine Street intersect each other, and onto the last block of Bridge Street, which ends at the steps of the Catholic church.

There was a small gathering at the end of the block, and out of curiosity, I decided to check it out. Monsignor Bartholomew, the parish priest, along with Crusoe Moise, Jean Claude Gaston, and some other boys were present.

I decided to join the gathering, but first I greeted the Monsignor with the respect he deserved, and then everyone collectively.

It was always good to be in the company of Monsignor Bartholomew, for there was always something of substance to learn. Moreover, lacking the arrogant and racist tendencies of his predecessor, Father "H," the Monsignor understood his role as a spiritual leader and always treated others of different faiths with great respect and tolerance.

Prior to the gathering tonight, we had had many good conversations that had helped to alter my negative perception of the Catholic Church. Although there are still some basic principles that I believe are designed to exploit the ignorance of our people, Roman Catholicism as presented by clerics like the St. Lucian Monsignor had a sense of humility to it that draws me closer and closer to my old faith.

The Monsignor was sitting on part of the ruins of an old wall that bordered the old convent and formed the northern boundary of the old school yard where George, Kennedy, Ronnie, and I once attended school and played. I took a seat beside some of the boys at the edge of the asphalt-covered street.

The discussion, centered on the missing youths, caught my interest immediately. Everyone was expressing sadness over the incident, but also spoke in terms that seemed to suggest that they were already dead.

The Monsignor did not agree, and I half-heartedly shared his optimism. We believed that they were still alive, and with God's will, would return safely ashore.

A rush of quiet emotion suddenly came over me, and I was unable to decide whether I wanted to cry or allow myself to be rendered comatose by this chilling conversation. Having shared so much with George and Kennedy made it feel as if it would be a betrayal to completely detach myself from their plight.

I had no escape, and as much as I tried my best to hold my emotions in check, I knew that having this terrible and constant nightmare on my mind was the price I had to pay for having befriended them as a child.

As the Monsignor calmly continued with his line of optimism, I reminisced on the good old days with George, Kennedy, and Ronnie, and the abundance of pleasure we had in that schoolyard.

I heard the words that the Monsignor was saying, but couldn't seem to keep my eyes focused on him. Sitting at the edge of the asphalt street, it was very difficult to keep my sights off that bare spot directly in front of me, which once housed two school buildings and the old convent. It was there that we had received our first serious education, played together during recess, and, at other times, listened to invigorating stories about the sea told by both George and Kennedy.

Those were really glorious days, when life seemed immeasurable, and the innocent ambitions and aspirations of every school child flowed like a rushing river to the sea. Nothing, absolutely nothing was impossible then. But now, looking back upon those days, in the glaring absence of those physical structures of education, just made my heart wither. Instead of preserving those structures for historical posterity, they had all been broken down and transported like meaningless matter to a dumping site called Choc. This lack of insight on the part of the powers that be left us searching.

Strangely, the more I thought about it, the angrier I became. For although the memories of yesterday continue to burn deeply in my psyche, there was no physical evidence to help me savor those memories.

My attention was again drawn to the conversation\ in which the Monsignor continued to advance a view of optimism. And in the process, he also altered the opinions of those who thought otherwise.

Jean Claude, who sits as a disciple at the feet of Monsignor Bartholomew, takes us back in time to a similar incident involving three older fishermen. T-Chame, Black Brother, and Headley had been lost at sea for over a week. I distinctly recalled the event, for it was a week or two before the commencement of the annual St.

Peter's Day festivities. When word of their disappearance hit the streets, many of the fishermen in the community had mounted a vigorous but disappointing search. By the time the feast of St. Peter arrived, with a general acceptance that they had perished at sea, the townspeople set a single wreath afloat upon the waters of the bay as a fitting farewell to fallen comrades. But in the end, they were finally rescued off the coast of Venezuela. The gathering finally broke at about 11:15 P.M., which was about the time that the Monsignor, taking stock of the time, begged to be excused for the night. In fact, tomorrow was Sunday and he had a very busy schedule ahead of him. Customarily on Sundays, he performed two masses in Gros Islet (a high and a low), and then traveled to the countryside to proclaim the gospel of faith to the loyal Roman Catholic following out there.

The weight of sleep was heavy in my eyes as I continued along the short journey back home. But even as I walked the streets, I couldn't help but have a little doubt about the sentiments of optimism with which the gathering had ended.

I would have liked to believe that all was well out there for the boys, but I also worried a lot about other things. I thought about the parents of George and Kennedy, and those of the other boys, and just couldn't begin to imagine the pain and anxiety that they must have been going through this evening.

Oh my God! This whole thing hurt.

At the corner of Parish and Notre Dame Streets, I was met by Puppy, the neighborhood dog. He was very happy to see me, and escorted me to my front door.

Once inside the house, I slipped quietly into my room, where the darkness of night swallowed me whole till the morning light.

The Chips Are Down

It must have been about 12:00 noon when I finally crawled out of bed. The chocolate tea, which my mother had prepared earlier, had grown cold in the pot. Even the charcoal from the first morning's fire had turned to ashes. I was deeply disappointed and wanted to start another fire, but decided against doing so. "Lazy! Lazy!" These are the words my mother might have said were she present. But who cared; she was not around to see.

Feeling the morning hunger screaming in the form of tiny gas bubbles in my stomach, I poured the cold chocolate in a cup and grabbed a loaf for breakfast. I made my way to the backyard to sit on a log that had been shielded from the murderous rays of the midday sun. With the winds rustling gently though the coconut palms above me, I began to enjoy a slow, contemplative breakfast. Out here, the air was fresh and clean, and it filtered through my nostrils with ease. From the yard behind me, where dry coconut palms act as a buffer between our property and that of the neighbor next door, the radio played a prerecorded broadcast of the morning Mass from the Roman Catholic cathedral in Castries. I began to think about the afternoon, but couldn't seem to come up with anything to do. The rugby match that had been scheduled for later that afternoon had been abruptly postponed till the following Sunday. Although I am not a rugby player, and have never attempted to play the sport, I have often occupied my Sundays by being supportive from the sidelines. On weekends when the game is played, I am the custodian of the first-aid kit, and also the Heinekens that are kept on ice for when the game is over.

My cousin Victor (Natty), who plays on the team, is a big favorite of mine. He is tall and well built, and loves to tackle his opponents without fear. I often worry about his safety, but he hardly has any concern for himself.

I'd been sitting under the coconut tree for well over an hour now. The shade had shifted a bit. *I've got to go*, I thought to myself, and proceeded out of the backyard.

In the small kitchen, which is detached from the main house, I noticed that my mom was present. She'd returned from her regular Sunday visit to her mother's house at 73 Marie Therese Street.

On a narrow shelf, which was covered with a Waverly table cover (commonly referred to as a "tappy" by the locals), was a blue bucket filled with fresh drinking water. A frozen chicken lay in a pot beside the bucket. Not too far off, on a second shelf beside the open window, a slow but steady fire burned in the coal pot.

My mother, quickly sensing my presence behind her, handed me a bowl of uncooked rice. She expected me to seek out all the chaff, which I called "debris," until it was safe for human consumption.

She could tell by my body language that I was displeased, but she decided to ignore me completely. I really hated that task, but

I am even angrier with the government for importing this filth from Guyana. I always thought our lives might have been easier despite the cost if Uncle Ben's rice were imported in larger quantities. I had occasionally sampled this rice and know the taste, and difference between Uncle Ben's long-grain rice and the baby teeth-sized rice from Guyana.

I was just about to step out of the kitchen when I heard the familiar voice of Mrs. Artinaz in the doorway. She was a distant relative of my mom who resided in the countryside, but preferred to travel to downtown Gros Islet in order to attend Mass. Sundays were always the happiest days of Mrs. Artinaz's life, since it was about the only day of the week that she could find someone with a receptive ear to listen to all of her complaints and worries about an ever-changing world. My mom is that kind of person, "the mother of all affliction." People like Mrs. Artinaz always came to her to lay their troubles at her feet.

As I made my way back into the back yard in search of a comfortable spot, I realized that the neighbor's radio had caught a bug. Those crackling sounds that interrupted the broadcast came across like the buzz of bumblebees in my ears. "Boomer!" I chuckled to myself, since it was common knowledge what made the radio sound this way.

Cheap radios from Taiwan, "Akai" are magnets for roach infestation. One needs to look no further than the back of the radio to discover the problem. There is something inviting in there which always attracts the St. Lucian roaches. Let them find an opening to the back of the Akai, and very soon they will not only lay their eggs inside, but they will also begin to play havoc with the wires.

I found a comfortable spot, but the task of cleaning the rice was proving to be very difficult, as usual. The bowl was filled with those little dark particles that seemed to outnumber the baby tooth-sized grains of sickly-looking rice. Compounding the problem was a dusty, powdery substance which covered my hands like latex gloves. It was quite some time before I was able to complete the grueling task, and then I headed towards the kitchen.

At the doorway that led into the kitchen, Mrs. Artinaz was now sitting on a chair with a cup of tea in her hands. Not wanting to appear rude, I begged to be excused and handed the bowl to my mother.

I entered the main house and stepped into my room for a change of clothes, but couldn't seem to decide on a choice of clothing. I reached into a cardboard box and grabbed an old pair of jeans, and a T-shirt with a faded political symbol.

I was just about to slip it on when the thought of who I might offend crossed my mind. There are always a few political zealots on the streets of Gros Islet, and caution must be exercised against those who love to curl their noses at other people. Although my family has always been supportive of the ruling party, and makes no apology for doing so, there are some who would prefer that we didn't. Thank God that our democracy is still strong, and that we have not reached the point of Jamaica or Haiti, where guns are used to silence opponents. I decided to wear my T-shirt. What harm could it do, except to suffocate those who wish to curl their nose at me?

It was about a quarter past two as I stepped out onto the streets. For a Sunday afternoon, the streets seemed quieter than usual. I headed in the direction of the bay area, where I hoped to gather the latest news on the boys.

From the homes on either side of the street, I could hear the regular Oldie Goldie Sunday afternoon music blaring from the radios. I guessed it was only natural for families who wanted to spend a perfect Sunday afternoon before returning to work and school on Monday.

As I quickly passed the first boathouse on my right, I noticed a few people under the boathouse. Therefore, without any hesitation, I decided that it might be a good idea to hang out there for while.

The conversation under the boathouse was about the missing youths, and of how Nourgearo had placed an urgent call to neighboring Martinique for assistance. In fact, my understanding of what was being discussed was that, a young woman by the name of Taylia Daniel (sister to Claudius and Terry Daniel) had talked Nourgearo into contacting her brother-in-law.

Monsieur Ejene, who is married to Morella, the eldest sister of Taylia, Claudius, and Terry, among others, is a very skillful fisherman with years of experience. His boat is well-equipped with two engines in the back and a number of pieces of state-of-the-art navigational equipment that would assist in locating the boys.

Interestingly, Monsieur Ejene had cultivated a very good relationship with George and Kennedy over the years. As a matter of fact, during most of their earlier visits to Martinique, the boys would often divide their vacation between the homes of Monsieur Ejene and Timotay.

I couldn't help but pay close attention to the conversation, especially the part when someone mentioned that Monsieur Ejene was due to arrive in St. Lucia at any moment now. I temporarily interrupted the conversation to inquire about this a bit. By their estimation, it would take monsieur Ejene, with two powerful engines in the back of his boat, no more than two and a half hours to get to St. Lucia.

The urgency which had been placed on Monsieur Ejene's getting to St. Lucia renewed my hopes. Suddenly, I felt a rush of excitement, which almost seemed to indicate that the afternoon might turn out all right.

I also thought of Monsignor Bartholomew and what he had said the night before. I guess he was right. There was always hope at the end of the tunnel, and even in the darkest of situations, one ought not to lose one's faith. A miracle was still possible, and if it were the will of God, George, Kennedy, Perry, Baby, Jones, and Peter would return ashore together.

Amidst all of the discussion that was going on, it was evident that all eyes were glued in the direction of Pigeon Island, from whence this benevolent French man and his boat would first appear. Any time, he and his boat would thunder into the Gros Islet Bay with a mighty roar.

Unfortunately, although I wanted to witness his grand entry into Gros Islet, I was not able to stick around for very long. I cursed to myself as Pairsheen appeared in a red pickup van. I had completely forgotten my promise to him since the rugby match had been postponed. I had offered to help out on his watermelon farm at Cas-En-Bas, and obviously, someone had told him that I was by the bay.

A promise is a promise. And since I have always felt a bond to the commitments that I make to others, I felt that it was important to join him in the van.

The scent inside was not only fresh, but the vehicle itself rode beautifully. Only days before, Pairsheen had purchased that van to help him transport building supplies, and naturally, to reap the full benefits of having enough space to carry his watermelons into town for sale.

As we drove towards the farm at Cas-en-bas, Pairsheen pulled up near an unfinished building which was the site for a proposed treatment center for alcoholics. Right there and then he began to explain an idea he had, but somehow I couldn't find myself receptive to it at all.

He tried very hard to convince me that this site was ideal for hosting a "Block-o-Rama" to benefit the band, but somehow I felt so detached from the conversation that I just could not listen. Frankly, I was still thinking about the boys and their families, and I just couldn't find a sensible reason why there was all this talk of a Block-o-Rama right now.

Somehow he finally caught my attention, and while I can't recall exactly what he said to reach me, I sort of fell in tune with the conversation when he said he felt that the spot was large enough, and that it could easily attract a huge number of people because of its close proximity to the highway.

That afternoon, I learned a valuable lesson from Pairsheen, which altogether made me see a new side to him: he was a very shrewd businessman. And his seeming lack of empathy for the boys did not mean that he didn't care. In fact, what I learnt from him was that in all the emotional feelings of sadness and grief, one couldn't afford to stop living by refusing to devise new means of putting bread on the table.

As we walked back to the van, I inquired a bit about his grand idea. My concerns were with getting electricity to the sound system, since there were no sources of electricity onsite. He managed a faint smile, and as we climbed back into the van he began to explain how he thought electricity could be carried over to the grounds.

It was simple; all he had to do was make an arrangement with Milo, who owned a small bar in the vicinity. He would run the wires from the bar across the road and onto the grounds. And if push came to shove, and this idea was unworkable, the next thing would be to rent a generator for the event. Strange but true, that event would become a reality weeks later.

The short ride to the farm took no more than a few minutes. Within moments of our arrival there, we wasted very little time getting to work.

Unlike the previous harvest, which had yielded a small crop, this one was far beyond Pairsheen's wildest imaginings. There were huge watermelons all over the ground, with countless smaller ones hiding under the clustered leaves. As we picked out the good ones and stacked them one by one in an area unobstructed by the leaves, the pile grew taller and taller until there was nowhere else to put them.

Our next task was to load them into the van, which proved to be very tedious. However, once this was completed, it became a funny sight to see the way the body of Pairsheen's van had dropped to the ground. "Wow!" I joked around with him. "It seems that your van has been impregnated by a good harvest of watermelons." To that, we both laughed a bit, and soon it was time to leave.

It must have been close to 6:00 P.M. when we finally left the farm and headed into town. There were several stops along the way due to the rockiness and occasional steep hills of the Cas-En-Bas region. But we managed the best that we could.

Upon our arrival in town, dusk had just about settled all over Gros Islet. As I watched the brightly-lit street lamps with the night insects hovering around them, I was convinced that they were giving credence to the deepening darkness to come.

The pickup came to a halt at the corner of St. John and St. George Street, and very soon, with the assistance of a few other guys, we had unloaded the watermelons from the van. They were then carried into the yard where some were stocked inside the small brick kitchen which was completely detached from the main house. It was at that point that I decided to bid good-bye to Pairsheen, and headed for home.

I didn't make any stops along the way, and within a few minutes I was home and in my room, sorting through the cardboard box for a clean towel. I desperately needed a shower and couldn't wait to wash the dirt off my body.

The water was warm and soothing as I stepped beneath the tap, which was surrounded by galvanized steel in the back yard. I was having fun, and was mesmerized by the sound of the water as it fell on my head, and onto the pebbles which we had gathered from the seashores.

Tonight, although the skies were covered with stars which cast light over the darkness, I had no intention of showering for very long. In fact, my idea was to get out as soon as possible, change into new clothes, have some dinner, and head right back out.

Within an hour I was out of the house and back on the streets. I wanted so badly to find Nourgearo, who I was certain would be able to shed some light on what had actually transpired that afternoon.

Fortunately, I did not have to go very far to find Nourgearo. He was standing at his favorite spot near York's Café, and with him was Placide (George and Kennedy's oldest brother), Martin Phulchere (who was not only my first cousin but also Nourgearo's), and an old chap by the name of Tommy, a.k.a. "Wire."

Monsieur Ejene had arrived in St. Lucia as expected, and had been accompanied out to sea by Nourgearo and Raphael "Shoalin" Pamphile, a bosom friend of mine.

That afternoon, after they had searched the entire area along the western cost of the island, they decided to return once more to the area where Nourgearo said that the boys had gone to set their nets. This time, although they found no traces of the missing crew, the search party was able to locate and recover the two nets from the sea.

As the afternoon dragged on, and the prevailing darkness spread itself like a blanket across the water, Monsieur Ejene called off the search and returned to shore. It was over. George, Kennedy, Perry, Jones, Baby, and Peter were now presumed to have perished at sea.

Calamity Looms At Sea

The presumption that they had perished at sea, and the time at which everyone thought they did, would months later prove untrue.

On Saturday, February 15, the second day of the ordeal at sea, hopes of being rescued remained high, but there was a cautious approach to the unfolding situation. This, and the weight of the uncertainty ahead, coupled with worries about the length of time it would take before they could be found, played havoc with their minds. Could it be possible that no one had noticed that they were not around? And if so, what could be done to prepare for an indefinite period at sea?

They looked ahead to devise a contingency plan to aid their survival. The main idea was to catch as many fish as possible and put them out to dry in the sun. Everyone was required to pitch in and work. They also thought that if they could remain focused, and not worry too much about the little stuff, that their chances for survival were good.

At about 10:30 that morning, after searching through the entire boat for a fishing line, Kennedy soon found one coiled up near the bow. He spent some time trying to untangle the line, and when he succeeded, a dry piece of bait was attached to the rusted hook and tossed into the ocean.

There was a long moment's wait before anything happened. However, once the first fish was caught, several others were added to the catch. They included red snappers, and, to their surprise, a few flying fish, which ordinarily would not have been caught with a fishing line. Each of the boys took turns with the fishing line, increasing the catch, till there was enough to last for days.

Following that period, there was a long silence aboard as George undertook the difficult task of scaling the fish and removing their intestines. Then, one by one, Perry reached over and soaked each fish in a bowl of seawater until they were sufficiently free of blood. The fishes were then laid out to dry on two empty seats near the bow, and suddenly it seemed as though learning to be patient in case of an extended period at sea was about the only thing required to carry them through.

The morning had expired without a single sign of rescue. As the powerful rays of the sun beat mercilessly upon them into the afternoon, they soon searched for ways to quench their thirst.

More than anyone else, it was a bit of a surprise to hear Perry complain about a painful lump in his throat. His last drink of water had been more than thirty-two hours ago. A creature of habit, he would gorge on water early in the morning and never think about it again during the course of the day. Unfortunately, his last drink had been at about 9:00 A.M. that fateful Friday.

Throughout the course of the afternoon, although everyone aboard seemed to be in good spirits, the desire to quench their thirst did not abate. George started an odd joke, and pretty soon everyone began to think seriously about it. In what was not meant to be anything but a joke, he had dared them to put their manhood to the test by gorging on a few gulps of pure seawater.

True to his defiant nature, Baby was the first to take on the challenge. He grabbed a small bowl, leaned over the side, and gathered enough water to quench his thirst and display his machismo. As he defiantly drank from the bowl, the rest of the crew simply looked upon him in stunned disbelief.

There was great triumph in his eyes when he was through. But the best part came when he claimed that the water had indeed quenched his thirst, but admitted that it was a hellish experience trying to get the water down.

His candid admission had not only done much to bring laughter to the faces of everyone, but it also provided the impetus to the others to indulge in a bit of free-spiritedness.

They all followed Baby's lead, even George, and joked of how the water hurt their taste buds. The fun became even more enjoyable when Jones mockingly dangled his tongue right out, as if to suggest that he had lost the ability to keep his tongue in his mouth. The laughter was loud and carefree, and at times even hysterical. But it was therapeutic in a sense.

Amidst all the laughter and fun, no one seemed to have noticed the fading sunset and the darkness of night approaching. But when they did, the laughter was silenced as the alarm bell of reality rang through their heads. The prospect of yet another night at sea had triggered frustration in everyone.

This whole nightmare, as far as they were concerned, was becoming more serious than anyone really wanted to admit. They had made preparations for the long haul, but weren't prepared mentally for the loneliness of night. And so, as the night progressed into a wilderness of darkness, they eventually buried their disappointment under the weight of sleep.

Sunday, February 16

There was a rude awakening on Sunday morning as tempestuous seas tossed the boat to and fro upon the expanse of water. With the exception of Friday evening, in the two days since the ordeal had started they had not really experienced the conniving nature of the ocean which George, Perry, and Kennedy knew so well.

Today, the only elements in sight are the sun, sea and sky. There isn't even a trace of seabirds hovering overhead, much less the cloudy images of St. Lucia which were still visible up to late Saturday afternoon.

The morning winds are strong and blustery for the most part, and the rippling effects of its velocity can be felt all over. No one has said a word, but the growing anxiety on their faces, particularly those of the younger crew, is not lost.

George has picked up a bit on their growing disposition, and feels the need to calm their fears. He suggests that what's happening out there is no big deal, and that it's something that occasionally occurs at sea. He entreats them to relax, assuring them that the storm will soon pass.

Perry

The daughter Perry never knew - Perry Anne-. She is now 18 years old.

For the next three to four hours, they endure the brutal ravages of the ocean. Their stomachs roll, and they suffer from the effects of the high splashing water, which stings their skin. As the cold morning winds continue to whip their naked backs, they shiver from a lack of warmth.

A calm finally comes at about 10:30 that morning, at which time Kennedy leads the crew in prayers. They thank God for his protection thus far, but also pray for the ordeal to come to an end. Then, after they are through with offering their supplication to heaven, the boys prepare for breakfast.

During the course of their slow, contemplative meal, Perry speaks quietly about life in general, including his own private expectations for the future. Something big is about to happen in his life, and he can't hide the joy that he feels inside. Any day now, his girlfriend Lydia will give birth to their very first child together.

For a moment, a genuine excitement overshadows all of the dangers ahead of them. Perry longs to be near Lydia and their unborn child, and wishes that the events which started last Friday afternoon had never occurred.

However, by the end of the breakfast that consists of raw fish and an occasional sip of seawater, the morning continues as it had the day before. Not a sign of rescue, but the boat continues to drift, and it chills the spirit.

Sun, sea, and sky are all that surrounds them. Collectively, they have resigned themselves to the fact that their fate is in the hands of a great God, who alone can protect them.

The morning is spent in quiet contemplation. But by the afternoon, something occurs that lifts their spirits.

In the hazy distance, the form of an unidentified landmass is spotted. There is a loud cheer on board, which quickly tempers into a kind of cautious optimism. They are happy to finally see the hazy image of land, but there are also concerns about the continuous flow of the current, which seems to pull the boat farther and farther away.

Half of their hearts feel a sense of disappointment, but the other is optimistic about this turn of events. They are hoping that at some point the current will stop its drifting motion, and perhaps guide them towards the landmass.

The moment seems like eternity. It is clear by late afternoon that not only has the current not changed its direction, but their patience has been severely tested. Frustrated, and fearing that they might have missed a chance at rescue, they attempt to row the boat towards the landmass.

Unfortunately, the tremendous distance, an unrelenting ocean current, and occasional high winds severely hamper their effort. The more they row, the more difficult it is. As it becomes increasingly obvious that the conditions do not favor massive effort being put forth, the idea is finally abandoned.

They regroup again after only a few hours. No one is satisfied with the idea of leaving their fate to chance. With worries of another evening at sea, and the probability that the landmass might once again disappear, they soon devise another plan.

Interestingly, everyone seems to have an idea of how to get there. As they discuss the various ideas among themselves, they finally settle on the one that has the likeliest chance of success.

The idea is from George, who suggests that a makeshift sail be constructed out of two cloaks that are on board. He is convinced that if the sail is constructed properly, there's a great chance of sailing the boat ashore.

They briefly go over the plan of how to construct the sail. And very soon, the cloaks are each cut into halves, the arms removed, and the pieces assembled at the edges with twine. It is then hoisted upon a wooden pole which is fastened near the stern.

For the next hour or so, they wait patiently for the winds to change, but nothing happens. In fact, the only movement above them is the noisy sound of the sail as it flaps loosely in the wind.

Soon there is a sense that things may not work as planned. As the currents pull the boat further and further away from the landmass, they see the last shimmering lights in the distance as darkness descends upon them.

Monday, February 17

At daybreak on Monday, although they awake to much calmer seas than they did the morning before, there is a great sense of disappointment upon discovering that the landmass has vanished. Once again, they find themselves surrounded by sun, sea, sky, and lots of unanswered questions about their future.

Throughout the early part of the morning, there isn't even a whisper on board. The silence has been amplified by the gentle sound of the breeze that seems to ignore their very existence.

Slowly, as the morning advances and the day becomes warmer, the icy mood that characterized the morning gives way to pleasant conversation and occasional laughter. At the top of the fun list is George's idea to construct a sail which never even caught the winds. They think it is a nuisance flapping in the wind, and joke a lot about how silly the idea was. Now they are out of a pair of rain cloaks, which could have proved handy in case of a storm. George himself does not take any offense to the jokes, and appears quite amused by them. If anything, not only does he enjoy the laughter and free-spiritedness, but he also relishes the quiet sense of optimism that comes with the laughter.

For the most part, they joke and talk about life in general, but never in a negative tone. All they want right now is to remain healthy, for this is the only way to beat the odds of survival at sea.

True to his old form, George recounts the story of T-Chame and company when they were lost at sea. He has to go into a lot more detail, since none of the boys below the age of fifteen were old enough to remember that incident.

He begins from the time they left Gros Islet to the time when the outboard motor refused to work. The experience of how they had ended up being stranded was very similar to their own experience. T-Chame and company had survived an entire week at sea, living on dry fish and seawater, until the day when they were fortunate enough to be spotted and rescued off the coast of Venezuela.

The mood continues to be light after George's recitation of the story. But as the twilight gives way to a fourth consecutive evening at sea, a somber mood quickly sets in. Although they have not lost their sense of optimism, they hate the darkness. They make no effort to hide the fact that the period of darkness is the most disconcerting part of the ordeal. The uncertainties of nighttime, and the occasional movement of large sea mammals in the water around them, make the night dreadful.

However, as the evening progresses under wraps of darkness, they witness an enchanting wonder, which could well be described as one of the greatest natural phenomena of all.

A full moon is slowly rising as if from beneath the sea, and it rises steadily towards the partially starry skies above. They gaze in amazement at the perfectly shaped sphere, which seems so close and yet so far. That great ball of light not only illuminates the ocean, but the image of it rising from the sea feels almost spiritual. As the evening finally matures into full night, they are convinced that God and his angels have visited them.

In their lifetime, they have seen a lot of the moon in the night skies, but none could compare to this one. It is like pure mysticism at sea, a thing that only a few men live to experience.

Later in the night, the magic that began with the rising of the full moon unfolds into other surprises. For the first time since the ordeal began, they watch in disbelief as the lights of a slow-moving vessel appear in the far distance.

Initially, they are mute with shock. But as the reality of the moment begins to set in, a euphoric mood of celebration breaks out on board.

"Look at this," someone shouts, "A boat! A boat! A boat!"

"Can you see it?"

"Yeah!" comes the response. "It's moving over there." "It's a boat."

For the next five minutes or so, although there are no lanterns or a flare aboard with which to send out an SOS, they are satisfied and thrilled to have witnessed the existence of other human life at sea.

However, as they settle down a bit, an enormous silence replaces the euphoric atmosphere. With the exception of the rocking motion of the boat and the gentle tap of the water against it, there is a dull silence.

Although the quiet of the evening has swallowed the air around them, no one dares to remove their gaze from the lighted vessel in the distance. Of course they aren't going to be rescued tonight, but they've had what they consider a thrilling and encouraging experience.

Through the moon's soft glare, they continue their vigil. The seconds turn to minutes, and the minutes to hours, but still no one flinches. But then, as the larger vessel continues along its steady course, and the distance between them grows greater and greater, the lights fade through the prevailing darkness like a thief in the night.

That evening, they continue to enjoy what is left of the night, while thinking a bit of the days ahead. So far, in spite of the frustrations of the last few days, everyone is feeling quite safe.

Tuesday, February 18

The morning begins with what is by now the ritual watch for the sunrise. But today, expectations of what the day might bring are much higher than the day before. There is faith and hope, and a longing to be rescued today. Could this be the day they have waited for? Or will they have to wait another day?

As the day breaks fully over the ocean and the first rays of the sunlight touch their faces, prayers are quietly offered to heaven. They individually thank the Lord for keeping a protective watch over them though the night; and they seek deliverance from unknown dangers.

There is a long pause after the prayers are over, during which time a couple more minutes are spent to reflect a bit upon their hearts' desires. Then afterwards, with the exception of Perry, everyone takes the time to feast upon the usual breakfast of raw fish until they meet their level of personal contentment.

Perry seems a bit withdrawn today, but no one makes much of it. They have all inquired of him, but he insists that he is okay, and that's all there is to it. His legs are stretched out to their full length, and he has both arms under his head. No one cares to disturb him again, and he is left alone for the moment.

Peter, Jones, and Baby are back to their usual selves, and they tease each other like naughty kids often do. About a seat away from Perry's feet, George sits quietly with his head bowed while Kennedy does a bit of fishing.

About that time, Perry decides to have some breakfast. After lazily stretching his muscles a bit, he reaches forward and grabs a fish from a rubber bowl. The fish is fully dried and has a golden tan from the abundance of sunshine these last few days. However, instead of sinking his teeth into it with all the ardor of a hungry man, he only nibbles on the flesh, then suddenly tosses it back into the bowl. He returns once more to his previous position, and shuts his eyes without a murmur.

Strange? You bet it is. For it is not like Perry to either ignore or refuse food. George is by now sitting upright, and has observed what just occurred. After Perry has returned to his position, George shifts over and whispers something to Kennedy.

As they watch him in silence, they are burdened with an urge to inquire of him again. Although it feels like the right thing to do at the time, they finally decide to respect Perry's unspoken wish to be left alone. Moreover, with Perry not complaining or having exhibiting any signs of illness, they assume that he is just going through a difficult phase, or a mood swing.

It is now close to midday, as they can tell by the position of the sun in the sky. It has unleashed its scorching rays upon them, and there's a general feeling of discomfort. Their skin is dry, and it feels as though they are slowly baking like a roast on an open barbecue. It is intense, but no one complains.

However, as the moments drag on and the feeling of discomfort grows stronger, Kennedy utters words which sound absolutely insane to everyone.

"I'm going to take a swim in the ocean," he says aloud.

"What!" George quickly responds. "Are you out of your mind?"

There's a sudden hush aboard, and even Perry has sat upright in his seat. He momentarily stares at the ocean, and then at Kennedy. As the expression of seriousness tightens around his face, it's as though he is screaming out the words: Crazy! Crazy! Crazy!

George has begun a gallant effort to dissuade Kennedy from taking that swim. He thinks that they are unfamiliar with this strange body of water that surrounds them, and fears that it might be infested with sharks. He also has strong reservations about the ocean currents, and fears its unpredictable motion. Moreover, after having quietly observed its magnetic strength, he is convinced of its sweeping powers.

As has become customary since the ordeal began, another long silence again prevails. Kennedy sits there with a sheepish grin, but no one knows for sure what is going through his mind.

Did they persuade him? And what is this grin all about? In fact, ever since last Friday evening, there's been a special bond between all of them. They've been so close that Perry's earlier "mood swing," and now Kennedy's talk of swimming in the ocean, seem a bit unsettling.

Kennedy has not changed his mind, and the afternoon sun has not helped one bit. It bears down on them with such intensity that it feels almost surreal. To Kennedy, risking a swim in the ocean is far less dangerous than being afflicted with sunstroke. Moreover, after days of being cramped in a boat, with the accompanying physical and psychological strain, a bit of exercise and refreshment outweighs the risk.

"I'm going to take that plunge," he insists loudly, "but the rest of you are free to do as you wish."

There's another long silence, which cuts through the intensity of the heat like a knife. In the back seat, where George and Perry are seated, there's a sigh of resignation. Over towards the front seats, there's not even a murmur from Jones, Baby, or Peter. In fact, their eyes are fixed upon George and Perry, hoping to hear them say or do something.

A great period of time elapses before Kennedy acts upon what he has just said. But when he finally decides, he ties a rope around his right wrist and fastens the other end to the boat.

The heat from the oppressive sun, coupled with anticipation of what might follow, seems to burn them alive. No one wants him to take that plunge, but they understand that Kennedy will not change his mind. This largely quiet fisherman with the lion's heart can be very difficult at times.

As he calmly steps on top of his seat, Kennedy leaves no doubt in their minds. He is now fully elevated, and before they can even manage a second breath, he's gone!

For the next thirty to thirty-five seconds, they wait breathlessly for him to resurface. And when he does, he quickly wipes the water off his face, gauges the distance between himself and the boat, and suddenly bursts into laughter.

In spite of its choppy appearance, the water is warm and comfortable. There isn't the even the slightest sign of sharks around, and their fears are eventually alleviated by Kennedy's relaxed appearance in the ocean. He remains there for the next ten or fifteen minutes, and by the time he decides to swim back to the boat, George is waiting to assist him aboard. Like a fish fresh out of the ocean, he is hauled into the boat, but he seems so satisfied to have taken that plunge.

Everything he ever did was always done with modesty. Therefore, when Baby and Jones begin to brag about his bravery, he does not think much of it. It was only a swim, and this is all there is to it.

It doesn't matter much to Jones or Baby that Kennedy makes light of their attempts to shower praise upon him. He is monolithic in their eyes, and they want so badly to experience the "high" of bravery, and the adulation that follows. Moreover, the heat of the sun doubling its strength upon them is all the urging they need.

Everyone who knows him understands full well that a tendency to flirting with danger has always been a part of Baby's psyche. He knows that also, and will not hesitate to show his defiance even though no one has challenged or dared him to take that plunge.

As he proceeds to fasten the rope around his right wrist, no one says a word. He steps up on the seat, moves closer to the edge, and takes a mighty leap into the ocean.

He lands feet first into the water, which brings a bit of laughter on board. However, although it wasn't really a dive in the sense of how Kennedy connected with the water, it doesn't seem to bother Baby, who basks in the opportunity to temporarily free himself from the bondage of the boat.

True to the comical side of his nature, he has to end his swim with a prank. After swimming in the ocean for less than five minutes, he becomes hysterical, and begins to swim like a man in distress towards the boat. "The sharks, the sharks, the sharks are coming!" he screams, and suddenly lets out a big laugh, to the relief of everyone.

He is beaming as they pull him aboard. Through the sparkling glare of his naturally white teeth and dazzling eyes, he looks quite content and very proud of himself.

Not only will Jones and Peter follow suit, but also George, and then later Perry will reluctantly join in. It is worth their while, and a perfect respite from a dangerous sun.

By nightfall, it is clear that they have come to the end of another day without a sign of rescue. However, unlike the other sunsets, when this night approaches, there isn't as much of a feeling of dread.

On two of the larger seats in the center of the boat, George and Kennedy are curled up side by side next to each other, having a little conversation. In the back, Perry has once again returned to his reclusive self, while the younger boys lie calmly on the remaining seats up front.

In the center seats, George and Kennedy's conversation is uninterrupted. It's a quiet reflection of the last few days. They are happy to be alive, and feel that it's a stroke of luck that has enabled them to survive thus far. But under the layer of humble acknowledgement is a quiet feeling of frustration that eats at their hearts.

They are worried about their mother Cecilia, and the emotional state that she is sure to be in right now. The thought of losing two sons at once, or even clinging to the hope that they might still be alive, must have destroyed her either way. Then there is the case of their father, Elton, and his brother "Cashow," who is Perry's father. What a triple blow this is for that side of their family: George, Kennedy, and then Perry.

Occasionally, they take pauses during the conversation to control their emotions, and they wish that none of this had ever happened. Then, turning their attention to things that are always in the backs of their minds, yet have not been discussed openly, they worry about the physical condition of everyone on board, and wonder why Perry has not been himself today.

George knows, and so does Kennedy, that Perry has not eaten at all today. Moreover, with the exception of the swim which he had in the ocean, he has spent the better part of the day dozing in the hot sun. What if he is sick, but is just too macho to admit it?

There is a period of calm, and the tapping of the water against the boat is all they hear. But somehow, although they are very much familiar with that sound, they feel drawn to its tranquil and lullaby-like effects.

Down in the boat's hull is a puddle of water. It's been sitting there for the last few days, but no one has even bothered to scoop it out. In fact, were it not for their conversation tonight, and Kennedy losing his balance while trying to move on the seat, it may not have ever come up at all.

Eventually they move on from that topic, and to another that was on their minds. They talk about the actual condition of the boat itself.

Yes, it had withstood the perilous seas, including that terrible storm on Sunday, but how much more could it handle? To the best of their knowledge, it was strongly built, but never before had it been tested on such a large expanse of uncharted water.

Throughout the course of the evening, they continue the pattern of moving from topic to topic. There are other things that they touch on, such as the absence of drinking water on board, and what should be done the next time it rains.

An idea is soon conceived. A portion of the makeshift sail will be folded into a gutter-like structure, thereby allowing the rain to flow through it and into the bottom half of a Clorox bottle, which holds only half a gallon of water if filled to capacity.

They again revisit the moment when their misfortune started off La Wash, and take the time to allow their minds to wander wildly.

What if they were rescued tomorrow? Wouldn't it be something to be back home, and to see the reaction of the people upon their return? Perhaps there would be throngs of people out in the streets, and among them a few that might simply hang out there for a chance to satisfy their curiosity. They will never ask any questions, and of course these are the kind of people you've got to be wary of. George and Kennedy let out a slight chuckle, and the conversation continues. Yeah, these are the kind of people who like to stand in the background, never ask any questions, but always have special twist to a story. There will be lots of stories to be told, and they each will go through the never-ending process of adding a twist. There's another chuckle, and they continue talking. They have conversed with each other for a while now, but there are plenty more things that George and Kennedy would like to talk about. Throughout all this time there isn't a whisper from Perry, or from the younger crew up in the front.

Tonight, unlike the other evening when the moon shone brightly across the ocean and appeared so close that they could almost reach out and grab it, the night is extremely dark. Although there isn't any doubt that they'd love to experience that evening again, there are no quarrels with the darkness that is tranquil and welcomes an early sleep. By the time the evening has reached the full maturity of night, they quietly check into a world where dreams are made of marshmallows and cotton candy, and where the hope of tomorrow awaits them.

Say It Ain't So

The peacefulness ends in the early hours after midnight. They awake to the soft groans of someone afflicted with pain.

Quietly, they listen, but not for too long. The disorienting effects of sleep drive them back to unconsciousness. They both awaken again, but this time the sounds which they heard before have a tone of reality.

In the darkness, their eardrums pop as they lie still, hoping to God that they are dreaming. The sounds continue unabated, and their excruciating tone immediately conveys the trouble ahead for them.

Their minds revert to Perry, and it isn't too long before they are convinced that he is in pain. It was just too suspicious, the way he carved an imaginary wall for himself in the back of the boat. He tried his best to camouflage his illness throughout the day, but can no longer tough it out unnoticed.

Treading carefully over a few seats in the dark, Kennedy feels his way along until he is able to reach Perry. "What's the matter?" he asks softly, but there is no immediate response. There's a brief moment of silence, as Perry, sensing Kennedy's presence, tries with difficulty to conceal his pain. He can't fool Kennedy, and his loud gasp for air gives his act away.

"What is hurting you?" Kennedy whispers softly in the dark.

There's another moment of silence, and then suddenly Perry replies in a muffled tone, "My body."

"What about it?" Kennedy entreats him further. "My entire body feels weak, my stomach is bloated, and my joints hurt badly."

There's a pause as Kennedy tries to figure things out. Then, unsure of how to proceed, he calls over to George to come quickly.

Baby and Jones have inched a bit closer to the center of the boat, but Peter remains glued in the dark to his seat. The boat begins to rock from the movement, which prompts George to politely request that Baby and Jones return to their seats. They do so without any rancor, and very soon George is able to join Kennedy in the back.

He is stunned at the degree of pain Perry is having in the dark. With Perry openly admitting to Kennedy that he is ill, there was no need for him to conceal his suffering from anyone.

Nothing could have prepared George for Perry's condition. Yes, there had been suspicions that something was wrong, but the evening had ended too perfectly for anyone to predict this sudden turn of events.

Therefore, as Kennedy attends to Perry, it is also obvious by George's silence, and his motionless form in the dark, that Perry's condition is both alarming and disconcerting to him. That moment speaks volumes, for it was never like George to be affected greatly by sad events. If anything, he has been a bulwark of strength throughout this ordeal, and in the back of Kennedy's mind, his sudden concern has registered.

Reaching in the dark in search of Perry's face, Kennedy feels a sudden rush of air coming from his nostrils. His breathing is much harder than he had originally thought, and there is also a steam of perspiration flowing from his temple.

Perry is as cold as ice, and the cold sweat that trickles through Kennedy's fingers says a lot about his condition. He also shivers from ague in the dark, and that sure frightens Kennedy. Maybe in the morning he will be able to make a clearer assessment of the situation. But for now, the morning seems too far away.

George has recuperated a bit from the initial shock, and together they try to stabilize Perry. They move him from the seat and lay him comfortably in the bottom of the boat. There isn't any water in the area, and a light float supports his head.

They take the time to comfort him, and for the next hour or so they keep a quiet vigil over him. Then gradually, as the pain subsides, he finally gets a chance to sleep.

For both George and Kennedy, that moment could not have come at more opportune time. With the morning not too far away, they crawl back to their space, hoping to catch some sleep.

However, for the next several hours preceding daybreak, except for an occasional catnap here and there, they can hardly sleep. Their internal peace has been totally shattered, and it's difficult to return to the state of mind they had left shortly before this awful episode reared its ugly head.

At the first sign of daybreak on Wednesday, both George and Kennedy creep quietly back to check on Perry. He is still lying in the bottom of the boat, but his physical appearance almost shocks the foundation from under their feet. Even the younger boys have crept closer for a peek, and they can also tell by the somber expression on the faces of both George and Kennedy that all is not well.

Perry's eyes are as glassy as the morning ocean, and he lies there as if he is locked in the embrace of death. His speech is slurred, and everything about him is troubling.

There are also some other gruesome reminders of what had transpired in the night. His chest is covered with a dark, dry vomit, and the foul odor it gives off, combined with the many bouts of diarrhea he appears to have had, leave a ghastly smell in the morning air.

Although the stench seems to choke their airways, neither George nor Kennedy can find it within themselves to walk away and leave Perry in this condition. George has begun a search of the boat, and he finds a bowl made out of a calabash. He leans over the side of the boat, gathers some water, and heads back to meet Kennedy and Perry in the back.

There is complete silence as George hastens to return. In the meantime, Peter, Baby, and Jones have quietly returned to their seats, and there seems to be a bit of soul-searching taking place on the part of Baby and Jones.

George hands the bowl to Kennedy, who keeps a firm grip on it until George has fully positioned himself. Once George finds a comfortable spot, Kennedy hands the bowl back to him and proceeds to gently lift Perry's legs.

After soaking an old piece of rag into the water, George reaches under Perry and wipes the feces off his buttocks and lower back. Kennedy sets him down a bit while George reaches over the side of the boat, empties the contents in the bowl, and draws some fresh water again.

He later hands the bowl over to Kennedy, who proceeds to wash Perry's face, his armpits, and vomit-covered chest. Once he is through, the float is rearranged under Perry's head, and he is left alone for a while.

A significant part of the morning has elapsed before they finally decide on breakfast. George has chopped some of the fish into tiny pieces for Perry, but he just can't eat any of it. Therefore, after eating their own breakfast, they check on him again, and later return to their seats.

On Wednesday, as the day grows warmer and eventually unbearable, they repeat some of the same things which they did the afternoon before. Only this time, with Perry lying gravely ill inside the boat, the laughter and fun has dissipated from the day.

As they each take turns swimming in the ocean, the only thing that keeps recurring in their minds is Perry's fate. It wasn't supposed to have turned out this way, and never in their wildest dreams did the thought ever cross their minds that something like this could ever happen to Perry. He is just too physically strong, and has too many years of experience at sea to have succumbed to such an illness. This just couldn't happen.

The thought continues to weigh heavily on their minds. And as the day progresses without a single sign of rescue, there isn't much to keep them hopeful. From here on, everything seems to unravel into a state of despair.

Over towards the front seat, Peter just sits there in a stoic posture. It's been very hard to tell what's been going on in his mind. Jones is not talking either; rather, he stares at the ocean as if hoping to find a place to hide himself. Baby is in a crouched position on the seat, but there's a deep-seated expression of fear on his face. He occasionally makes eye contact with George and Kennedy, but never looks directly at where Perry is lying.

A bit later in the afternoon, George and Kennedy return to check on Perry. But what they discover makes their hearts sink. He has slipped into a coma, and is having difficulty breathing. With his eyes closed dead shut, and phlegm blocking his airway, he can't respond when they call out his name. Indeed, the dark shadow of death is knocking on Perry's door, and it has chosen to do so on a day when the sun is out in full force and the ocean shows its gentle self.

George cannot stomach the thought, but Kennedy proves for once that he has greater courage than George. He feels the need to do something for Perry, and decides to immediately act upon the impulse. After drawing some water from the ocean in the calabash, he sprinkles it over Perry. At least if it was the last thing that he did for him, he hoped to offer Perry some comfort.

The air feels heavy around them by the time they finally return to their seats. As both George and Kennedy try to control the effects of the pain that has imploded inside of them, the feelings of vulnerability and fear, which were hidden under the façade of bravery and courage, show in their facial expressions.

It is a moment of great sadness and horror as both Jones and Baby, too overcome by their emotions, simply break down and cry. George and Kennedy can't help them either, for they are too distraught to offer any words of comfort. Therefore, with a bit of time on their own with their emotions, both Jones and Baby learn to calm themselves down.

With the silence comes a deep moment of reflection and prayer, as Kennedy, sensing rattled nerves, silently prays to God to give them the courage to accept the things that they can't change.

He is also concerned about Peter. His lack of emotion, and his seeming disconnection from everything and everyone, greatly trouble Kennedy. Increasingly, it is becoming harder and harder to read his frame of mind. What could he be thinking?

Prior to joining the expedition on February 14, Kennedy did not have much interaction with Peter. Baby and Jones he knew, but even they surprised him by breaking down and crying.

However, as Kennedy ponders a bit on things, he eventually draws some striking parallels between himself and Peter. In many ways, Peter is a lot like him. Behind the veneer of an occasional smile that he has managed since the ordeal began, there may be lots of secret thoughts that are stored in a special compartment of his brain. He is easygoing and speaks only when there is a need to. And although he may have already adapted to the conditions around him, he thinks that if anything, he will survive.

On the other hand, Jones is a lot like Baby. He never thinks before acting. For example, if something came to mind, he would just say or do it, and suffer the consequences later if it turned out to be bad.

At fourteen years old, although Jones has a very skinny frame, few of his peers have ever dared to challenge him to a fight. The boy is tall, approaching six feet, and is a warrior at heart. Interestingly, he is among the lot who can barely contain their emotions when the going gets tough.

Another hour or two has passed, and George and Kennedy regain the courage to return to Perry's side. His condition has not changed, and his eyes remain glued shut. Again, except for the faint sounds coming from his mouth and nostrils, there aren't any visible signs of life left in his body. Every passing minute seems like his last, and the silence grows and grows around them.

With the progression of the afternoon, it is evident that another rainstorm is about to sweep the ocean. The fading sunlight is now being replaced by a blanket of dark clouds, and the winds slash through the choppy waters with considerable force.

A light drizzle has begun, and it steadily grows into a torrential rainfall. It is packed with dangerous thunder and lightning, scattered about like fireworks in the skies and over the ocean below. Reaching under one of the seats, George quickly pulls out part of the makeshift sail and hands it to Kennedy, who covers Perry's body with it. The other half is folded into a gutter-like structure which ends at the mouth of the Clorox bottle. With that done, and Perry secured under the wraps of the sail, they quickly return to their seats to weather the storm.

Throughout the storm, they endure the whipping effects of the rain as it is splattered by the winds against the boat and their bodies. Then there is the occasional violent rocking that sends shock waves exploding like dynamite inside of them. This continues for the better part of two hours, and is all over as dusk approaches.

Now, with the sea storm safely behind them, Kennedy wastes little time in checking on Perry. But then, as he lifts the sail from his body, the reality they have fought so hard to reject lies solidly before him.

Perry is dead!

His eyes, which were shut throughout the coma, are wide open, and they communicate everything Kennedy needs to know. Perry did not die without a fight. The sad expression upon his face is indicative of a young man with plenty of misgivings about dying. After all, he was only twenty-one, and who could ever blame him for questioning death?

But then, as Kennedy continues staring at his remains there in the stillness, the coincidence of how Perry was taken away from them during the rainstorm is mystifying in itself. Somehow, he feels as though Perry's spirit is still hovering around, and that the restlessness and defiance in his eyes must have been about the unborn child he will never live to see.

George is over by now, and like Kennedy, he too is speechless. He simply stares at Perry's body, as if trying to make sense out of what really happened here. As George tries to regain his composure, Kennedy places his hands over his dead cousin's forehead, strokes his brow, and gently shuts his eyes for the last time.

Then, turning to face George and the other three boys who have quietly gathered near, they weep silently over Perry's passing.

For the rest of the evening, and through Thursday morning, not a word is uttered. The new batch of fish, which had been laid out to dry for consumption, still remains untouched. And as their melancholy and great sadness continues to ravage their senses of self, the future grows bleaker.

By late Thursday afternoon, as Perry's body lies there exposed to the extreme heat, something has to be done. They know that they can't just sit there with the corpse without devising a plan of what to do next. Moreover, the unexpected number of flies that it has suddenly attracted is additional cause for concern.

Then comes the painful decision of how and when to dispose of the body. Initially, they want to leave it aboard for a few days, in case of rescue, but soon they can no longer stand the buzzing sounds of the flies which at times land on their lips and other parts of their bodies. Therefore, with the sun descending slowly, they decide to arrange an impromptu sea burial for Perry, with all the respect and dignity that can be afforded to him under the circumstances. But they will wait just a little longer.

It is a moment of great dread. In Kennedy's mind, and perhaps in the minds of the others, this could not possibly be happening. Kennedy's thoughts go back to his childhood days, when the concept of someone receiving a burial at sea was virtually unheard of. Perry did not die by drowning, and the fact that they are about to take matters into their own hands and dispose of his body in the sea weighs heavily on his mind.

To date, the only man known to them who has ever been buried at sea was an old German scientist by the name of Swank. For many years, he lived in seclusion at Pigeon Island, and gained a reputation for chasing visitors off the island. Although very little was known of his past, there was always great suspicion among the locals that he might have been a former Nazi who had fled Germany after the Second World War.

In fact, the precious few who got close to Swank were the handful of local workers who were employed by Mrs. Josset Agnes Legh, or "Ma Snowball," as she was known to native St. Lucians. Josset was a British former actress who, way back in 1937, had leased the island from the British government for ninety-nine years.

Those who knew Swank knew only two things about him. He claimed to have invented foam rubber and always reminded everyone that he was to have a sea burial in the event of his death.

Back then this was the talk of the town, since the custom in St. Lucia was to bury our dead in cemeteries. With the exception of those who had died at sea, and in keeping with our people's strong Roman Catholic beliefs, we held our funerals in churches, and the remains were interred in the ground.

The tears have begun to stream down Kennedy's cheeks, as the thought becomes overwhelming. The ocean is a place that

Perry loved, but the thought of a sea burial seems almost sacrilegious. However, with a little time to reconcile things in his mind, he is able to get over that thought.

By the time they are gathered together for Perry's burial, the last traces of daylight are just lingering over the ocean. It is a moment punctuated by intrigue that chills the nervous system. There is not a single movement or whisper on board as they think of how to begin.

For next two to three minutes, no one is able to muster any courage to lead the others in prayer. Then suddenly, breaking the silence, George begins a slow recitation of the "Our Father," in which everyone joins. They also recite the "Hail Mary," followed by the symbolic Sign of the Cross which signals the end of the service.

Perry's lifeless body is slowly lifted from the bottom of the boat, placed temporarily on the seat, and with a slight lift, it is rolled over the left side of the boat.

For a very brief moment, the body remains afloat on the water. Then gradually, as if to emulate the setting sun, it begins a slow descent to the bottom of the ocean.

Learning to Move On

In the aftermath of Perry's death, life becomes even more difficult for everyone. In fact, not only are they afflicted by the emotional scars, but there are also the psychological ones that they are forced to bear.

There is a common fear in everyone, and that is the fear of death. We are haunted by it, and the horror it unleashes when it is about to claim its victims leaves a lot on their mind.

A period of grieving, confusion, and reflection occupies the three days following Perry's burial, but then they gradually regain the courage to move on. It is time to concentrate on hope, and no one really wants to be left out.

Life out here will have to be focused on survival. This means returning to the state of things prior to Perry's illness and death. They understand that trying to remain focused in the face of the fresh memories will be difficult. But then, starving themselves and wallowing in self-pity while the sun plays havoc with their bodies will not help their situation at all. Perry is dead, and there is nothing that they could have done to save him. There will be time enough to mourn him properly in the future, but for now, it is more important to think of their own survival.

For the next few days no one speaks of Perry. And before long, it is as though he never existed. This new attitude no doubt helps to boost their morale, and daily they try their best to keep things this way. But just as it seems as though the worst is over, they are dealt another blow.

On Tuesday, February 24, Baby becomes afflicted with a serious illness. Not only did no one see it coming, but it happens in the most unusual of ways. After spending most of the morning laughing and joking around with the other members of the crew, he suddenly lowers himself to the floor of the boat and complains about severe pain in his abdomen. He begins to weep inconsolably, which deeply moves everyone onboard. The groans of agony from his unbearable pain pierce their hearts like a shining dagger.

It doesn't take very long for George and Kennedy to come to his aid. That's when it hits them: Although Baby is conscious of his surroundings at the moment, his illness bears a striking resemblance to Perry's.

A flood of perspiration pours from his brow, and the heavy stench of human waste in the air tells the tale of a young man who has involuntarily defecated in his pants. His looks are piercing, and his eyes convey the deep fear he feels inside. They seem about to leap from their sockets. In a desperate effort to free himself from the burden of his fear, he gently grabs onto George's arm and asks, "Do you think I'm going to die?"

There's a silence as he releases his hold on George, and his hands drop to his sides. He is visibly weak, and he falls to the deck in a fetal position.

George draws closer to him, but still can't find the right words to say. It's clearly a question for which he does not have the answer, but he can't run away from the pressure that he is under.

"You are going to be alright," he quietly says to Baby. Then slowly turning to face Kennedy and the other boys, and seeing the blank stares on their faces, he bows his head in deep sadness.

There's a lot going through Kennedy's head, and it's awfully hard to erase the memories of what befell Perry. Moreover, it sends shivers through their bodies to hear Baby, once a buoyant and playfully mischievous lad, inquire about his own mortality.

In fact, the thoughts that continue to flow through their minds are driven by their own fear of death. All of a sudden they can't seem to make sense of anything. Baby continues to suffer, but he does so with quiet groans. They can hear him, but they can't seem to reach him.

That moment soon passes. And it isn't long before they are able to continue with their original plan to aid Baby. Initially, there is a bit of discomfort as they try to remove his feces-filled pants. But they do. And Kennedy leans over the side of the boat and washes it all out in the ocean. He spreads the pants out on the seat to dry, then returns to George's side to assist further with Baby.

Both Jones and Peter are awfully quiet. They are so quiet that it's impossible not to notice. Baby has always been the spark that lit their fire, and without him they are as cold as ice.

George is very busy trying to make conversation with Baby. He whispers softly to him, and Baby whispers back in kind. The pain is severe and his responses are at times inaudible. George, sensing the kind of pain that Baby is in, decides to keep quiet for a bit but does not leave his side.

There's a long silence as Baby curls further into a fetal position. His body trembles violently with ague, and the sound of his teeth as they knock forcefully against each other underscores his anguish.

George is by now positioned near his head, and he cradles it in his hands. Then gradually, as George helps Baby into a comfortable position, he withdraws his hand from beneath Baby's head, and Baby responds with a deep sigh of relief.

George is visibly troubled, but he can't find a way to express it. There's just too much going on in his mind to think optimistically. He sees that Baby is gravely ill, and there is nothing that he can do to stop the cycle of bad luck. The reality of Perry's death, still fresh on his mind, is not helpful to him at all. His facial expression is painted with the picture of despondency, and God alone knows the kind of pain he feels inside.

In fact, ever since the moment that Baby complained about feeling ill, things have gone into a tailspin on board. He continues to suffer without relief, which prompts George to speculate about his illness.

He is convinced that the dried-out fish and seawater that they were forced to consume these last few days was responsible for Perry's death, and now Baby's illness. He shares his thoughts with Kennedy, and suddenly silence falls.

There's a long pause as Kennedy turns to look at Baby on the floor. *He's probably dying now,* he thinks to himself, but he still can't seem to get over the quick progression of Baby's illness. At least Perry had a chance to linger for a day or two while hopes were still high for rescue. But the way Baby is declining seems to indicate that it could all end for him very quickly.

It is nearing sundown, and after leaving him alone for several hours, they return to check on him before the incoming darkness. His body is cold and stiff, and as George whispers his name, and touches his hands and face, there is no response. He has died. Baby has expired without a word.

While it is true that Baby's death takes a massive toll on everyone, no one is more affected than Peter. For the next fifteen or twenty minutes, Peter weeps inconsolably over the passing of his cousin and best friend. But even with all the tears that are streaming down his face, he does not scream or say anything at all. His arms are folded and pressed against his stomach, as if to contain the growing pain inside. His sudden burst of emotions further shakes both George and Kennedy. At last, the boy with the emotions of steel has bared his feelings for everyone to see.

However, there is something strange about Jones's behavior. He appears spaced out, and seems to have climbed into a natural high. As he sits there undaunted by Peter's emotional distress, anyone might swear that he had never known Baby before.

George has not fared well either, as once again he is speechless. He looks numb, and the expression on his face mirrors the emptiness he feels inside.

A lot is also going through Kennedy's mind, but strangely he has a bit of courage inside, which seems to prompt him to defy the moment. He can't allow death to have dominion over his thoughts, and he struggles hard not to get to where George is heading at the moment. Secretly, he has vowed to survive at all odds. And so, instead of thinking of all the bad things, he prefers to think of the days to come.

For Kennedy, it is all about survival, and what better time to show some inner strength than at this very moment? He's got to do something to wrestle George out of this melancholy mindset, and decides to politely inquire what he was thinking of.

George is slow in responding, but when he does, he drives directly to the heart of the matter. He is resolute in his belief that the fish and seawater were responsible for the deaths of both Perry and Baby. He has decided also that he wants no part of it, and is prepared to carry on without any food.

"Are you out of your mind?" Kennedy demands of him.

"No, I'm not!" he responds right back.

They go back and forth for a while, but in the end, Kennedy is able to knock some sense into George's head. George's idea, which would have resulted in starving himself to death, is certainly not a wise option. Besides, with the exceptions of Perry and Baby, who had succumbed to an unknown illness, everyone else is physically all right.

Baby's body is left on board for the night. But by morning, they accord to him the same rites and respects that Perry received for his burial. Without any fanfare, but with great sadness, Baby's body is interred into the ocean.

Wednesday, February 25

Although Wednesday, February 25 is by no means the best of days, it is certainly not the worst. George has eaten for the day, but he still has not regained his confidence. There is still something eating at his heart, and it continues to manifest itself in the form of depression.

Kennedy again cautions George about the dangers of dwelling on things of the past, for he knows that it is capable of destroying him. Therefore, for the better part of Wednesday, he tries to engage the rest of them in quiet conversations to uplift their sprits. Similar to the days before, there is no talk of Perry, or even Baby, whose body they have just interred into the ocean. They need insulation from the past, and Kennedy succeeds in establishing that environment.

By afternoon, they manage to work up the courage for a swim. It is enjoyable and offers them some respite from the burning sun. As the afternoon drags on, there is less of a preoccupation with time, or with how long it's been since they suffered the loss of Baby.

With the afternoon growing into night, they rest comfortably on board. There isn't much conversation between them, but it seems that everyone is doing just fine. Sleep will come to each of them that evening, and unlike the night before, when they tossed and turned in anticipation of the morning when they would dispose of Baby's body, they sleep peacefully through the night.

There are good days ahead, but every day seems to end without the slightest chance of rescue. They are not fazed by this, and feel that someday a stroke of luck will come. Except for the familiar settings on board, and the sea, sun, skies, and darkness, there is nothing in view. The boat has continued its slow drift over the vast expanse of water, without any foreseen or conceivable threats to their safety.

That calm, that peace, that cautious hope for a stroke of luck, will disappear without warning. And when it does, it comes with a physical trauma that not even the deaths of Perry and Baby combined inflicted upon them. Poor Jones has suffered a nervous breakdown, but evidence of this mental condition was not apparent until now. To everyone's astonishment, he leaps on Peter and begin to punch and kick him like a soccer ball.

Poor Peter, now fully understanding what is happening to Jones, fights back as vigorously as he can. George and Kennedy move over to intervene, but even they have much difficulty subduing Jones. He is kicking, punching, spitting, and saying a host of dirty curse words, until they are finally able to subdue him. George holds firmly to his upper body as Kennedy takes a grip on his feet. Then slowly, as he is released, Jones lies peacefully in the bottom of the boat, as if he had nothing to do with what had just transpired. They continue to keep a watchful eye on him, for fear that he might again act violently, but that moment never comes. He has chosen instead to ignore everyone, and will not respond even when they attempt to have a conversation with him.

The only picture left of Jones

By now, a few hours have passed, but Jones is still lying unrestricted in the bottom of the boat. Kennedy attempts to coax him to eat, but he refuses. He is left alone to his will, but they begin to worry that he might eventually starve himself to death.

It is now shortly past noon, as they can tell by the sun's position directly over them. As the afternoon grows warmer, and the rays of the sun begin to beat upon them with impunity, less and less attention is paid to Jones. They are of the opinion that the worst is over, and that it was very likely that they might have gotten through to Jones, even if he pretended to ignore them.

They haven't, and proof of Jones's state of derangement is just about to play out in the most painful of ways. Suddenly he is up on his feet and banging on the sides of the boat, and threatening to throw himself overboard. His eyes are lit with an unnatural fire which seems to have opened up a passageway for a peek into his disappearing consciousness.

Both George and Kennedy inch closer to him, but they are mindful not to alarm him further. With their hearts racing and legs trembling beneath them, they try their best to cope with the situation at hand.

The boat rocks from side to side, as Jones continues to scream frantically and bang on everything around him. George and Kennedy lose their balance and stop at times, but never for more than a few seconds. George finally gets within an arm's length of Jones, who by now has jumped on top of the seat. George isn't sure whether Jones is really about to jump, but he is determined to not take chances. Therefore, reaching forward with lightning speed, he grabs onto Jones's trousers and forcefully pulls him backwards. In the process, Jones bangs his head on the side of the boat, but it does not matter now, since all they want to do is restrain him.

It is a furious struggle, as George tries his best to keep Jones down. He is screaming, kicking, punching, and biting, but with the help of Kennedy, George is finally able to restrain him.

This time, they do not intend to take any chances, since it is very obvious that Jones has become a menace to himself and probably to others on board. Therefore, not wanting to give Jones an opportunity to carry out his death wish, they make the painful decision to bind him with a rope. After they are successful in doing so, Jones remains in confinement through the afternoon and into the evening.

That evening, no one can bring himself to open up a discussion, or to even whisper softly. The thought of what transpired during the course of the day is just too painful to invite words. With that weighing heavily on their minds, they each retire to bed, hoping that at least by morning, Jones will have returned to his senses.

On the following day, as the morning breaks over the horizon with the fresh scent of the ocean rising into their nostrils, they awake to find Jones looking dazed and tired. Obviously, he did not sleep at all, and in his present state of derangement there is no doubt that his mind has wandered. He has become a keeper of the night. It is sad, but true; Jones has finally lost the essence of his existence.

As each member of the crew munches on a portion of dried fish for breakfast, they try in vain to persuade Jones to eat, but he refuses. He wants no part of anything on board, and refuses to communicate with them. The morning finally passes, and Jones's occasional conversations with himself tell them that Jones is sinking deeper and deeper into an abyss of mental anguish and depression.

He remains this way for the next few days, and as each day comes and goes, the progressive deterioration of his physical and mental condition worries everyone on board.

It has a serious effect on George, who feels so much pity for Jones that he can not bear to see him bound. He wants to set the poor boy free, but Kennedy is worried about the consequences that might follow.

For the next several hours, George occasionally leaves his seat to check on Jones, but whenever he returns, there is always great sadness on this face. He has had plenty of opportunity to study Jones, and knows that he is serious about continuing his hunger strike. Moreover, Jones' fragile-looking body and quickly fading complexion cause George to fear that the situation is getting out of hand.

The dreaded image of Jones starving himself to death haunts and torments George. Unable to live with the thought any more, he is prepared to risk all other dangers by releasing Jones from what he feels is an inhumane imprisonment.

The decision is made, and Jones is freed from his bondage. Then, in a slow retreat away from Jones, George and Kennedy take seats near Peter in the center of the boat, leaving Jones alone in the front seat to decide his own fate.

Jones sits upright on the seat. He gazes at his surroundings, which might appear a bit strange to his eye. Still he does not acknowledge their presence, not even when George calls out his name. Jones has found a place in his mind where the actual state of reality is hidden by delusion.

The quiet whispers on board give way to gentle sighs of relief. Jones has not acted violently, nor has he attempted to leave his seat. And this continues to please everyone, even as they watch him guardedly. With each passing moment, there is a calming docility about him. Their confidence soars, leading them to believe that Jones might have just been protesting his temporary bondage, and might continue to be harmless, and perhaps even help himself to some food. But none of this will ever materialize.

Suddenly, there is a violent shuffle, causing the boat to move from side to side. Jones has sprung up with lightning speed off his seat. And before they can even fully understand what is happening, he has landed in the ocean with a mighty force.

There is utter chaos both on board and in the water, as they shuffle back and forth in panic. Jones has struck a realm of reality, and is splashing violently in the water, trying his best to keep afloat in what is definitely a fast-moving current.

They all yell out his name and toss a rope to him. Somehow in the tightening current, despite his efforts to grab hold of the rope, he misses it repeatedly. With each passing second, the odds are stacked up more highly against him. He finally perishes as the force of the current submerges him into a watery grave below.

This is one of the saddest moments of all. For not only did mental illness rob Jones of the ability to think rationally, but it also forced him to eventually contemplate suicide, and to take his own life.

In fact, if the traumatic experiences of Perry's and Baby's deaths had not totally killed whatever was left of their spirit, then the horror of Jones's death may have done so. The spectacle of his death forces them to come to grips once again with their own mortality, and gives rise to a most frightening thought: out of an original party of six, three have perished so far. The haunting question of who could be next keeps recurring in their minds.

Silence, the great commander on board since February 15, finds a way once again to work its magic. Resignation, depression, and fear threaten to end their dreams of returning home alive.

Losing George

In the days following Jones's suicide, the pressure builds. The intense mood of apathy and resignation causes them to completely lose track of time. Night and day are one and the same, and the essence of living is lost.

This period takes a greater toll on George than on anyone else. During the course of these very long days, which go by unrecorded, George has begun to unravel. He is thrown into temporary mood swings, but always does his best to control it.

Peter's sudden loss of independence, which is manifested in the way he clings to and relies on George and Kennedy, does not help either. It is an added burden for them, especially for George, and the whole situation is worrisome for Kennedy.

Peter might have already decided that the key to avoiding his own tragic end is to cling firmly to George and Kennedy. He has made them his rock, and in them he seeks psychological shelter from the haunting images that he has seen.

For Kennedy and George, it takes a painful amount of courage to appear strong for Peter. But it is more so with Kennedy, who tries to be strong for both George and Peter. As the days linger on, he tries gallantly to give the impression that things have returned to normal.

It works for while and, though reluctant at first to ease into the comfort zone Kennedy has created, George finally does.

My friend George. He is in a very contemplative mood, with his back towards the Caribbean Sea which he loved so much.

Mornings are once again spent fishing, following the routine of the earlier days of the ordeal. With the exception of swimming in the ocean, which they abandoned some time ago, they find peace and comfort by attempting to engage each other in pleasant conversation.

This has also done Peter a world of good, and very soon, he is able to combat his fear of death. As he gradually lessens his dependence on both George and Kennedy, it seems for a moment that they have finally gotten over the worst.

It is not meant to be. As the days progress, and the mornings turn into afternoons, and afternoons into evenings, the broken sprit George has tried so hard to camouflage is now in the open.

In what is to be a recurring experience of personal nightmare for Kennedy and Peter, one morning George suddenly begins to isolate himself from the other boys. He retreats to the stern of the boat and refuses to make conversation with anyone. He stops eating, and for great periods at a time he sits with his arms upon his lap, his head bowed in deep thought.

The worst comes one morning, when Peter arises from his sleep to witness George talking to himself. Frightened out of his wits, not sure of what to do, he creeps to where Kennedy is still lying fast asleep and informs him of the situation.

Quietly they listen, as George speaks to himself like a madman would. Then there is the occasional laughter, which simply blows their minds, but especially Kennedy's. He feels compelled to act.

Unable to bear the pain of George's mental breakdown, Kennedy feels that the best way to approach the situation is to knock some sense into George. He just can't accept that the brother whom he has loved so much, has succumbed to mental illness.

Kennedy tries, but George simply stares right through him, as if he never existed.

That really hurts, and for the rest of the day, Kennedy goes through a kind of grieving process, which is both personal and lonesome. He indeed tried his best to save George from harm, but succeeded only to a point. Looking back at the events that led to this moment, he painfully wonders whether there was something that he could have done differently. What if he had tried talking more forcefully to George in the early days of his illness? Would he have been able to save his brother, friend, and closest confidante?

That question continues to haunt Kennedy during the course of the day, and by evening, with the shadows creeping over the ocean, it's clear that this will make for a difficult night. This also brings his mind back to Jones, and the difficulties he and George had encountered in controlling him. With the fresh memories of the violence that characterized Jones's illness, Kennedy prays silently that they will never have to experience the same with George.

It will nonetheless be an evening as never before seen. After he falls asleep unannounced, the fury of George's frustration, which led him into depression and caused his mental break-down, lights up the night.

While Kennedy and Peter sleep, George moves over to where Kennedy was lying and begins to physically attack his brother. He is screaming his guts out, accusing Kennedy of maliciously steering the boat away from the shore.

The ensuing moments are ones of fierce struggle and pain, as Kennedy fights desperately to shield himself from the heavy blows that George, in his state of fury and mental illness, is inflicting upon him. The whole moment is truly distressing for

Kennedy, but he has no choice but to fight back with what energy he has left, hoping that George will finally leave him alone.

By the time the intense struggle finally abates, George and Kennedy lie in the bottom of the boat, gasping for air. But then, in the state of exhaustion that follows, George breathlessly asks Kennedy the following question:

"Tell me the truth, and please don't lie. Don't you see that landmass over there?"

"No," Kennedy replies quietly.

And then there is total silence.

For hours afterward, it seems as though Kennedy's reply to George must have appeased him. He remains lying there for a while, and later returns to his seat and the isolation that he has imposed upon himself these last few days.

However, at daybreak, shortly before the horizon fully ushers in the new day, George is acting up again. This time, instead of physically attacking Kennedy, he is exhibiting more powerful signs that have come to characterize his state of delusion.

His face is adorned with an expression of great anxiety, and he has begun to point to something he thinks he sees in the far distance. The landmass he claimed to see in the dark has once again appeared in his mind. He is hinting, and he seems to mean it, that it is time for them to attempt to swim towards shore.

Fearing the worst, both Kennedy and Peter brace themselves for trouble. Knowing that they have no intention of following George's suggestion, they hope to God that this scene will not erupt in violence.

A lot rushes through Kennedy's mind as he sits there helplessly thinking of what to do next. He has experienced the pain of how this ordeal has tried to shatter them, but that is nothing compared to the physical paralysis that he feels right now. Any move to physically subdue George is bound to end in a blood-bath, given George's size and physical strength, coupled with the state of mind that he is in. Kennedy understands that such an attempt could well prove to be not only a daunting task, but also a grave mistake.

George's behavior has also had a profound effect on Peter, who has taken a seat in the extreme bow of the boat. He is no doubt scared, and chooses to stay clear of George's path. Peter avoids all eye contact with him, and neither will he say or do anything that could draw George's attention to him.

Concerned for the safety of everyone on board, including George, Kennedy eventually works up the courage to try to get through to him. That old magic has worked a few times before, and he prays that he can convince George that the only thing in the distance is a gray firmament of sea and clouds.

Without leaving his seat, he calls out George's name. But Kennedy's attempt to persuade George is met with cold silence. There is defiance on George's part, and it can be seen in the way he continues to gaze intently in the direction toward which he perceives the landmass to be.

With each passing moment, it becomes increasingly clear to Kennedy that there is nothing he can say or do to draw George out of the world he is locked into. Therefore, accepting the fact that it just might be too late to save George from himself, he stares at him with pity, believing in the back of his mind that this may well be their final moment together.

The next several minutes bring an uneasy calm. Not a word is uttered as Kennedy prays hopelessly that George will be guided by reason. Although not fully satisfied, he accepts for what it is worth the notion that he has done all in his power to keep his brother safe. Now it is all left to George, and perhaps divine intervention, to avert what seems sure to come.

Although George is still sitting on his seat, every movement, from the gentle breeze that blows to the tapping of the water against the boat, greatly increases Kennedy's anxiety. In his mind, there is a recorder that replays a horrific scene: the vivid memory of Jones's sudden leap into the ocean.

During the tense silence, George's fascination with his illusion continues. He smiles to himself at times, and then suddenly turns serious or contemplative. This is clearly the behavior of a madman, and it kills Kennedy to see him this way.

In the front, Peter continues in his self-imposed exile. He neither speaks to Kennedy, for fear of alerting George of his presence, nor does he look at him. The boy is so terrified of George that fear has caused him to cower for his own survival.

There is a momentary lapse in George's gaze at the horizon. He has now turned his focus to searching for something aboard, but Kennedy isn't sure what he is after.

George is a bit impatient and agitated as he does so, which raises Kennedy's internal alarm. Perhaps he is just going through the motions of his deranged state. However, before Kennedy is fully able to understand what George is up to, he grabs a float that is wedged under the seat, and in the twinkle of an eye, George lands in the ocean with a huge splash.

Kennedy and Peter watch in horror and disbelief. George momentarily loses the float, but quickly reclaims it. He draws it close to his chest, and begins to slowly drift away from the boat. In the absence of the dangerous currents that wasted little time in claiming Jones, George begins his journey towards the "shore."

During the course of all these unbelievable events, never once does he look back. George is determined to make it there alive, and seems proud to have finally been able to leave behind all of the physical and psychological traumas that this ordeal has unleashed upon him. He is going back home, to a place where life has a semblance of normality.

Gradually, as he continues to swim towards the "landmass," the distance between them grows wider. He is an experienced swimmer, and even in his state of delusion, it shows. Both Kennedy and Peter, shocked to the bone and trying to understand what has just occurred, simply watch intently as George drifts further and further away, until the image of him fades.

Not a word is spoken as Kennedy eventually turns to face Peter. He feels cold inside, and although the morning sun has begun to warm the day, he is unable to feel its heat. There is a dizziness in the air, and his ears ring as if a loud cymbal has struck them. He does not feel like crying, as crying seems so odd right now. He can not explain the feeling that he has right now. He loved George, and has always so profoundly idolized him. They were always inseparable throughout their childhood and teenage years, and now what?

Lord, this really hurts.

Surviving George

Not much is said in the days following George's departure, yet Kennedy and Peter are inherently focused on survival. But how many times have they followed that recipe, only to have their hopes dashed by another tragedy? When it's not physical illness, it's mental breakdown. Death, it seems, always comes in pairs—first to Perry and Baby, who died of a similar disease, and then to Jones and George, whose demises came as a result of mental breakdown.

But then, are there any lessons to be learnt here, or are they doomed to suffer the same fate? It is hard to be hopeful, especially when the concept of death remains an enigma. But they will try.

With each passing day it becomes a bit easier, as their desire to live grows stronger. They have learned to cultivate patience, coupled with an unwavering faith that survival is indeed possible. Mindful of the effects that negative thoughts can have on the mind, they talk neither of the past nor of things to come. They live for the moment, and this is exactly how each day is spent at sea.

One evening, their lives change. Under a blanket of stars, Kennedy awakens during the night to relieve himself over the side of the boat. He has not noticed anything, and proceeds as usual. A few days ago, he began to feel weakness in his legs. Now there is a bit of that as he struggles to maintain his balance, but so far he is able to overcome that problem for the moment.

Around him, the coolness of the night breeze makes him shiver like a leaf, and although it has brushed away some of the sleep from his eyes, he can't wait to return to his favorite spot for the night.

He is almost done now, and he gazes at the night skies for a last look. As he gently turns his heard around, something catches his attention.

It's the formation of a landmass, with lights fading in the distance. He can't believe what he sees, and panics at the thought that, like George, he might have begun to hallucinate. Quickly setting himself down upon the seat, he rubs his hands into his eyes, hoping to fight off the dangerous effects of hallucination. But when he looks again, the images are still there in the distance, and he is convinced that it is for real.

Unable to contain himself, he howls out to Peter, who is fast asleep in the bottom of the boat. "Wake up, wake up, Peter, wake up," he cries, but Peter is too deep in sleep to hear him.

Moving clumsily over the row of seats ahead of him, he makes his way to the spot where Peter fell asleep for the night. "Peter, Peter," he calls out aloud, and shakes him a bit.

Peter is half awake, but does not fully comprehend what Kennedy is up to. Still not able to make any sense of what is going on, he pulls away as fast as he can from Kennedy, and takes on a defensive posture. Then slowly, as he awakes and calms himself a bit, he rises to his feet to stare in awe at the twinkling lights in the distance.

It is a wonder that he has waited weeks to see. The signs of life in the distance on a clear night make him thankful to be alive.

Throughout the course of the night, they hope and pray that the boat will continue its slow drift towards the landmass, and that perhaps by daybreak they will have a clearer sense of what it looks like. However, this is not meant to be.

By daybreak, instead of catching a close and breathtaking view of the landmass, they are disappointed as the current pulls the boat away from it. But even so, all is not lost, since the incoming sunlight allows them to have a distant view of it.

For one thing, what they had first perceived to be another Caribbean island in the night has the formation of what might well be a continent. It is covered with rolling hills and mountains which rise steadily into the clouds, and for miles upon miles on each side it stretches to distances beyond the range of the naked eye.

However, as the morning progresses, impatience settles in. Unable to think rationally, they attempt to row the boat towards the landmass. That effort is a huge lesson in futility, as the many days and nights of exposure to the elements, coupled with poor nourishment, have sapped the energy from their bodies. They eventually hang their heads in frustration and physical exhaustion, understanding that they gave it their best.

For the rest of the morning and into the afternoon, they gaze in awe at the magnificent scenery that, in effect, erases the sun, sea, and sky that they have grown accustomed to. It is an inspiration, fueling their hopes for survival. Although it is unattainable at the moment, there is hope as long as the image is present.

As night falls upon them, they each take up similar positions. With their backs resting comfortably against the side of the boat, and legs stretched out the entire length of the seats, they unwind to a perfect evening, which later gives way to restful sleep and hope for the morning to come.

After a night that concludes with a fairy tale ending, the morning holds promise that Perry, Baby, George, and Jones will never see. The first rays of sunrise creep over the horizon, forcing their eyes to open slowly to greet the new day. As they finally wake up, each at his own individual pace, there stands before them a head-spinning image of a country so close, but covered with such a dense forest, that it almost seems uninhabitable. A lot has happened overnight. For even as they slept in the arms of darkness, the ocean currents vigorously pushed the boat closer and closer towards the landmass.

This new glimmer of hope is by far the most reassuring signal that perhaps they might finally escape their misery at sea. The many quiet nights on the ocean, the sometimes-turbulent force of the ocean's waves, the isolation and despair, are all about to come to a grinding halt.

There is hope! And even in their weakened physical state, they are assured by their presence of mind that was never held captive by the perilous days that are now behind them.

Later that morning, as they quietly survey the unique features of the vast wilderness before them, Kennedy takes the time to remind Peter of the virtues of patience. He has observed Peter's eagerness to get ashore, and wants to be certain that Peter understands the risks of swimming towards the jagged edges of a landmass that is unknown to them.

In his usual quiet manner, Peter seems to have understood. Looking at him now, and seeing the amount of weight he has lost these last few weeks, convinces Kennedy that there is no way that Peter would ever attempt such a thing.

By nightfall, the distance they've covered has brought them closer and closer to the landmass. In addition to this encouraging sight is the fresh scent of seaweed in the atmosphere, which ignites their senses.

It may soon be possible to attempt their escape, but for tonight they will wait under the cover of darkness until the morning, when the shore will be nearer still.

Vanished in the Night

Except for the soft rustling sounds of the morning breeze, and the gentle taps of the ocean against the boat, an eerie silence punctuates the morning air. Stretching out a bit, while feeling a tremendous sense of appreciation for life, Kennedy feels ready for the challenges ahead.

A long moment elapses, then he finally notices that Peter has not awakened. Normally, Peter is always the first to catch the sunrise, but has not done so on this morning that matters most.

A cold chill sweeps over Kennedy's body, and he softly calls out Peter's name. He calls again, a bit louder, but there is no response at all.

There is a sinking feeling in his chest as his mind races to recall the words of caution he gave to Peter only yesterday. He prays in his heart that what he fears is not so. If there is anyone who deserves to have made it, then it would have to be poor Peter. That boy has been through a lot, and after weeks of fighting to remain alive at sea, it would be a devastating blow if anything has befallen him now.

From the position where Kennedy sits, he can't tell whether Peter is still lying on the boat's floor. Incapacitated by physical weakness, he drags himself over the row of seats until he finally makes it there.

His mind explodes upon the realization that Peter has vanished. With the blood racing through his veins, contracting the muscles of his heart, his stomach twists with pain as his heartbeat grows louder and louder. He feels the oxygen depleting from his lungs, and a feeling of dizziness forces him to lie down on the seat. But even in his momentary sickness, his mind reverts to his last words of caution to Peter.

Certainly Peter could never have contemplated suicide, and neither will Kennedy accept that he attempted to swim alone towards the shore. There was simply no reason to, since the dangers were already discussed yesterday. There is only one thing that could have happened.

Kennedy thought that at some point during the night, Peter might have awakened to ease his bowels. As he stooped on the side of the boat, half asleep, defecating into the ocean, he might have fallen over and drowned.

For the rest of the morning and into the early afternoon, despite his unique abilities to block tragedy and negative thoughts, Kennedy experiences a profound feeling of depression and sadness over Peter's loss. He knows that Peter at times had a fear of dying like everyone else, but he was always moved by the courage he had seen Peter exhibit throughout most of the ordeal. Like Moses, Peter lived to see the promised land for which they had waited for so many days, but he will never get the chance to enter.

Late into the afternoon, the weight of all these sad and depressing events finally push Kennedy once again to firm up his resolve to survive. Only this time, his decision is driven less by patience than by a determination to take matters into his own hands.

For some strange reason, he is suddenly convinced that if he is to make it through this ordeal alive, the time is right to plan his escape. As he ponders his fate, the urge to swim towards the shore builds inside him with great speed. He is finally going to defy death, and the thought that he is going to do it for his brother George, and his cousin Perry, and for Baby, Jones, and Peter, is more of a reason to act now.

In fact, for the first time since the idea came to him the evening before, it all seems possible now. The distance between the boat and the huge landmass is now several miles. As he continues to stare at the vast country, with its natural vegetation over rolling mountains, it becomes time for him to make that move.

However, as he struggles to lift himself to his feet, he realizes that it will take more than sheer will to accomplish his goal. The many weeks of dehydration and malnutrition have not only left him physically weak, but have impeded the movement in his joints. Yet he believes that once he hits the water, the strength and the experience that he cultivated as a swimmer will return.

As he slowly struggles to detach one of the wooden seats from the boat, he becomes breathless, and is forced to take pauses in his efforts. Huffing and puffing, he takes in large gulps of air until he finally succeeds.

Now totally exhausted, and badly needing some rest, he sits on the floor of the boat, his head tilting forward between his knees, hoping to catch his breath. After a moment, he is able to lift himself up while holding on to the wooden seat in his hands.

That moment on his feet is a dizzying experience in itself. He takes a couple more deep breaths to stabilize himself, then slowly tosses the wooden seat into the ocean.

Just as he is about to lower himself over the side, he observes some rather strange movement in the water beneath him. Frozen, he watches as a large gray monster climbs to the surface, and with jagged teeth, bites off a large chunk of the seat.

Like magic, the blood shoots to his head, and his reflexes spring into action. Pulling quickly away from the brink of gravity, he stumbles backwards, hitting his head against a two by four brace in the bottom of the boat. He loses consciousness. For the next few days, or perhaps a week, he remains in that state, before miraculously regaining his senses.

Landfall

The next time he awakens, Kennedy comes face to face with a reality that the men and boys who had set out to sea with him on that fateful Friday had hoped for, but never saw. The boat has finally made it ashore, but it's quite some time before the realization sinks in. Fearing that, like George and Jones, he might be hallucinating, he repeatedly rubs his fingers over his eyes, hoping that this moment will pass. As he lies down in the bottom of the boat, still unsure of who he really is, he falls asleep again, without any fear of the destructive rays of the sun. But the next time he awakes, he has a greater sense of who he is.

With the boat banging hard against the sand amidst the rush of the tide, his eardrums pop, and the impact sounds off in his head like thunder. It is time for him to get out of here, and with every fiber in his body he is prepared to do so.

His very first attempt to lift himself is a personal struggle. After repeated falls to the deck, he decides to take a rest. However, being the kind of guy that he is, Kennedy refuses to accept any limitations that have to do with his physical condition. Having the presence of mind to understand that his life is at stake if he dares remain in the boat a moment longer, he tries again.

It is not easy, and the occasional jamming of the boat against the sand by the incoming tide means that he has to double his efforts.

Still lying face-up in the bottom of the boat, he lifts himself to a seated position and grabs onto one side of the boat. He is determined, and even if it means crawling out of the boat, Kennedy is prepared for the challenge ahead. Slowly, gathering all of his strength, he literally crawls out of the boat.

The very first time his feet touch the ground, he collapses. He attempts to lift himself up again, but has the very same results.

Struggling to keep his head above the knee-high water, he drags himself along until he is safe on the sand. Once there, he lies down on the sand for a while, overcome by exhaustion but thankful to be alive.

A moment passes before he is finally able to gather his strength again. And when he does, he struggles to sit on the sand to observe his new surroundings.

All around him is a deserted beach, bordered by a dense forest which seems to extend miles and miles inland. The scenery is horrifying, and it isn't long before he is consumed with fear.

A lot of thoughts pour into his mind, as the uncertainties of the future unravel like a blanket before his eyes. After enduring so many brutal days of physical and psychological battering, Kennedy does not think that he has much left in him to continue. Unsure of what do next, he quietly prays, hoping to God that he will be spared further hardship in this strange land that fate has brought him to.

Fearing the worst, he crawls over the sand and towards the bushes ahead, in search of a safe area. He finds a place among some shrubs, and not too long after, falls into a deep sleep.

Unsure of how long he might have slept, he suddenly awakes to the sounds of strange movement in the bushes around him. Someone, something, perhaps a wild animal, is walking over some dry twigs in the area where he lay down. He is petrified, but the worst of his fear is yet to come.

Standing directly over him are what appear to be human beings. He is able to tell by the formation of their feet and their chipped toenails that they are used to walking barefoot in the dirt.

Although they have not said a word, it seems as though they have been standing there for a while. Unsure of how to react, he shivers with fear as he struggles hard to assume a defensive posture. He is going to fight for his life, even if it is the last thing he ever does.

A few seconds later, after he gathers the courage to lift this head off the ground, he makes visual contact with the strange people standing over him. Most of them are half-clad, with stocky builds, and have features resembling those of native Indians.

The last time he saw anyone remotely close in appearance to these people hovering over him was in a television documentary sponsored by National Geographic. Today, years later, he is looking at them in person.

There is a dead chill in his blood as his heart races, stops, and finally takes off again. For although the documentary did not label those people as being cannibalistic, there were other stories that he had heard about the peaceful Arawaks and fierce Carib people who once inhabited St. Lucia before the arrival of Christopher Columbus in the West Indies. There is no way for Kennedy to know that these men have no intention to harm him.

Therefore, while acknowledging inwardly his defenseless state, his outward demeanor of hostility remains.

A few more seconds pass, and still the brutal and ferocious attack that Kennedy expects does not occur. In its place, he receives empathy and compassion, as one of the men, determined to alleviate his fears, stoops slowly to the ground and pats him on the head.

Kennedy releases a deep sigh of relief as the man attempts to engage him in conversation. But although his body language is easily understandable, his spoken language is not recognizable to Kennedy.

One of the men in the party catches on to what is happening, and tries to communicate with Kennedy through a sort of reenactment. His motions describe in great detail how Kennedy painfully climbed out of the boat and eventually crawled over the sand. When he is done, it is clear to Kennedy that they had been watching him all along from the bushes.

The first man who stooped to have a conversation with him looks upon him like a father. There is great trustworthiness in his eyes, something that Kennedy has always been good at detecting. He introduces the entire party to Kennedy, and a quiet debate among them follows.

Although he does not understand the words they say to each other, it is clear to him that they are trying to decide how best to deal with the situation. There are a few sharp words, evident by the occasional tone of their voices and the gestures they make while talking. Then, finally, when they seem to arrive at a consensus, two of the men follow a narrow footpath that leads deep into the forest, while the others remain with Kennedy. From the hand gestures they use to communicate with him, he understands that the others have gone to seek help or perhaps fetch something. As they sit beside him on the ground, they converse with each other, occasionally attempting to engage Kennedy in conversation. After forty-five minutes to an hour, two of the men who departed earlier return with a few more people and a wheelbarrow carved out of bamboo and flat wood. They lift him gently into the wheelbarrow, and are on their way.

Kennedy is wheeled along a narrow path, lined with huge trees and shrubs on either side. On occasion they stop to take turns at pushing, until they finally make it into a tiny village.

That evening, Kennedy is taken into one of the homes. The woman of the house, presumably the wife of the man who took him in, attends to Kennedy and feeds him warm milk. She prepares a bed for him, where he will spend his first night in comfort since the beginning of the ordeal.

After she leaves him alone in the room, he closes his eyes without any concern for the past, or for the days to come. All he ever wants to do is sleep. And that he does.

Driven Away

On the following morning, Kennedy awoke to the loud voices of the villagers outside. Curious to see what was going on, he struggled to take a peek through a narrow window that was directly above the bed.

There was a somewhat heated argument going on outside, and one of the men involved in the shouting match was his host. He seemed visibly upset, but he had much control of himself.

Unsure of what was going on, Kennedy wearily pulled himself away from the window, dropping his head gently on the fiber-filled pillow and hoping to God that his presence had not caused any ill feelings or dissent within the community.

There was a knock on the door, and in came Kennedy's host and three other men. They greeted him politely, but due to the cramped space in the room, two of the men were forced to make way for the woman of the house, who followed immediately after them.

She had in one hand an aluminum cup, and in the other a wet rag. She and her husband helped Kennedy into a seated position. Then with great care, she wiped his face with the rag and handed him the aluminum cup, which contained warm milk. As she slowly stepped back to allow him an opportunity to drink from the cup, she smiled at him warmly, in the caring fashion of a mother.

Given his fragile state, it was a while before he could finish the milk. But once he was through, she hurried forward to take the cup away from him.

Once he was again lying on his back she wiped his face again and then anointed his brow with a sweet-smelling ointment. She used the rest to massage his arms and legs.

This was very comforting to Kennedy, who was grateful to have received nothing but compassion since the moment he came into contact with these villagers. This morning was even more special, as the compassion that they had shown towards him echoed far beyond the cultural and language barriers between them.

She left the room looking downwards, at which point the men reentered and stood there with gazes of wonder. Until this morning, he had not seen them before. And in the silence that filled the room upon their return, his mind quickly reverted to the heated argument outside the house.

A lot more could be said about the rest of the morning, for it was punctuated with suspicious thoughts that Kennedy could not hide. And even as he tried to appear comfortable with the men in the room, this strange sense that something was about to happen left a sunken feeling in the pit of his stomach.

The men all left the room again, only to return momentarily. And then, without a single word, they gently lifted him off the bed, carried him out of the bedroom, and finally out of the house.

On a dusty road not too far from the row of small houses, an old bus was idling in wait. The man at the wheel seemed familiar. In fact, he had been among those who had stepped into his room earlier that morning.

The air outside was tense as he was helped into the bus. Whatever lay ahead for him, God only knew. The thought of having survived the ordeal at sea, only to be subjected to a further life of fear, consumed Kennedy. Thoughts of whether he was better off dead began to encircle his mind. It was made even worse by the teary looks in the eyes of the family that had hosted him the night before. They looked visibly shaken, and did not seem to be able to hide their emotions. As the bus began its slow acceleration, the waving of hands like the flapping of swallows in the air was all he could remember.

For the next several miles or so, close to about an hour, there was silence aboard as they drove along some rather rough terrain and unpaved roads. For Kennedy, the only solace was the loud sounds of the engine, which, at times, distracted him from his fear.

He had moments when thoughts of throwing himself off the moving vehicle and perhaps escaping into the dense woods along the way crossed his mind. But how was this possible, when the many weeks at sea had caused so much physical weakness that it had even restricted his movement? And come to think of it, how was he going to escape in a strange country, the name of which he did not even know? As he pondered upon those things, the vivid realities, coupled with the need to survive, finally caused him to dispel these ideas.

Throughout the course of the long journey the driver did not attempt to communicate with Kennedy at all, but it did not bother him very much. There was one thing on his mind, and as long as the silence meant that there were no plans to subject him to any physical harm or danger, it was alright with him.

Hours later, at the end of what seemed like a ride from eternity, the bus finally exited the rough and dusty highway and made its way into a small town of no more than twenty-five hundred inhabitants. The homes along the narrow streets, though not quite middle-class, were far more modern than those which he had left behind in the sparsely populated coastal village.

The bus eventually came to a halt right in front of a small, unpainted concrete building. There were several people standing outside, and some of them helped carry Kennedy inside.

Once inside, his fears dissipated upon discovering the clever arrangement that his host had made on his behalf. Realizing that Kennedy required more care than they were able to give him, they had arranged to have him taken to this small medical facility or health center.

There was gratitude in Kennedy's heart as he pondered on the generosity and kindness of his hosts. For while they could not explain to him the reason why he had to be taken away from their home, the proof of their good intentions was now very clear to him.

The first to attend to him was a young doctor and nurse, no more than thirty to thirty-five years of age. They began by asking him some questions, which of course he did not understand. As they continued to press him for answers, frustration built up inside of him.

At one point, he was tempted to say something in English, but decided against it. He did not want to complicate things, and felt that there was no way that these people, who spoke a strange language, would ever understand anything in English.

He wanted to tell them about himself, and of the horrible circumstances that had brought him to their shores. But he finally decided that it was useless.

For the next several minutes or so, there was a battle of wills. They were not giving up on their strange language, and Kennedy refused to engage them in English. But all of that came to an end as Kennedy, filled with frustration, finally managed to say the following:

"I don't understand you! But if you understand me, I am from St. Lucia."

There was a moment of silence afterwards, as the nurse stared hard into his face. She had caught a bit of what he had just said, and drew her hands over her mouth. With her eyes popping in astonishment, she said something to the doctor in their native language, which gave Kennedy the impression that either one or both had understood him.

Their initial attempt to communicate in English seemed very difficult for them. For a while, their words sounded like Cracker Jacks jumping horribly from a box. But that didn't matter much to Kennedy, as what was most important now was the fact that he had finally established part of his identity through the use of the English language.

All at once, the state of frustration and anxiety that had gripped him for many weeks dissipated altogether. The mere fact they understood that he was from a place called St. Lucia, although they did not know its precise location, meant there was hope for him. He was determined to work their broken English to his advantage, with the hope of impressing upon their minds his great desire to return home.

Through the course of the difficult conversation between them, he also learned some things of interest, while jogging his memory for other things that he had heard over the radio back home. In fact, the landmass he and Peter had spotted from the ocean, and on which he had finally been able to set foot, was no longer a mystery.

After weeks at sea, Kennedy had finally landed in the South American country of Colombia, somewhere between Barranquilla and Santa Marta, roughly a thousand miles away from St. Lucia. The mountain range he and Peter had looked at from the sea in awe was the famous Andes. It was also a region where poor peasants, or *campesinos*, cultivated illicit drugs, and where the feared Medellin Cartel operated with impunity.

Colombia, a Land of Intrigue

Kennedy's days in Colombia were mostly spent in a hospital and later in an army barracks. They were long days of anticipation, suspicion, and sometimes frustration and fear.

Less than a week after his arrival at the small medical facility, he was transferred to a large hospital several miles away. It was equipped with a professional staff who had a good understanding of medicine, and who eventually contributed immensely to his recovery.

Getting better was a priority for him. But wanting to get in touch with his mother back home was of equal importance. In fact, one of the first things he requested upon arrival there was for some way to contact his mom. He made his wishes known to everyone with whom he came into contact, and he hoped that they would eventually do something to help him out.

A whole week went by, but still there was no word from his mother, said the nurses or the doctor who had been assigned to treat him. In fact, on the occasions when he reminded them, the reply was always that the hospital administrator was looking into it.

Then suddenly, one morning, the original staff who were assigned to treat him did not show up at all. They had been replaced by a new nurse, and later a doctor who seemed to care little about interacting.

Fortunately for Kennedy, the new nurse who had taken over the job turned out to be different. She was also one of the prettiest women that he had laid eyes upon since his arrival in Colombia. The attention that she gave to him, and the polite manner in which she treated him, reinforced his initial impression of her as a good person. Through her spotless face, and the lovely curve of her eyelids that projected softly over her deep brown eyes, he could see a level of profound sincerity. As the bond of trust between them grew, he finally amassed the courage to request in earnest that she personally contact his mother on his behalf.

Indeed, his wishes came true, or so it seemed at the time. For in spite of the fact that her limited English did not allow her to communicate with him at length, she understood somewhat and was willing to assist him as best as she could.

She briefly left the room, only to return later with a man with East Indian features. He had gold plastered on two of his front teeth, and he was very polite as he introduced himself in English with an accent that was somewhat familiar to Kennedy.

He revealed to Kennedy that he was originally from Guyana, but he had lived and worked for many years in Colombia. Three years previous, he had accepted a job as a janitor in this hospital, were he had worked since then.

He was here to serve as a translator for the nurse, which meant that Kennedy was now free to communicate to him everything that he wanted the nurse to know. With the purpose of his presence established, the whole truth could now be told.

It was a bittersweet moment for Kennedy as he began the story of how he had ended up in Colombia. And as he did, he could not help but notice the sympathetic reaction on the face of his translator, and also on the face of the nurse as she heard the translation to Spanish. When he was through, there were tears in her eyes, and Kennedy felt relieved that he was finally able to communicate his story to someone.

For an undetermined period, a great silence engulfed the room. Both the interpreter and the nurse, struggling to come to terms with what they had just heard, stood there as if they had been frozen in time. What they had just been told was horrifying, but it was also amazing to think of Kennedy as having been able to make it though the ordeal.

As the conversation resumed, Kennedy expressed through the interpreter his desire to speak to his mom, or, failing that, whether the nurse would be willing to do so on his behalf. The nurse gave him assurances that she would do all in her power to assist him, but there were a few hospital procedures she would have to follow. Given the circumstances under which Kennedy had arrived in Colombia, she would first have to relay the information to the doctor in charge, who would then have to relay it to the Hospital Administrator, who would then contact the appropriate authorities in Colombia. They would then proceed to contact the St. Lucian Government, who in turn would contact his mother.

What a tangled bureaucratic nightmare! But these were the added frustrations that Kennedy was forced to deal with.

Several days after his conversation with the nurse and the janitor, no word had arrived from St. Lucia. He never again heard from the janitor, who had offered to assist him independently of the hospital. Although the Janitor had never asked

Kennedy for a telephone number to contact his home, he had, unknown to the nurse, sneaked in this promise to Kennedy.

The days that followed were days of great frustration. Every day was like a never-ending wait, filled with suspicion of the answers he was always given. In fact, when they grew tired of him asking, he was always given the line that everything was fine, and that he would be going home as soon as he had fully recovered.

Towards the latter part of his third week in Colombia, although his health had improved to the point where he was now able to sit up on his own and even ride around the hospital in a wheelchair, there was still no word on whether anyone had contacted his mom, or even when he would be able to finally go home. This and other things, such as his repeated attempts to practice walking without the aid of the wheelchair, only to lose his balance and fall right back in the seat, fueled his anger and the frustration that kept eating at the walls of this stomach.

During the course of that long and difficult period of recovery, he would often employ a mental process of escape, which often came in the form of the visualization of a glorious day when he would finally make his journey back to St. Lucia.

But in spite of his ability to find a way of escape in his mind, there were always times when he could not control the thoughts that took him back to the horrifying events that had begun on February 14, and had concluded in death for everyone except him.

The mysterious way in which the engine had suddenly cut off, the never-ending drifting upon the open seas, the images of Perry's and Baby's deaths, followed by the terrible hallucinations that eventually led to Jones's and George's demises at sea, Peter's sudden disappearance, and finally Kennedy's arrival in Colombia, made him feel as though he had just woken up from a bad dream. When his mind was drawn into that cycle, even though he was never able to understand or control what triggered it, he always had the ability to squash those unhappy memories right away.

Then there were the times when he was able to think a lot about George, separately from the bad experiences. He often thought of George in the present tense, and marveled at the life that they had had together. He loved and missed him very much, but would never allow himself to go beyond that.

Towards the end of the fourth week in Colombia, Kennedy was riding high on the back of destiny. The many weeks of frustration, as he waited for the day when he would be able to walk without the aid of the wheelchair, had finally come to an end.

His very first steps were quite memorable, and the smile upon his face was a reflection of the joy that he felt inside. It was also important for other reasons; it meant that he would soon be able to go back home to St. Lucia, as promised.

Often, he would inquire about going home, only to receive answers that really did not make any sense at all. Hospital officials were very evasive, and even though he had never met directly with any government officials in Colombia, he was always told that the government was still working on resolving the situation.

Those long weeks of frustration and waiting finally bred Kennedy's suspicion and distrust. He often worried, and could never seem to understand why he had not been allowed to at least talk to his mother while the government tried to sort things through.

The moment of truth finally arrived one morning when he was removed from the general hospital and taken back to the small medical facility. His heart raced as he stepped into the center, where a man whom he had never met before was there to greet him.

"*Señor*," the man called out in Spanish, and then proceeded to communicate in broken English to Kennedy. "I'm here to help you, *Señor*. I take you to Aruba, and you go to your country from there. But now, you don't say nothin' to nobody, until I tell you some more."

There was stunned silence as Kennedy did his best to process what he had just been told. As he quickly raced through the words in his mind, his meeting with the stranger fueled both optimism and suspicion. It was the first time in weeks that he had ever been given a clearly defined idea as to how they planned to get him home. Yet, at the same time, the stranger had not mentioned when that would be, and had also insisted the he not talk to anyone about it.

What is the game plan here? Kennedy thought to himself. If it were really true that plans were under way for his return to St. Lucia, why would this supposed representative of the Colombian government want to keep it a secret?

However, not wanting to appear apprehensive about what he had just been told, Kennedy did his best to remain calm, while at the same time trying to make sense of all of these strange occurrences since his arrival in Colombia.

After the man had departed, Kennedy again thought very hard about their meeting. There was something fishy about this whole thing, enough to trigger much discomfort in him. He just could not understand why they had removed him from the general hospital and taken him back to the small medical facility. He had a lot of unanswered questions, and his thoughts suddenly took off again, raging in a state of restlessness.

The answers would finally come to him in the days ahead, and when they did, it was with a brutal reality. Almost three days after his return to the medical facility, he finally came face to face with the "real" representatives of the Colombian government in a meeting that would change his life.

In fact, they had come to arrest him! Two uniformed military personnel drove him to an army barracks, where they interrogated and questioned him about his relations to the drug trafficking trade.

Stunned, unable to even respond to the question, Kennedy just sat there with a blank stare, as one of the officers informed him that there were sufficient reasons to believe that he worked as a "mule" for one of the Colombian cartels. He was also accused of falsifying his claim as to how he had arrived in Colombia, and was informed that the authorities did not believe his story. They said they would have to detain him for an indefinite period of time, pending further investigation into his background.

The length of the interrogation took its toll on him. Not only did he understand the serious nature of the accusations against him, but he knew very well that if he couldn't find a way to establish his innocence, there was the possibility of his spending the rest of his life languishing in a Colombian prison.

This sudden twist of events, and the uncertainty over his future, made him feel as though he was reliving the dreadful circumstances that had brought him to the shores of Colombia.

It was sad, but even sadder was his perception that the people at the general hospital had betrayed him. In his mind, he had begun to put the pieces together, and soon there was no way to rule out their participation in this great evil that had befallen him. There was just too much intrigue since his arrival there, and armed with this feeling, his mind wandered further.

Looking back at his lengthy period of recovery convinced him even further that instead of genuinely trying to arrange for his return back to St. Lucia, certain people in the Colombian government must have been quietly conducting an investigation into his background. It was all a conspiracy, and the evasive behavior of the doctors and nurses meant that they must have been party to what was going on. His mind was also drawn back to the Guyanese man who had briefly acted as his translator. He never heard from him again, and whatever had happened to him was a mystery.

He also had his doubts about those who had arrested him, and secretly questioned their true identity. For example, if they really wanted to confirm his story, why didn't they contact the authorities in St. Lucia? As he sat there in a state of sadness and confusion, he finally gathered the courage to pose the same question to them. Of course, consistent with everything that had occurred since his arrival into Colombia, he could not get a direct answer from them.

Several days passed after his interrogation, but still no one could tell him how long they intended to keep him in detention. He had not been charged, and while they never subjected him to any physical abuse or torture, he wanted so badly to have an idea of what was going on their minds.

His curiosity was further fueled by the fact that they had not locked him up in any cell, and had not in any way restricted his movement in the barracks. Even if he walked out, which nobody was preventing him from doing, he had absolutely nowhere to go. His interrogation was the only thing that seemed remotely close to trouble with the law. And even that process, when it was over, felt as though they had finally found the answers they were looking for. But then, the burning question remained trapped in Kennedy's mind: what were those answers?

As the first days of his detention stretched into a week, Kennedy tried his best to fight anxiety and to settle down. He befriended a few of the soldiers who were convinced of his innocence. By the following week, he was being treated as if he were one of them. He was fed well, and given clean clothes to wear. Most evenings, when the lights were turned on in the barracks, they would invite him into a small hall where they played dominoes and treated him to good Colombian beer and coffee. His mind was always away from all his troubles whenever he was with them. But then, as soon as he was alone, his thoughts reverted right back to the reality of what had brought him to Colombia, and reminded him of his deep yearning to return home. Thinking of St. Lucia was his way of escape, and that special feeling, along with the kindness of the soldiers in the barracks, was exactly what held him together both physically and mentally.

Freedom at Last

The morning of April 27, 1985, saw a reversal of the bad fortunes that had followed him since the middle of February. He was summoned into a waiting room, where a soldier (perhaps a sergeant) apologized for the circumstances that had led to his detention, and informed him that arrangements were currently underway for his safe return to St. Lucia.

Kennedy's body went numb as the words fell on his ears. He had heard those words before, and wasn't quite sure how to react. The last time he was told that arrangements were being made for his return to St. Lucia, he was arrested and taken into detention.

There was a tense moment of silence as he struggled to make sense of everything. The sergeant, quickly noticing what a bittersweet moment this was for him, laid his hand on Kennedy's shoulder as if to reassure him that what he had been told was the truth.

The sergeant continued talking to Kennedy, informing him of his release tomorrow morning. There was another silence, followed by words of gratitude on Kennedy's part. He finally left the room with a smile, but mindful of keeping his newfound happiness under wraps.

He hardly slept that night, and when he was able to close his eyes, he did so with unease. Right now, all he could think about was the morning, and what may or may not be in store for him. It also gave him some time to reflect a bit on the life of intrigue he had lived in Columbia, including the ordeal that had brought him here in the first place.

Suddenly, he could not stop thinking about it, while at the same time afraid to revisit the experience in depth. In fact, whenever his thoughts came to the point of replaying how the ordeal had blown George's mind and in effect forced him to take his own life, his defenses shot up like a missile, quickly shooting down his acceptance of George's final fate. He knew there would be enough time in the future to mourn George's passing, and also to put the tragic endings of the other boys in perspective. But for now, he needed all the strength that he could muster in order to survive the long and uncertain journey back to St. Lucia.

The morning was slow in coming, but by the time the first light broke through the barracks, he was ready to leave.

Two soldiers escorted him out of the barracks and into a waiting bus outside. The bus was to take him to a place he thought sounded like Port Australia, where he would meet a man who had been entrusted with the responsibility of taking him to Aruba. Once there, other arrangements would be made for his safe return to St. Lucia.

With no passport or travel documents in his hands, his nerves rattled as he bade goodbye to the soldiers. The air that he had just inhaled seemed loaded with anxiety and suspicion.

As the bus finally pulled out of the yard and onto winding roads ahead, Kennedy found himself confronted by more questions than answers. The abruptness of the decision to free him, and the secretive arrangements that had been made for his entry into Aruba, did not seem to conform to the norm. For example, if the government of Colombia had indeed sanctioned his release, why was there such a systematic effort to conceal his departure? Couldn't they have instead flown him directly to St. Lucia, instead of going to all the trouble of getting him into Aruba?

Those thoughts pervaded his entire being. Throughout the entire journey to Port Australia, which lasted for several hours, all he did was pray to God to watch over him.

However, in spite of his guarded disposition, he entertained thoughts of brighter days ahead. He thought of his mother and father, his eldest brother Placide, his youngest sister Jackie, and what it would be like to see them all again.

They arrived in Port Australia some thirteen hours later, and were quickly introduced to the man who was assigned to take him to Aruba. He was tall, with broad shoulders, and he had patches of gray in his hair. There were bags under his eyes, a sign of the kind of life that he might have lived. His complexion was pale, not like one would expect of someone who had lived in the tropics. The man had arrived in Port Australia several days before Kennedy's arrival there, but he had been forced to remain there a bit longer to wait for Kennedy. They would have to hang around the port for a day or two, since they had missed the boat to Aruba by a few days. It was a tough experience, but so was the rest of this business.

For the next few days, they kept a quiet vigil near the docks. The man paid close attention to every single vessel that entered and left the port, and at times reacted with a sigh of frustration when the vessel he was watching for hadn't arrived. Something strange was going on, and it certainly was not legitimate at all. But then, having been left to the mercy of everyone else that he had come into contact with in Colombia, Kennedy had no choice but to accept the risk that came with his supposed return to St. Lucia.

A mysterious vessel finally arrived on the evening of April 30, and through the thick darkness that had long ago fallen over the docks, someone from the dimly lit vessel signaled with a torch-light in their direction. That moment was like a scene from an espionage movie. The blood began to race through Kennedy's veins, and the only thing he remembered was the moment when the beam of light fell dead on his face. Next thing he knew, they were moving hastily to the area where the vessel had just docked, and with every step forward his thoughts exploded.

A man whose face he could not see in the dark helped him aboard. And just as quickly as they had walked towards the boat, everything was in place for a fast departure on what was to be the first leg of his journey back to St. Lucia.

Aruba

There were a few unsettling things about Kennedy's debarkation in Aruba. The boat's crew never bothered to take him to the customs or immigration authorities, and had likewise avoided going there themselves.

They disembarked in a remote and darkened inlet, where the formation of the landmass shielded anyone with the desire to indulge in clandestine activities. From the look of things, it seemed as though they had made that run many times before. The men knew and understood that area, and were undaunted by whatever risks were involved.

But not Kennedy. His thoughts swirled with many questions as the gripping effects of fear continued to toy with his emotions. They had smuggled him out of Colombia and into Aruba without a single travel document, and what lay ahead for him in a country that was supposedly Aruba?

Trying his best to remain vigilant for any other instructions that were to be given to him, his mind temporarily drifted back to some of the mysterious circumstances that had characterized his stay in Colombia. Obviously, he had been lied to. But then, while it was clear to him that the government of Colombia had no direct knowledge of his presence in the country, he was troubled by the question of why a group of shadowy figures would go through the painstaking hassle of returning him back to St. Lucia. Could there have been a larger plan other than a benevolent gesture on the part of strangers?

Those questions, and the belief that he had found himself at the center of an illegal operation, fueled his imagination. As far as he knew, the real Colombian authorities did not even know that he was no longer being detained in their country, the Arubian government did not have a clue that he was here, and the St. Lucian government must have thought by now that he was dead!

The more he thought about all the things that had transpired between his arrival in and eventual departure from Colombia, the more complicated his thoughts became. Therefore, not wishing to compound his mental confusion, he made his way out of the vessel, hoping that his sojourn with darkness would soon come to an end.

Later that night, despite having made it safely into Aruba, Kennedy was certain that all was not well. As a matter of fact, things took a turn for the worse when the woman in whose home in he was supposed to have stayed pending new arrangements for his final return to St. Lucia, suddenly became too frightened and decided to back out of the agreement. She was so scared that she would not even entertain the idea of having Kennedy in her home for one evening.

A testy argument erupted between the woman and Kennedy's guide, and it soon became apparent to Kennedy that they were dumping insults on each other. Then there was a moment of calm, and the visibly upset gentleman informed Kennedy that it was time to leave.

The streetlights, which occasionally lifted the darkness from their faces, revealed signs of their worry. The gentleman seemed clueless, but he wanted desperately to unburden himself of the responsibility of being in charge of Kennedy. This was becoming increasingly evident to Kennedy with each passing moment. After almost fifteen minutes, the gentleman had had enough. He had grown somewhat irritable and perhaps even nervous. Being out on the streets, unsure of what to do next, he seemed to feel exposed to some kind of danger. Clearly, he wanted to be on his own, but felt guilty about wanting to leave Kennedy out on the streets alone.

Suddenly, he had an idea, which was to direct Kennedy to the nearest police station. Kennedy would walk on his own into the precinct, giving the authorities a distorted account of how he had been rescued on the high seas by a group of local fishermen who had taken him to Aruba. He was to refrain from making any reference to Colombia, and hope that they would believe his story and perhaps expedite his return to St. Lucia.

Frankly, it was easier said than done. The thought of turning himself over to the Arubian authorities had a chilling effect upon Kennedy's mind. What if they did not accept his story, and decided to jail him instead? He had seen everything go wrong for him in Colombia, and was not certain that he had the strength to undergo further interrogation. Moreover, given his fragile emotional state, how would he be able to stand up under such intense scrutiny?

Kennedy wholeheartedly pleaded with the gentleman to spare him that experience. Unsure of how much the gentleman had really been told about him, Kennedy proceeded to recount the entire story of how he had ended up in Colombia. In the process, he tried his best to communicate, though not in so many words, that he was not connected in any way, shape, or form to any illegal business.

There was a brief silence when he was through, and by the expression of awe on the man's face, Kennedy could tell that he was greatly moved. In the process, Kennedy had also changed the man's mind, and with that came a new idea.

Several months ago, the man told Kennedy, he had be-friended an elderly woman at the local market. Her good deeds of charity were common knowledge to everyone. Weeks later, he had performed some repair services for her at her house, and now he felt that she might be receptive to accommodating Kennedy for a few days, or at least the evening.

They arrived there shortly before 11:30 P.M. The two proceeded up a flight of steps and onto an L-shaped balcony. The outside lamp, glowing dimly from above the front door, cast shadows over the balcony. Then, in what seemed like a moment of hesitation, the man ran his fingers through his hair, bit on his nails, and then hesitantly tapped on the door.

After a second or two, they heard footsteps coming towards the door. Someone behind the curtains peeked though the glass window, and soon the door was slightly ajar.

The man seemed to utter a greeting in a language which was certainly not Spanish. He was personable and intelligent, and aside from the strange business he was no doubt involved with, he came across to Kennedy as a man who had mastered several languages.

There was a bit of hesitation on the part of the woman who had come to answer the door, and from her unenthusiastic response it was clear that she intended to maintain her distance from them. The gentleman sensed this and said something else to her, and within a few seconds she had invited them in.

"What brings you here?" she seemed to say in the language in which he had communicated to her. He then said a few words to her, at which point she invited them to have a seat.

Although Kennedy had no knowledge or understanding of the language they spoke, he could tell by their body language that he was the subject of discussion. They continued their exchange for a little while longer, until out of the clear blue sky, the woman turned to Kennedy and said: "*Oho say jean Ste Lecee?*"

And all of a sudden, his mind seemed to have exploded. She had actually spoken to him in St. Lucian Creole, something that he had thought he would never hear again.

After taking a few moments to compose himself, he managed to say, "Oui," to even the astonishment of the gentleman. He must have told her that Kennedy was from the island of St. Lucia, but the St. Lucian Creole was something that his linguistic abilities did not quite extend to.

"I am also St. Lucian," she said in Creole. "But I've never been back home since arriving in this country some thirty-five years ago. Your friend here thinks that I am from Aruba." With those words, she turned to the gentleman and said something in the language which they both spoke.

He looked stupefied with shock as he raised his hands to his mouth. Then slowly, he withdrew his hands, said something to her, and gave a smile of relief.

She explained to Kennedy that she had arrived in Aruba during the early fifties, during the era of mass exodus to the Dutch-controlled islands of Curacao and Aruba. Most of those who came were from the English-speaking Caribbean Islands, most notably St. Lucia. They had found work in the oil refineries, which had at that time formed part of a booming industry in both Curacao and Aruba. She was once married, but her husband had since passed. They had one child together, a boy, who had since grown up to be a man.

And at that point of the conversation, as if to show off her motherly affection for her son, she spread her arms in the air, and told him what a good boy her son had been.

There was a pause, which alerted Kennedy to the fact that his presence had delighted her immensely. She stared at him in disbelief, unable to process how fate had led him to her doorstep.

The conversation resumed, and very soon she was inquiring about a man by the name of Willie Volney, who had also hailed from Kennedy's hometown of Gros Islet. Apparently, she had met him in either Aruba or Curacao, where Willie Volney had worked as a young man. Unlike Volney, and many other immigrant workers who had returned home (and in the case of Willie Volney, had gone on to establish a lucrative business of selling gas), she had decided that her place was in Aruba.

They spoke a bit about Willie Volney, and she was told of how he had become the undisputed king of the gas business in the northern part of St. Lucia. His rise to financial power and political influence had made him an icon in the minds of many people.

With the evening winding down, and interest in Volney waning, Kennedy's escort into Aruba politely begged to be excused. He had had a very long day, and needed to get some rest.

After he had left the house, the conversation between Kennedy and his new host resumed. She had moved on to talk about her earlier years in St. Lucia, and of the many people she had known during that era. Of course, Kennedy knew none of the other people whom she had mentioned personally, but he did not give her the slightest impression that he did not have an interest in what she had to say.

For Kennedy, the thought that he had found hospitality in the home of a fellow St. Lucian was indeed a source of relief. For the first time in weeks, he began to release himself from thoughts of future uncertainties. Listening to her recollections of life in St. Lucia under British rule, when it was a sugar-producing colony, was something of a change from the life he had been forced to live these last few months.

Evidently, her many years of absence from St. Lucia had blinded her to the kind of development that had occurred there since. She was still stuck in the primitive years when an over-bearing system of poverty, aided by British Colonialism, had wreaked havoc on the people of our country and region. Memories of the era when every blasted English aristocrat had fattened himself at the expense of St. Lucia's people of color gave her a distaste for returning home.

The clock on the wall struck 1:00 A.M., which suddenly alerted her to how late it was. She directed Kennedy towards one of the back rooms, and promised that that by morning, when her son returned from the graveyard shift which he normally worked, some arrangement would be made for him to speak to his relatives back home.

The morning was fast in coming, and although he slept well, the first light of day made him feel like he had never gone to bed. Therefore, hoping to catch some more sleep before the morning filled the room, he slipped the covers over his head and did just that.

The next time he awoke, the morning had completely erased the remaining darkness in the room. He gave himself a bit of time to acclimate to his new surroundings before getting off the bed.

Later, as he stepped out of the bedroom and into the narrow hallway which led into the living room, he almost tiptoed until he was there. He was hoping not to disturb anyone if they were still sleeping, and with this in mind, he tried very hard.

Out in the open, the sweet aroma of morning coffee filled the air, and with every breath he took he wished for the taste of coffee on his tongue. Kennedy quietly took a seat on the chair which he had occupied the night before, and hoped that whoever had prepared the early morning brew would come out soon.

There was someone in the kitchen, by the sound of squeaking floors and drawers. A moment later, he found out who it was, as a tall, slender young man walked into the living room.

"Good morning!" he said in accented English. And with a smile, he walked over to Kennedy to introduce himself. His mother had already briefed him about Kennedy and his situation, and they seemed from the onset to hit it off nicely.

They conversed with each other for a long time without any interruption, except for a brief moment when he went to the kitchen to fetch some coffee for Kennedy. It was thrilling for both boys, but it seemed even more captivating for the young man, who felt himself privileged to be able to help someone in need from his ancestral homeland of St. Lucia.

Later that morning, after the two had spoken candidly about the unfortunate circumstance that had first brought Kennedy to Colombia and then Aruba, it seemed that there would be no further need for the escort into whose care he had been entrusted. Whatever other business he was into, his job involving Kennedy was over.

Things were now going well for Kennedy, because by virtue of his new friend working for the National Telephone and Telegraph Company, he would soon be able to tell his family and the rest of the world that he was still alive.

Kennedy had suffered a great deal, and that suffering was excruciating. It had caused him both physical and psychological pain, but, praise God, he had not lost his mind or his determination to live.

His friend grabbed a pen and paper, and eagerly asked for his telephone number back home. However, once Kennedy had informed him that his mom did not have the luxury of owning a telephone, he decided that a telegram would work best. He would also do some research at work, and find the listing for the police in St. Lucia. Acting upon Kennedy's advice, the telegram was to be addressed to:

Stanislaus Phulchere (alias Nourgearo)
C/O The Gros Islet Police Station,
Gros Islet, St. Lucia, West Indies

For reasons unexplained, Kennedy had not chosen to address the telegram to his mother. However, there was no doubt in his mind that Nourgearo would deliver the contents of the telegraph to his mother. Not only did he trust Nourgearo as a friend, but he always knew that just as he had done so many times before, Nourgearo would come through for him again. He needed him now more than ever, and together with his eldest brother Placide, he believed that the two would be able to offer his mother a lot of comfort once the message was received.

The News Hits Gros Islet

In days that preceded the arrival of Kennedy's telegram, it seemed that life in Gros Islet had already returned to normal. In fact, from the looks of things, the period of mourning was all but over. Wanting to put the bad memories behind us, we as a people did the best we could to move on with our lives.

Nourgearo was busy enjoying a game of cricket at the Gros Islet playing field when the telegram arrived that afternoon. It was handed to him by a police officer, which almost led him to believe that he had just been issued a summons.

Initially, he just looked at the piece of mail with great suspicion, and then at the officer, who continued on his way without a word. These "Babylons" (a local term for the police) had always been viewed with suspicion.

As he tore through the perforation to view what was written inside, he almost lost his balance as he read the contents:

Kennedy is alive, and is currently in Aruba. Please call…

In shock and disbelief over what he had just read, Nourgearo stood there, unable to decide what to do next. It was a moment that was so surreal that he was eventually forced to take a seat on the ground. He took another peek at the contents of the telegram, and suddenly there were wheels under his feet as he raced from the playing field like a madman.

He was heading in the direction of his mother's house, and did not even take the time to stop for any oncoming traffic. There was a weight on his shoulders, one that he had not asked for, but one that he just could not let go of until he was able to have someone else confirm what he had just read.

Within minutes, he stormed breathlessly into the house and quickly handed the telegram to one of his sisters, who could not understand what was going on. "Read this," he said, looking intently at her.

She read the contents, and like Nourgearo had, she just stood there unsure of what to say. Then suddenly, as though waking up from sleep, she suggested that they go to the police station, where they could make a telephone call to verify the authenticity of the telegram before breaking the news to Kennedy's mom. Moreover, since the telegram had not said much except that Kennedy was alive, they wanted to clear the air as to whether everyone was safe.

Together they dashed out of the house and onto the streets. They headed up Dauphine Street, towards the Gros Islet Police Station, which is located just a few blocks away.

Breathlessly, they entered the precinct and immediately informed the young officer at the desk of the nature of their visit. They handed the officer the telegram, and after reading it he reached for the telephone and began to dial.

His hands shook nervously when he touched the dial on the rotary phone. Then, as they waited for the call to go though, he handed the receiver to Nourgearo, who by now had tears streaming down his face.

There was a woman's voice at the other end, and Nourgearo quickly responded to her greetings: "Hello, may I please speak to Kennedy?" Then there was silence.

A long, drawn-out silence filtered through the receiver as he waited, and then suddenly he heard a calm and gentle voice saying, "Hello?" at the other end.

"Kennedy! Is that you?"

"Yes." came the reply.

"My God!" said Nourgearo, "I can't believe that I am talking to you."

"Nourgearo, It is me, I made it!" And then came a brief pause.

"What happened to Dis-Yute?" Nourgearo asked, using George's nickname.

"He did not make it," Kennedy replied in a somber tone, and then there was another silence.

"Jah!" said Nourgearo in a voice full of grief and shock. Choking temporarily on his words, he exhaled through his mouth, while trying his best to appear strong.

He eventually was able to compose himself, and Kennedy told him a bit about the tragedy. For the next five minutes or so, Nourgearo listened intently as Kennedy spoke, not wanting to miss a word of what he had to say. By the time the conversation finally came to an end, Nourgearo and his sister promised to inform his mom about their conversation and make arrangements for them to speak.

The sun was setting outside as they left the station house. They hastened their steps as the mighty weight of disclosing the good and bad news to Kennedy's mother pressed upon them like a ton of steel.

The front door was slightly ajar when they arrived there. As was customary, given their close relationship with Kennedy's mom, they simply knocked once, called out her name, and walked right in.

She was lying down on a sofa in the living room, but slowly rose into a seated position. She gave them the usual St. Lucian greeting of "*Sa-Ka-Fet*" (what's up), not expecting to hear much from them aside from the usual happenings in and around Gros Islet.

There was silence as they both sat there staring at her, unable to give the message which they had come to deliver. "What is it?" she said with a bit of apprehension, still not thinking that it had anything to do with her sons or the other boys.

"We just spoke to Kennedy," said Nourgearo calmly.

"You just spoke to Kennedy?" replied Cecilia, in a tone that seemed almost dismissive of what Nourgearo had just said.

"Yes, we did," said Nourgearo's sister, who then went on to explain what had just happened.

Cecilia was by then on the edge of the seat, but soon fell back, resting her head against her sofa. There was a stunned expression of disbelief on her face, and they could tell that she was still trying to come to terms with what she had just been told.

Understandably, the many weeks of personal anguish had left her drained. And whereas the news of Kennedy's survival was perhaps the best thing she had been told in weeks, the news that George and other boys had perished also had a profound effect upon her.

Rising slowly to her feet, she begged to be excused for a moment, then entered the master bedroom for a change of clothes.

She returned clutching a purse in her hands, and she asked them to accompany her to the home of Ms. Cynthia Hodge, another close friend and confidante.

The journey to Cynthia's house by bus is roughly ten to fifteen minutes. They were there not too long after. They were fortunate that she was home, and as usual, they were welcomed into her house. They broke the news to her, and without any hesitation, Ms. Hodge had the telephone in hand to dial the number.

There was complete silence in the living room as Ms. Hodge took her fingers off the dial. This was a moving moment for Cecilia, one in which she would finally talk to her son for the first time since February 14, 1985.

There were visible tears in her eyes as she accepted the receiver and placed it over her ears.

"Kennedy?" she said, and when she heard his voice at the other end, she choked on her words to him. She was gently comforted by Ms. Hodge, who placed her hand on Cecilia's shoulders. Finally having worked up the courage to speak to her son, she proceeded.

She seemed satisfied and relieved when she handed the phone to Ms. Hodge again. At the other end, after he had talked with Ms. Hodge a bit, Kennedy handed the phone to his friend, who along with Ms. Hodge, and later St. Lucia's Foreign Ministry, settled on a tentative date for Kennedy's return to St. Lucia. They settled on May 4, 1985, and unless something drastic happened, this was the target date.

When the news finally broke on the streets of Gros Islet, huge crowds of people amassed on several street corners. Everyone was giving their own conflicting versions of what had actually transpired, and the story seemed to take on a life of its own.

In fact, my first brush with the misinformation, which was circulating like wildfire, was at the corner of Bay and Parish streets. I was taken aback by the large numbers of people who had gathered there, and decided out of curiosity to stop for a while.

I was glad I did, but the news was both happy and sad. The story here was that everyone with the exception of George and Kennedy had made it, something which I found almost difficult to believe.

I was sick to my stomach, and felt that it was not possible that both George and Kennedy had not survived. I knew the boys, and I also understood their abilities when it came to the sea, and I felt that this just couldn't be true. It was as if I was reliving the whole episode again. I really thought that I had already accepted the reality of their deaths several weeks before. But now, it seemed like I was entering a second round of grieving. *Oh, Lord*, I thought!

Towards the later part of the evening, I decided to pay an impromptu visit to the Phillips' home on Notre Dame Street. Upon my arrival there, I greeted Kennedy's mom with the usual courtesy and respect, as if she were my own mother.

There was a small gathering of personal friends in the living room, people whom I was very well acquainted with, and who also knew me personally. After acknowledging everyone present, I took a seat beside one of the women while trying to work my way into the conversation that had been going on when I arrived.

I soon discovered the inaccuracy of the story that had been given to me. In fact, contrary to the news that were more survivors, I learnt that everyone aboard, with the exception of Kennedy, had perished. He had made it to Aruba, and would soon be home.

Those present in the Phillips' home talked a great deal about George and the other boys. And as the conversation continued in circles, it was ended again on Kennedy. The momentum and anticipation of the date for his return to St. Lucia was building quietly, and every second that I spent there seemed like a countdown.

Later that evening, as I left the Phillips' family home, I felt a mixture of sadness and joy. While I was extremely happy that Kennedy had survived the ordeal, I also felt profound sadness for all the lives that had ended at sea. And while it was true that I did not have any actual knowledge of the circumstances that brought about their deaths, I felt a burning intuition that closure would only come when I was able to see Kennedy face to face.

Home Sweet Home

Kennedy's journey back home began on Saturday, May 4, 1985. He was dressed in a pair of white jeans and a T-shirt, and he wore a wide-brimmed straw hat with the national emblem of Aruba pasted on it. Holding tightly onto a small satchel which contained some money and souvenirs, Kennedy was ready for his trip back home.

After he tearfully thanked his host, who only the night before had extended an invitation for him to stay longer in Aruba if he so desired, he proceeded through the security gates and into a small lounge from whence he finally proceeded to board the aircraft.

As he climbed up the stairs and quietly took his assigned seat, there was a feeling of personal triumph, one that caused him to look back on the experiences he had just had and marvel at how he was able to make it.

This flight would take him to Antigua, from where he would continue on to St. Lucia on a Leeward Island Air Transport (LIAT) carrier.

The flight took off from Aruba on schedule, and climbed into the clear Caribbean skies above. Kennedy peeked through the windows for a last glimpse of Aruba, thankful for all of the goodness and compassion he had received there. His mind was now dead set on Antigua, one less island, and then St. Lucia.

After his aircraft landed safely in Antigua, he proceeded into the main terminal and into a waiting room. Kennedy spent several agonizing hours there while awaiting his flight, which was not scheduled for departure until the evening.

That evening, as he boarded the tiny aircraft for the final leg of his journey to St. Lucia, he felt a great burst of excitement, something that he had not felt these last few months. Indeed, he was going home, and hearing the flight destination read by the flight attendant over the intercom caused him to lie back, resting his head comfortably on the seat.

In fact, the emotion of that moment grew much stronger than he had anticipated. He was resting comfortably on the seat, yet sweat poured from his brow like a running stream. As the aircraft finally took off, his heartbeat thundered with every blast of the engine.

Strangely, as the plane began its descent towards Vigie Airport (now George F. L. Charles Airport) on the Island of St. Lucia, the burst of excitement that had characterized his departure from Antigua suddenly changed to a feeling of mild depression. Like a cassette player rewinding, he thought of the days gone by, and of those who did not make it home alive. There were lots of regrets, and things that he wished he could have done differently. Then, looking through the window into the darkness outside, he slowly brushed away the tears, hoping that this would finally bring closure to his long ordeal.

Kennedy's first glimpse of St. Lucia from the sky was of a sparsely-lit island. But then, as the aircraft dropped lower and lower, he stared in awe at the bright city lights that illuminated the night below.

Not very long after, there was a sudden jolt. The wheels had finally touched the small concrete airstrip beneath them, carrying the aircraft forward until it came to a grinding halt. He was back home in St. Lucia, but the reality had yet to fully descend upon him.

As the passengers began filing out of the aircraft, Kennedy remained in his seat. Still unsure of himself, he looked intently through the window and saw some uniformed people standing on the tarmac. They glanced at each passenger as they went by, something that seemed quite normal at the airport.

It would soon be his turn to leave, and grabbing his satchel from the overhead compartment, he walked slowly through the narrow aisle, passed the two smiling flight attendants near the exit, and stepped out in the open.

It was something of a rebirth to inhale the sweet, fresh, St. Lucian air, which quickly brought him to the reality that he was back home in St. Lucia.

At the foot of the stairs, he was politely greeted by two police officers, who then directed him through an open gate. To his amazement, a crowd of people were waiting outside, and they greeted him with loud cheers and jubilation.

Among those present were Peter Phillip (no relation to George and Kennedy), the district representative of Gros Islet; members of Gros Islet's local government; the incomparable mayor of Gros Islet, Mr. Yoke Felicien; and popular radio host Mr. Marcellus Miller.

Behind them, the thunderous cheers and well wishes continued. These were people who had traveled all the way from his hometown of Gros Islet to greet him. However, while he was deeply moved and appreciative of the tremendous welcome that he had received, nothing was more profoundly touching than the moment when he heard the voices of Nourgearo and his brother Placide among the crowd. He could not see them, but he could hear them. They were yelling out his name at the top of their lungs.

As he made his way into the crowd, almost blinded by the tears that streamed steadily down his face, he walked straight into the open arms of his mother Cecilia and his sister Jackie, who quickly wrapped their arms around him and cried inconsolably on his shoulders.

Our Meeting—The Conclusion

Circumstances of a personal nature had made it impossible for me to be at the airport. But I was determined to see my old friend on the following day.

At about 7:30 A.M. on Sunday, I paid a visit to the family's residence in the upper section of Notre Dame Street, hoping that he would be there. As I made my way up the sandy portion of Notre Dame Street and onto the paved section that starts at the intersection of Church Street, I crossed paths with a great number of Sunday worshippers on their way to Mass. We exchanged pleasant good mornings while watching out for the incoming traffic that was coming south on Notre Dame and from the left on Church Street.

I was at the Phillips' house just moments after, and proceeded to knock upon the door. I waited a while, and when I did not hear anyone respond, I decided to knock again. No one came to the door, which led me to believe that I had gotten there too early, or that there was simply no one home.

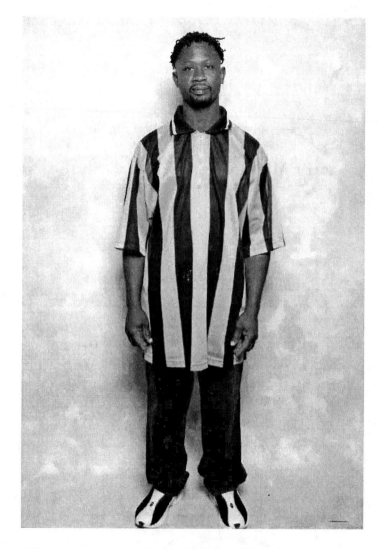

The most recent picture of Kennedy taken this year (2004).

I had another idea, and that was to head over to the family's old residence at Bay Street, where as a child I had spent time in the yard with George and Kennedy. Although not all of the family had actually resided there in the last year or so, my guess was that they might have decided to have Kennedy stay there instead.

That guess was wrong. For after I inquired from a group of people who had gathered outside the home on Bay Street, I was left with the impression that none of them knew exactly where Kennedy was or where he had spent the night.

I was a bit disappointed, but felt that there were lots of days ahead to speak to my old friend. Besides, after such a long time away, and all that he had gone through, I felt certain that wherever they had taken him after he had left the airport, it was for his own good. He needed that rest, and although I felt a selfish desire to impose myself on his right to privacy, I felt contented that at least he was finally safe back home.

However, as fate would have it, I bumped into Kennedy's mother at the corner of Dauphine and Notre Dame Street, a few feet from Mr. Herbert Scott's German Bar. I was glad that she recognized me right away. What a magical and pleasing moment for me.

I guess my many years of association with both George and Kennedy had convinced her that our friendship was sincere. They were my friends, and I was theirs. And so, like family, I did not have to ask the question about Kennedy's whereabouts. She volunteered.

"You can see him right now," she said quietly. "He is over at Cynthia Hodges' place. There are a few people over there right now, and I am sure he will be happy to see you."

At that point, I anxiously bid goodbye to her and walked briskly to the bus stop, which was only a stone's throw away. Within minutes I was on a bus headed for Mongirud, a middle-class suburb of the old town of Gros Islet.

The air was uncharacteristically cool by the time I got off the bus. Without any concern for the incoming traffic that sped along the road, I was soon over on the other side of the highway, and up the steep and narrow path that leads to Ms. Hodge's residence.

By now, the adrenaline was pumping through my veins. With every step forward, my heart pounded like a drum, filling my chest with uneasiness. I was gasping for air, but it did not matter much. I was going to see my friend, and this was the only thing that mattered. It was, for me, an unparalleled experience, for I had never known anyone who had gone through so much and yet could live to one day talk about it.

Suddenly, I was standing below a towering balcony, without the slightest idea of where to find the entrance. I was lost, really lost, until a voice from upstairs directed me towards the entrance.

It was Ms. Hodge, and I was grateful that she had allowed me into her home. As I tiptoed across the room and onto the balcony, my mind just exploded with joy when I saw Kennedy.

He was sitting in a chair, with one arm on the balcony's column and the other pressed against his temple. He looked a bit frail to me, but there was something about him that said a lot. Some say that miracles never happen, but the soul that I saw sitting on that chair was a product of one.

I knew him, and he knew my heart!

And so, as he stood up to embrace me in friendship, I thought of the good times, and of the days when we were boys, George, Kennedy, Ronnie, and I.

Epilogue

In the years since the ordeal, many changes have occurred. Today, although Kennedy still resides in Gros Islet, fishing is no longer the backbone of his economic survival.

Kennedy never did discover the true reasons behind his arrest and detention in Colombia. If any attempt was ever made by the Colombian government to locate or pursue him after his departure, he is not aware of it. As for his hosts in Aruba, he communicated with them for several months after his return home, then lost touch with them.

In the years after, he acquired greater knowledge in carpentry, from which he earns a modest living. He has also tried his hand as a proprietor, operating a small pub which he named the "The Fisherman's Bar." It is located on Marie Therese Street, just moments away from the Caribbean Sea. And though it is not as successful as it was in the early years, the structures still stand as a testament of his innovative sprit and effort.

There is no doubt that a lot has changed in Kennedy's life since the unfortunate experiences of February 14 through May 4 of 1985. To say that this experience has left an indelible mark on Kennedy is something of an understatement.

During the course of our interview together in 1994, which was conducted in a convenient spot along a stretch of beaches that concludes at Pigeon Point (formerly Pigeon Island), Kennedy tried desperately to fight back the tears. This occurred on several occasions, whenever I was forced to evoke George's name in our conversation.

Although it's been years, George is still the missing puzzle piece in Kennedy's life. While it is obvious that Kennedy has learnt to cultivate a quiet sense of independence without George, I couldn't ignore the tremendous affection that he still has for George's memory, including the abundance of influence George still has over him in death. "There are certain things that I have undertaken since then, that if George was alive, they may have been different." Those words from Kennedy, strong and compelling, will never escape my mind.

Throughout the chapters in this book I mentioned the names of certain individuals who, by virtue of their association with either George or Kennedy, became integral characters in this story. Therefore, in keeping with the purpose of this epilogue to provide an update, I wish to continue along those lines.

Stanislaus "Nourgearo" Phulchere: Nourgearo still resides in Gros Islet. He is a carpenter by trade, but in the years following the tragedy, he has debuted on the musical scene as a Calypsonian. He remains today a good friend of Kennedy and his family and one whom I have kept a good relationship with.

Ronnie Maxius: The last time I saw Ronnie was in the summer of 1983. It was his very first visit to St. Lucia since departing for Barbados in the late 1970s, and we sure had a good time. I am sure that it would please him to know that I have documented the early part of our lives together in this book.

Sylvester (Lala-leel) Eugene: Prior to visiting St. Lucia in 1997, I hadn't seen my childhood pal in almost thirteen years. I guess we both were fortunate to have been in St. Lucia at the same time. Lala-leel now resides in Barbados, and he has not lost his good nature.

Augustine "Cork-A-Bet" Joseph: Cork-A-Bet was brutally executed by the St. Lucian police in 1996. Their actions that day were not justified by the offence which they alleged that he committed. He is buried at the Gros Islet cemetery, the same one that overlooked our old playground.

Francis "Ba-ba-lew/Boom-Boom" Lord: The old acolyte has fallen from grace. The dangerous road, which started at experimentation with marijuana and which he followed further during the incoming age of cocaine, transformed him into an addict. It hurts, and I pray that one day the old acolyte will get the help that he deserves to set his life straight again.

Claudius and Terry Daniel (former Seagulls teammates of both George and Kennedy): Both are still very close friends of both Kennedy and Nourgearo. For a few years Claudius worked for the former district representative of Gros Islet, Peter Phillip, but has since left his employ to pursue other opportunities. Terry, on occasion, works as a carpenter with Nourgearo.

The McPhee brothers: Most of the McPhee brothers are still in Gros Islet. They are employed in a variety of fields and have done the best that they could with their lives. Skey is married, and resides in neighboring St. Vincent.

My cousins: My cousins Kenneth, Cheryl, and Fedora are all in the United States. Victor lives in Canada.

Sandra Modeste: Our childhood friend and neighbor, Sandra Modeste, resides in the United States.

David Moise: I still share a close friendship with Dave, but sadly his brother Crusoe, after years of battling sickle cell anemia, passed away a few years ago. He is buried in the Gros Islet Cemetery.

I could not end this epilogue if I did not give you an honest update on life in Gros Islet, along with some of the changes that have occurred in the Catholic Church since then.

Today, although Gros Islet has gone through a period of modernization, one can still find remnants of the Gros Islet of old. Some of the old houses are still standing, and the fishing industry, though it has declined a bit, remains to this day the economic bloodline of some of our people. However, if you were to ask me about one aspect of Gros Islet that has not undergone any changes in over years, I would smile and say that it is no doubt *POLITICS*. The political drought of homegrown candidates to represent Gros Islet in St. Lucia's House of Parliament continues.

Moreover, with the influx of new people who have come to reside in Gros Islet, they may well have reduced our people to the status of minority by now. Gros Islet has become a melting pot, which makes political aspirations for "homegrown" candidates irrelevant. In fact, if any indigenous Gros Islian is ever successful in breaking that political curse, it would have to be an individual who is able and willing to shed the stigma of being "homegrown," and who will instead pander to the diversion of views in the micro-constituencies that today make up the political district of Gros Islet.

Although much has not changed in the area of politics in Gros Islet, I am pleased to announce that a lot has changed in the Catholic Church since my childhood. The Church today is more tolerant of others with opposing religious views, and has gone a long way to seek redemption for its tainted past.

Today, many of the sermons coming from the pulpit are evangelical in nature, and geared towards an enlightened congregation. The church has also learnt to adapt to our culture, and it may be safe to say that it has finally found its St. Lucian identity. In addition, while most of our people are proud members of the international family of Catholics, they are no longer subjected to the overbearing European influences and racism that characterized the church's earliest operations in St. Lucia.

In recent years, although there have been some cases of misconduct by clergymen, we have overcome the days when children were slapped or humiliated in public by white clerics. Other forms of punishments, such as requiring a child to kneel in church for the duration of the mass, could never again occur in our community. Today, our children go to church because they love to, and not for reasons that derive from fears of a priest, Limbo, Purgatory, or Hell that so terrified the children of my day.

I too have come of age, and while my views on Christianity have gone through some radical changes, I feel perfectly at home worshipping among Catholics, Adventists, Jews, Muslims, and members of many other religious faiths of the world.

Writing this book has been a very difficult process for me. It brought back wonderful memories of things I had forgotten, along with things I'd wished to forget. However, despite of all the bad memories, I am proud to have been able to work up the courage to be as candid as I could in this book. I am also delighted to have been a friend to both George and Kennedy, for it was out of our long-standing personal friendship that the idea for this book came along.

Acknowledgments

I wish to give special thanks to my friend Kennedy Phillip for allowing me the opportunity to write this book. I am certain that without your approval and undeniable cooperation, my efforts could not have come to fruition.

I also wish to thank Stanislaus "Nourgearo" Phulchere for sharing with me the many valuable details that enabled me to piece this story together. Your encouragement and endorsement of my idea to write this book was a source of inspiration so rarely found in our community.

I do not believe that I could have fully envisioned the perilous conditions that the victims (George, Kennedy, Perry, Jones, Peter, and Baby) endured at sea, if it weren't for the help of a good friend and master fisherman who hails from St. Lucia, but now resides in New York. Therefore, I wish to thank Antoine "Pharaoh" Joseph for inspiring my efforts to candidly reenact the events at sea. To Elizabeth "Darling" Deterville, Albert Gomez, Rollins "Coco" Joseph, Juliana "Julie" Perez, and Jeremiah Hyacinth: thanks for the immeasurable support along the way. To Jenny and Harold Gopaul: thanks for generosity of your friendship.

I also wish to express gratitude to Lenard Montoute for his contribution to this story. While in New York, and casually talking about the ongoing project, I learnt from Mr. Montoute that he was Baby's teacher and football coach in school. Once again, Spider, thanks for the tidbit.

Some of my best friends are still in Gros Islet. They are friends like Raphael "Shoalin" Pamphile, Thomas St. Hill, Embert Chouloute, James Dupal, Urban and Corretta Augustine, Worrel Phulchere, Anthony "Ananee" Defage, Victor "Tottor" Albert, the "Mighty Octopus," and others to numerous to mention. You guys have always understood me as a person, and have never sought to judge me in ways that are unfair. You have always shown respect for the God-given talents I possess, and have done everything humanly possible to defend and support me along the way. Thank you!

I also wish to give special thanks to my editor, Mr. Jeff Alexander. Your wisdom, accommodating attitude, skills, and professional outlook are responsible for guiding me towards the finale of this huge accomplishment.

To my aunts Paulina Philips and Suzette Prudent, my uncles, Clement "T-Boy" Prudent, Hobson Prudent and Llewlyn McCauldy, thanks for the love that you have always shown.

To my mother, Frances Prudent (*nee* Morille): thanks for being the guiding light throughout my life. To my father, Mr. James Prudent: Dad, the best years of our life are here and counting. Thanks for the support.

To my brothers Philip, Enoch, and Lew: my aim is to make you proud.

To my dear grandmother, Ms. Irene Morille; my aunt, Theresa Merring; Merle and Alfred Hinds; Michelle, Irene,

Fedora, Cheryl, Victor, and Kenny; and my dear cousin Kim McPhee: thanks for the immeasurable support.

To Evis and Ken Dubois: Thanks!

To the loving memory of my grandmother, Mrs. Houston Prudent, and my adopted aunt "Saco": I wish that you both were alive to catch a glimpse of *Glory Days and Tragedy*.

To all my relatives, specifically The Prudent, Morille, and Montoute families, and countless other friends in England, St. Lucia, Canada, and the USA, thanks for believing in me.

Finally, I will be always be eternally grateful to the love of my life (Phyllis), for being patient with me during most of that process. Thanks for reading, and thanks for always watching my back. You, more than anyone, made it happen!

About the Author

Therold Prudent is an avid traveler who has crisscrossed the globe during business and personal travel. He is also a progressive thinker who likes reading, writing, teaching, music, and politics. Mr. Prudent holds a master's degree in government and politics, and a graduate certificate in international law and diplomacy from Saint John's University. He also attended Adelphi University, where he received a bachelor of science in management and communications. Therold Prudent lives in Queens, New York, and is already at work on another book. In the future, he has plans to release an album of original songs. Mr. Prudent has been an accomplished guitarist for over sixteen years.